Beyond & Within

THIS WAY LIES MADNESS

Short Stories from the Edge of Darkness

Edited by Lee Murray & Dave Jeffery

Beyond & Within

THIS WAY LIES MADNESS

Short Stories from the Edge of Darkness

Edited by Lee Murray & Dave Jeffery

FLAME TREE
PUBLISHING

Publisher & Creative Director: Nick Wells
Senior Project Editor: Gillian Whitaker

FLAME TREE PUBLISHING
6 Melbray Mews, Fulham,
London SW6 3NS, United Kingdom
www.flametreepublishing.com

First published 2025

25 27 29 28 26
1 3 5 7 9 10 8 6 4 2

Hardback ISBN: 978-1-80417-906-2
ebook ISBN: 978-1-80417-907-9

The cover is created by Flame Tree Studio. Frontispiece illustration is based on *Metamorphosis* © Greg Chapman 2025.

Attributions for the story 'A Note for William Cowper' by Sara Larner:
Coleridge, Samuel T., 'The Rime of the Ancient Mariner' from *Lyrical Ballads*, J. & A. Arch, Great Britain, 1797–98
Cowper, William, 'The Castaway', 1799–1800, *The Works of William Cowper*, J. Haddon, London, 1849
Service, Robert W., 'The Cremation of Sam McGee' from *Songs of a Sourdough*, Canada, 1907
Poe, Edgar A., 'Annabel Lee', *Sartain's Union Magazine*, John Sartain, USA, 1850

A copy of the CIP data for this book is available from the British Library.

Printed and bound in China

Trigger Warning:

This book portrays aspects of mental illness, including associated themes and symptoms.

Table of Contents

Introduction

Lee Murray & Dave Jeffery

I heard all things in the heaven and in the earth.
I heard many things in hell. How, then, am I mad?
Hearken! and observe how healthily – how calmly
I can tell you the whole story.
– Edgar Allan Poe, 'The Tell-tale Heart', 1843

There is a recurrent spot where the pattern lolls
like a broken neck and two bulbous eyes stare
at you upside down. I get positively angry with
the impertinence of it and the everlastingness.
Up and down and sideways they crawl, and
those absurd, unblinking eyes are everywhere.
– Charlotte Perkins Stetson Gilman,
'The Yellow Wallpaper', 1892

THE BOOK YOU HOLD in your hands has weight. Not just in a physical sense, but in the gravity of its purpose. That it exists at all is testament to its uniqueness:

a horror work that defies convention by bringing together authentic, sensitive portrayals of mental illness in a genre that has notoriously lacked such tenets.

For its editors, this book had its first twinklings in 2016 when we co-wrote an article on the topic, although, as long-term advocates for reducing societal stigma of mental illness, it is fair to say this ethos was already crystalised in our bones. We had our own experiences of mental illness, of course: Lee with her lived experience of anxiety and depression, and Dave with thirty-five years as a practitioner in the UK's National Health Service. Our shared desire to put an end to damaging portrayals of mental illness in horror narratives led us to the Horror Writers Association (HWA) and a three-year tenure as co-chairs of the HWA Wellness Committee, during which time we conceived, developed, and delivered the organisation's Mental Health Initiative, a suite of programmes and resources designed to promote positive mental health through creativity, and to challenge stigma. Activities included groundbreaking virtual and face-to-face panels held at major genre conventions such as StokerCon and FantasyCon, forums which generated open, informed discussion between creatives and horror lovers. The response to these, and other events, was both humbling and uplifting, with horror authors sharing stories of how writing helped them cope with, and recover from, mental illness, addiction, and grief. It became clear to us that by reframing how we talk about mental illness in horror, by eliminating harmful, stigmatising language and demeaning narratives, there can be catharsis for both writers and readers.

Through this work, we also recognised that there was a hunger for stories and poems which represented people's authentic lived experiences, powerful, empowering fiction that didn't flinch from the truth, but which did so with compassion. This became the premise of our anthology. And since insights and understanding can be gained from contextualising how stories take shape, each tale in *This Way Lies Madness* is accompanied by a vignette written by its author, revealing aspects of their personal experience as a survivor, carer, or practitioner.

In these pages, you will discover tales of trauma, dissociation, body dysmorphia, psychosis, depression, anxiety, and more, captured in all forms of horror from the extreme to the nuanced. There is jaw-dropping violence, skin-crawling body horror, and quirky dark humour, alongside the quiet, heartbreaking introspections of people spiralling into madness. Yet all the stories and poems in this volume are framed so that the insensitive, stereotypical presentations of mental illness commonly found in horror are resoundingly and appropriately absent. Our authors have achieved this in a number of ways. As well as drawing on lived experience and careful research, they have all made effective and inventive use of metaphor; a conceit also employed by horror masters like Poe and Gilman, to explore the complex effects that mental illness can have on a person. Conjuring ghosts and poltergeists, vampires, haunted houses, and other unnerving manifestations, our authors have punctuated their tales with powerful symbolism, startling imagery, and compelling, and often confronting, intimacy. For a moment, we are living in the minds of their protagonists, obliged to experience their psychoses first hand, to listen to their reasoning, to see the inexorable lengths they will go to survive. We are forced to watch the horrific loss of *self*.

"…unblinking eyes are everywhere."

But we have also learned that horror literature has the power to bring people together. It gives voice to our fears, allowing us to explore difficult topics, while providing a vent for emotional trauma and a buffer for the loneliness so often associated with mental illness.

This book has weight because it proves that horror *can* do better. With a little belief and some commitment, change is possible. Language – literature – is important: it can weaponise or neutralise stereotypes, it can isolate or, as our bold and pioneering contributors have shown here, it can inspire creativity, forge connections, and foster hope. We are proud to welcome readers to this brave new world. Turn the page, for *This Way Lies Madness*…

Lee Murray & Dave Jeffery
Tauranga, New Zealand &
Bromsgrove, United Kingdom, 2025

TBR

Kayleigh Dobbs

HOW MUCH LONGER must I sit here, hoping to be chosen? To be unknown hurts, but it's not just that she doesn't know me that causes me to wither. It's that she doesn't even *want* to know me. I wait among the others, watching silently each time she appears, ablaze with excitement at the mere possibility that she'll honour me with more than just a passing glance, that her long fingers will finally reach for me.

But it's always one of the others she wants.

When I first met her, I fell in love. She scooped me up, enamoured with how I looked. She smiled and stroked my face, her brown eyes sweeping every inch of my being, and then she clutched me to her chest. I was special. Out of thousands of others, it was me who she saw value in, me who was given a home with her. I thought that finally, someone saw enough in my outward appearance to want to know what was inside. I have so much to tell and so much to give, so much I want to communicate. Ideas, dreams, personality, joy to give. That's what I am; it's all I'm for.

She took me home, and at her side I swayed, dizzy with the glee of acceptance. A key in a lock, the sounds of her kicking off her boots – so carefree! – her socked feet padding up carpeted stairs. The creak of floorboards as she took me to my new room. I was giddy with wonder: would she cradle me as she had when she found me, wandering these creaky floorboards, too engrossed with our silent conversation to notice the wear in the wood? I just couldn't wait to open myself up to her after a lifetime of having no one to share with, not a single person paying me any mind, that wretched torment was done.

But she shelved me.

That was over two decades ago.

And so here I sit.

I used to long for her presence – despite myself, I still do – and I lived just for those glimpses of her. The door brushing the carpet as she entered the room roused me, and then there she'd be, all brown curls and loose shirts and glistening eyes. She'd stare, sometimes for what felt like expansive lengths of time, but not just at me. Her eyes would sweep over us all as she mulled over who she deemed worthy. Her fingers would flutter around her lips when she couldn't decide. She'd mutter things like, "Must stop buying books" and "The never-ending TBR." She'd pensively reach out and pluck one of the others and scan them. Sometimes she'd nod and brush her fingers over their faces – how I long for her to touch me like that again! – and disappear with them clutched to her chest, just like she'd clutched me as she took me from that charity shop. Other times, she'd sigh and purse her lips and then return them to their place on the shelf, snatching up one of the others with no consideration whatsoever and just stalking out of the room without so much as reading the title.

The more she does this, the more I break. It's as though she's ripping me apart, one page at a time. I love her, but as the years have passed, as the dust of neglect settled on me, as I've watched small lines etch themselves into her pretty face and noticed white strands of hair growing and twisting into her brown curls, as age has started to take me too, I've also grown to hate her.

Why did she ever choose me in the first place? Why did she rescue me from that hideous place of disregard only to bring me here and reject me? Sometimes I wish she'd just left me there. There'd been no hope there either, but at least the promise of connection wasn't dangled in front of me like this all the time. And – and please forgive my vanity – at least there, I was something unique. 'Like new, never read'. I sat among others of my kind that were faded and worn and ripped, their edges twisting, their spines cracked, their sheen gone. Teddy bears and dolls with splitting seams and missing eyes, and jigsaw puzzles and board games with coffee stains and pieces lost. I was perfect. Pretty, even.

She'd seen something in me once, seen value. I was worth something to her that day. It changed so quickly, but why? What did I do to turn her against me? Why does she, week after week, continue to ignore me in favour of others? I've not changed. I don't understand.

There was a deluded time that I thought she was perhaps saving me for something special. Perhaps there was a reason that she held back. Perhaps I'd be whisked away with her on a holiday and read on a beach, like the one waiting to be read between my pages. I wanted to talk to her so badly, to make her happy, but I could wait. I knew that our time was coming.

But with each appearance and disappearance from her, my faith diminished. I realised that it was not just I that had been brought home with her and promptly forgotten – there are others just like me here, others that are older, that have surrendered to their lonely, closed-off fates. But I'm a romantic and I can't help but hope, even now, even still.

Two years ago, she selected me. But I was still angry. I messed it up.

Five years ago, she came into the room with a box and declared, "I'm sorry but I've run out of shelf space, so some of you have to go!" I thought I would die. I wanted to. I wanted to lean into the sunlight that was just out of reach and linger in it until I became kindling. The thought of going back to that charity shop, that wasteland of things with no value – I couldn't stand it. I wasn't the only one. Among us, there were those who screamed, howled, cried, but of course, she couldn't hear us. Her kind can't unless they bother to look inside, unless they care to know what lies within. In her oblivion, she neither cared nor knew of the horror she inflicted.

It wasn't easy for her to decide which of us to discard – it took her hours. But I could not sympathise with *her* plight, because mine – ours – was so severe. She tossed some of us like rags into that box with little or no consideration. Once loved, now trashed, and no reason shared for any of those decisions. How could she love us one moment and then toss us out? How could she get rid of those to whom she hadn't even given a chance?

When she looked directly at me, it was the first time I didn't want her to. How ironic that every other time I'd seen her, I was dying for her to see me back, and now here she was seeing me, and it was the most horrible moment of my existence. I tried to throw myself into that beam of burning sunlight. I couldn't, of course. That's the problem with having no agency or autonomy and being at the mercy of those more powerful.

Existence requiring manipulation. Needing them while being paralysed, and they don't see you and

don't want you and don't even care that their apathy hurts it hurts so much what changed why doesn't she love me why doesn't she care why

and for just a second, because I couldn't move myself, I willed her to fall into the sunlight instead of me and for it to burn her up. I envisioned her hair catching fire first. I fancied I could even smell it. I heard her screams and saw the flames reflected in her lovely brown eyes and I – I am ashamed to admit – desired it. I yearned for her to light up and light us all up with her, and then we'd all finally just be together, and there'd be no more waiting and wondering and hurting.

That was the first imagery I ever conjured, the first picture I concocted that wasn't gifted to me by a scribe. But so lost was I in the horror of the moment, of thinking she was about to toss me into that wretched box, that I didn't realise the shifting nature of my own sentience.

"Hmm." She flipped me over in her hand and half-read my back, and then pondered me as she gazed upon my face again. Do you have any idea how it feels to be trapped inside yourself as the one you love so openly and brazenly mulls over whether or not you're worth anything to them? "I think I probably will get around to you," she said, and I hated myself for being so happy to see that dangling carrot after so long of barely a passing glance. “This weekend,” she said, and slid me back into my place.

I was invigorated, renewed. The place I’d inhabited for years suddenly felt warmer, more comfortable, because now it was temporary. In just a matter of days, I’d be carried away again and she’d finally get to know the real me, and we’d spend that intimate time together, a private experience that nothing and no one else in the world would ever be a party to.

But then the weekend came and went, and so did she, and she didn’t pick me. She sauntered in like she was royalty and the rest of us peasants, and with an upturned nose, chose another. Right in front of me. I swear she even smirked in my direction as she did so.

I hated her. I raged. But my rage was impotent because I was still paralysed and I could do nothing but stew, locked inside myself, with only myself, and I no longer wanted my own company. After all, she didn’t. I went back and forth, unable to decide who I hated more between she and I. Perhaps the problem wasn’t her at all. Perhaps it was me.

Perhaps it always had been me. My fault. After all, she wasn’t the first person to consider and then reject me, to give me hope and then dash it like a wave against rocks. She wasn’t the first to stroke my face and tease me with the allure of touch, only to have no interest in my contents. She wasn’t the first to decide I wasn’t worth her time.

I wondered if my story was even that interesting after all. I thought my characters rich and my imagery beautiful, and my ideas and themes worth exploring, but perhaps that was just my vanity all along. Perhaps it was self-delusion. Perhaps I truly was only a pretty cover, and apparently not even *that* pretty. Perhaps all I really had to offer *was* on the outside, and in a world of thousands – hundreds of thousands – millions – more beautiful than I, the one thing I did have was worthless anyway.

I was nothing.

I was nothing.

I am nothing.

For two years after that day of the dreaded box, I withdrew completely inside the shelter of my covers, and there I stayed. I examined my story, re-examined, re-interpreted what was written within. I no longer liked it, and I understood why she wasn't compelled to experience it. I conjured more of my own pictures, more of my own ideas, wondering if I could change my narrative and become something desirable. Perhaps if I worked from the inside out, my face would eventually reflect the new me within. In time, she'd finally see it. She'd know I'd done this for her. She'd see me.

But I couldn't remake myself. The ink was etched too thick, and it ran too deeply. I found I could reshape some of the words, but not the ones of real substance, not the real hook of my being. I couldn't unravel my own plot and write something new. I was stuck with how I was, and I hated what I was, and that pain circled me back around to hating her for inciting this desire to change in the first place.

And then she came back and she headed straight for me, and instead of being elated – this is what I'd been dreaming of for over twenty years! – I was angry. As she reached for me, I wanted to smack her hands away, I wanted to fend her off and let her know it was too late. Her time was up – I would not wriggle on this hook forever. I would not simply fold now, just because she'd finally deigned me worthy.

"Time to give you a whirl," she said, smiling. I no longer loved her smile and no longer wished her to direct it at me. "Nice little bathtime read." But even as she said that, she was looking elsewhere, no doubt wondering if perhaps there was a better bathtime read. And that was another thing – bathtime read? So, she'd decided to 'get around' to me after all this time, only to willingly damage me with hot steam and, even worse, risk dropping and soaking me – certain death.

I wanted to bite her, and I tried. How dare she, after all this time I'd waited for her, pay me this little consideration? I was finally good enough to be given 'a whirl', but not even with the dignity of being read in a place where I wasn't in mortal peril. No. I wanted to hurt her like she was hurting me, wanted to inflict, I wanted to…

"Oof!" She almost dropped me but didn't. Instead, she slapped me facedown on the shelf. In any other circumstance, I would have been devastated by such an indignity, but there was the blood. I had no teeth to bite her, but I'd cut her – she didn't need to say it and I didn't need to see her bring her bleeding finger to her mouth. I could taste it. It seeped into my edges, and I drank.

I drank it all up.

I thrummed with a pulse for the first time. I suddenly felt like I not only had real eyes but that they were open for the first time. It was fleeting, lasting only as long as it took for the blood to dry. But even after I'd pulled that metallic life as far as I could into myself, even after it dried, I could still taste it, still gnaw on it. As she hissed and fussed over her papercut, I moved. Only a little. Just the tiniest lift of my back jacket, the tiniest ruffle of my pages – something that could be explained away by a harsh breeze, should one be free to enter.

I felt guilty knowing I'd hurt her, and guiltier because I'd been trying to. I wanted to tell her I was sorry. I screamed internally at my stupidity – she'd finally given me what I wanted, and my impulse was to attack her? How could I be so stupid, so awful? She didn't deserve to bleed. But then she left me facedown there. She left me *again*. The guilt subsided.

She deserved it.

She deserved it, and I'd done it, and I was able to do it because I'd envisioned it and desired it. I'd not known before then that I was capable. I felt powerful and the intensity of that hitherto unknown feeling was monumental – it eclipsed the love I felt for her a thousand times over. Or, perhaps, this *was* love? I'd only learned about the concept from what now felt like the silly story scribbled onto my pages. Characters that I once liked but now seemed vapid and shallow. Juvenile.

Lies, really.

This is the truth of love and devotion, the reality. She doesn't see me unless I make her see me.

I can feel the change in me now. I can feel my story dissolving. I don't know what will form in its place, but anything is better than the old me. The weak me. I don't want to be invisible and unwanted anymore. I want to be known. I want her to see me.

I shuffle.

I practise when the lights are out, when she's not here. I move in the dark. I imagine other things moving – an ornament, a stack of papers, her desk chair. Sometimes they move too. How powerful the imagination can be.

Her dried blood still tastes good, but I miss that pulse. I want it. A matter of time, that's all it is. I'm so strong now. She doesn't even know how much

I control around her. When the bath tap gushes, when the lights go out, when her phone battery suddenly drains.

Just a little more time, and I won't just hold power over what's around her.

I want her.

And the blood.

Author Note

I've been joking for a while that my TBR pile is so large it's gaining sentience, and the books on the bottom are probably pretty mad about how long they've been waiting there. I thought there might be a story in that, but I didn't realise how far into myself I would be able to reach to work it into what I hope is an effective metaphor for the psychological effects of prolonged rejection and trauma.

I don't mind sharing that as a child, I was bullied for being 'weird', and time after time my fear that I didn't belong was confirmed by my peers. My romantic life from my teens into my late twenties was a disaster because I feared rejection so much that I would put up with any amount of neglect, dismissal, and sometimes emotional abuse, just for the 'safety' of having a boyfriend. Then I met a man who was like me, who'd also experienced rejection and neglect, but instead of becoming more compassionate towards others, he weaponised the empathy and grace he received. He was controlling and abusive because he was afraid, and if I'd had an angrier streak to my personality, that could have been how I treated others too. That could have been me being controlling and possessive and employing tactics to make my partner feel unworthy and overly grateful for any kind attention. A wonderful mental health professional helped me with that insight years later.

The protagonist of this story is an amalgamation of how I spent years feeling, my unhealthy attachment style (which, thankfully, I have now worked past), and as sincere a reflection as I was capable of drawing of how awful feeling so irrelevant for so long can be. The character is also a reflection of what I could have become, drawn from the entitled, possessive behaviour I endured from others, who were also suffering their own traumas.

The Scarlet Angels of Regret

Jonathan Maberry

"I AM THE KING of the world!" he shouted. Screaming it at the top of his lungs.

To no one.

No one at all.

* * *

He wasn't really sure he was ever actually *destined* to do what he did or be what he was. That was a question to be answered. Not satisfactorily. Not definitively.

But he was pretty damn sure that his parents were largely to blame.

Mind you, there were a couple of chances for them to steer the ship into safer waters, but instead they decided to steer right for the shoals. Upon his birth – the result of a dim understanding of the rhythm method and appalling math skills – he was saddled with the absolutely unfortunate name of Osgood Poppleton.

Actual name.

The first name wasn't too bad. Osgood. Had his parents nicknamed him Oz or Ozzie or something kind of cool, trendy, catchy, or at least ironic, they might have set him on a different path. Instead they called him Goodie.

Goodie Poppleton.

Bit of a challenge, really. People wouldn't even name a dog Goodie, unless they didn't like the mutt.

As he saw it, it all started there.

As for Poppleton...well, there's no way to walk back from that unscathed. There was no path to being normal with that kind of name, unless you hosted a kids' show on Nickelodeon, wrote silly picture books, or had a job like CPA or used car salesman. Otherwise, it's just a license for the whole world to take shots. Free, with no apologies. The bullies didn't even have to hit him. They merely mocked, and no one in the history of unkindness has ever been more biting or accurate in that regard than school kids.

His father had it maybe a little worse, being a proctologist, but Goodie had no sympathy for him.

Mom taught pre-K, so she was safe.

The only relative he had who managed to make the name work was Uncle Joey, who spent years doing dirty little jobs for a second-string mobster in South Jersey. Down there he was known by the vaguely threatening name of Joey Pops. That worked. You hear about a connected guy named Joey Pops and you put a whole different slant on what that '*Pop*' implied. Even people who didn't know what a button-man was understood that Joey Pops was likely someone with whom fucking around was a bad call. Also, Uncle Joey played the role well – velour sweatsuits to hide some flab, and a little belly gun tucked out of sight. Hawaiian shirts for fancier gigs, and cheeks so pitted from childhood acne that his face looked like an eroded wall.

But *Goodie* Pops sounded like an off-brand breakfast cereal, the kind with lots of unpronounceable ingredients and no nutritional value of any sort. A three-year-old would want his parents to buy Goodie Pops at the grocery store, but no one else would. By the time any kid was four, the name would have passed from cute to stupid with zero chance of recovery.

Not that Oz Pops would have been better, Goodie realized. Sounded like an attempt to cash in on the *Wizard of Oz* or the *Wicked* movies, without actually having something to say.

Goodie was pretty sure that the first time he was introduced to other kids in first grade and had to endure the laughter, things were set on a certain course. A jury wouldn't convict him if he'd set the school on fire. After all, first grade is when kids are six, and by then mockery, unkindness, and a desire to hurt with words was baked in. In preschool that kind of name was merely cute and funny, but the shelf life on that was short-dated and was gone by the time the numbered school years began.

He wrestled with accepting the name. Sure, it would have been great if Goodie was an eccentric painter, a standup comic, or a writer of strange little novels.

It was wildly inappropriate for someone who wanted to conquer the world.

He could not conceive of anyone who would take Goodie Poppleton seriously. Even *he* would not have done so.

So, of course he turned to evil.

* * *

Going full evil wasn't because he had a worldview knocked askew by trauma. Nothing that dramatic.

His parents had not tried to hurt him with the name or the nickname. They weren't corrupt, malicious, vicious or cruel. Had they been, he could have *used* that kind of upbringing to justify everything and maybe even garner some support. There are, after all, people who would leap to his defense and try to explain his actions as an inevitable outcome of parental villainy.

But no. His parents had none of that. They were merely idiots.

His desire to pursue evil was not something passed down. He was not trying address cultural, ideological, or religious issues. This was purely existential and, as far as he was concerned, no one else's existence really mattered. His sure as hell hadn't mattered to anyone.

So…evil. It was simple, comfortable, even imperative.

Evil masterminds, he decided one windy autumn morning, did not need to be liked. Hell, it's not like he was starting a cult. None of that personal exploitation of charisma. He didn't have to go all Jim Jones and give long-winded speeches. He didn't have to justify his actions to followers and then encourage them to buy in. He didn't need to build a compound somewhere and convince the sheep to turn over their money to him and let him screw their wives or any of that nonsense. Please. He had self-respect, even if no one else respected him. Nope. He went for evil mastermind and leaned into that hard. His bachelor's was a dual major – organic chemistry and robotics. Goodie reckoned that no good could ever come of those two sciences, and 'no good' was what he was up to.

For his master's he again split, going to molecular biology and applied robotics. Again, aiming at a target all the way.

He didn't have the money to get his PhD, and was self-aware enough to know that he could never play academic politics in a useful way. What he craved was knowledge, and he had a bagful of it.

Once he made the decision to do only harm, things started to fall into place.

The kickoff was when his parents accomplished their only real bit of what he viewed as *good parenting* by dying. And not just dying – they were cut down when a disease broke out on a cruise liner and killed them within the first forty-eight hours, leaving behind a couple of huge life insurance policies and solid grounds for a massive lawsuit. He got really good lawyers – meaning they were clearly as evil as he intended to be – and they sued the top five layers of flesh from everyone who owned shares in the cruise line company. The actual dollar amount he banked, after lawyers' fees and taxes, was – to use precise accounting terms – a shit-ton.

Not just millions, but *many* millions.

He did not use the money to pay off his college debt because (a) fuck that, and (b) he expected to outlive everyone who could possibly come after him for either principal or interest.

Goodie committed one act of unfiltered good, though. He had his parents moved from cheap graves to a snazzy mausoleum in one of the better cemeteries in Los Angeles. He even visited a couple of times. Not to bring flowers, because that was a bridge too far. But to talk to them, to tell them the truth about what he was planning. And to let them know it was their fault.

Sometimes he imagined that he saw their ghosts standing nearby, faces appalled at what he was saying. Goodie wasn't sure he was imagining it, either. The ghosts looked very real. But when they spoke to him, there was no sound. Only the quiet of the grave. Over time he could no longer tell if he was imagining it, was actually *seeing* ghosts, or if he had become a true *mad* scientist in point of fact.

He went with option three, though he believed option two to be likely. Despite being a scientist, he read a lot of books on metaphysics and was more than half convinced that ghosts were real, but part of an area of science that no one had yet figured out how to quantify.

Goodie never went back to the cemetery. Seeing them talk without sound was creepy as hell, and he had more important things to occupy his attention.

* * *

Looking back, his first real evil plot was to learn enough about computers to research those people who'd ruined so much of his life.

His first target was the credit card company that let an eighteen-year-old dig himself that deeply in debt. Next was the credit company that bought the debt so they could jack the interest up to 34 per cent the first year alone, then kept upping it as if crushing someone with debt who was already unable to pay made any kind of sense. And also the piranhas who worked for the collection agency that bought the unfulfilled debt from the previous company.

All of them were corrupt down to their mitochondria.

Once he identified the culprits, Goodie decided to use his knowledge of chemistry to add some oomph to anthrax and have it delivered as gift baskets. The irony of using what he learned in the school they were trying to make it impossible to pay for was not lost on him. Not even a little bit. That was his actual *point*.

When those people started dying, it took weeks before the authorities sussed out the connection between the various victims. Goodie bit his nails to the quick waiting for the big announcement that there was a domestic terrorist targeting people in the collections industry to hit the mainstream news. And then the bigger bounce when it all exploded into social media. During the wait, he penned a manifesto that was, at first, published anonymously from a variety of email accounts that were false.

For about three full days he was a goddamn internet hero.

Someone targeting bloodsucking debt ghouls was the stuff of legend. And, sure, there were plenty of times when – looking back – he realized that he could have stopped there. Could, and maybe *should* have. But the debt collectors were too small a target for him. They were faceless assholes who had not laughed at him all the way through school.

A couple of times after those deaths he caught glimpses of people he was sure were the ones he'd just killed. He'd done the research to know each of them from their social media pages and the pictures in the obituaries. These people would be standing there, speaking or even yelling at him – but without sound.

Very creepy.

Just as he was beginning research into the social media accounts of people who'd harassed him in school, social media turned and bit him.

Hard.

The problem was that a reporter doing a human-interest story on the inhuman debt-collecting bastards wrote a heart-rending piece about how the children of one of the most vile collections guys caught the anthrax and also died. The backlash against Goodie was immediate and it was massive. He was now a fiend, a heartless bastard, a vile monster who should be pilloried and then whipped to death.

Blah, blah, blah.

"What the actual hell?" he yelled, scaring his five cats so badly they hid for two days. "They're only kids. Rugrats. Ankle-biters. People don't even *like* kids. Ask any comedian. They complain about them all the time. What I did was a freaking public service."

Goodie was completely convinced that he was the wronged party here. Those were the kids of bad people. Seriously...did anyone really expect them to grow up to be decent human beings? How could they? He used his own upbringing – both nature and nurture – to justify those deaths. At worst, he reckoned, it was acceptable collateral damage. The cost of doing the business of removing real scumbags from the world. And yet everyone with a Facebook, Instagram, X, TikTok, Snapchat, Threads, or Bluesky account begged to differ.

It was on day eight or nine of the unrelenting vilification of the 'Evil Anthrax Child-Killer' that he realized there was no making some people happy. So, fuck it.

"You want evil?" he bellowed at the flatscreen TV on the wall. "You just watch. I'll ***show you*** evil."

* * *

He went with robots next.

Okay, well, drones. But robots sounded cooler.

Anyone with a master's in applied robotics can build a drone. A moderately bright hamster could build a drone. There was nothing challenging about it.

Attaching a high-capacity spray dispenser with enough oomph to project a viral medium downward and outward at a useful rate...? Yeah, that took brains, and Goodie had brains by the bagful.

He spent seven months buying the raw materials, two to increase lift capacity to compensate for the extra payload, and another four to get the sprayers working just right. The virus itself took some time. He had to spend nearly sixty-five thousand dollars in bribes, but hey, larceny is only a number, right? Everyone has a price, and he had millions in the bank and more millions in Bitcoin, which had finally come out of its slump. In the end, the person he bought came through, and Goodie considered that a bargain. Money very well spent.

Goodie remembered standing in his living room, holding up a newly delivered vial of Marburg. It looked like tinted water, and he refused to wire the balance of the bribe money until after he'd looked at it under the microscope.

Yup, Marburg. One of the most contagious and lethal viruses known to man.

He paid the guy, issued a few credible threats, but also dangled the promise of more cash, and that kept his man silent.

Even so, it took Goodie another fourteen months to tweak the Marburg. The CFR – case fatality rate – of the virus was in the 24–88 per cent range. Nasty, but not diligent enough. A lot of it depended on the level of medical attention sufferers had available. Currently, anyone with good medical coverage – and the money to insure only the best – were the ones most likely to survive. That seemed unfair to him, because only the poor would die.

So, he bribed his guy over and over again until he had a lot of samples of RSV, Covid, and several kinds of influenza. The top three.

He paid the man and praised him for his attention to detail. The anthrax Goodie slipped into the man's pockets before returning the guy's jacket to him was just natural tidiness.

Goodie spent months playing with the viruses, forcing them to mutate, building on the most energetic strains. Those viruses were the perfect delivery system for Marburg. They would guarantee a fast spread and an unnaturally quick onset to a global pandemic.

And he was right.

It would be really fast and it would hit really damn hard.

By the time he was ready, Goodie had nearly five hundred thousand drones. He'd invested in a 'sports drone' manufacturing company and mass-produced his single-use sprayer drones. Or – as he thought of them – spitters.

Goodie drove back and forth across America releasing the spitters. He shipped hundreds to very bad people in other countries – folks he found on the Dark Web – and paid these bad actors to carry out the releases. He told the ones in the Arab countries that the diseases were designed to work exclusively on the Jews. He told the Jews they'd work only on Arabs. He had similar campaigns for every group that hated another group enough to want to see some bodies fall. It was the same viral cocktail in every drone. He was an equal-opportunity mass murderer.

While he waited for it all to start, he paid very careful attention to the refinement of the series of antivirals with which he injected himself. It occurred to him at one point – a little late in the game – that had he shared his antiviral drugs with the world, he might have become the greatest hero who ever lived. They'd have actually stopped the yearly flu epidemics, all of the Covid variants, and even the common cold. To hell with Salk, Jenner, Koch, Pasteur, or Fleming.

But Goodie Poppleton was past that point.

Well past.

He locked the doors of his mansion, released the hounds – well, spitters – and waited.

* * *

It took exactly seventy-seven days.

The TV news went off the air around day forty.

The internet shut down nineteen days later.

All power was out a month later.

And the world went very, very quiet.

* * *

He loved that quietness.

It was so beautiful.

No talking heads nattering on about bullshit on the tube. No car horns. No noisy kids playing noisy games. No phones ringing. No emails.

Nothing but quiet.

Oh, there was birdsong and the rustle of wind through the trees. The hiss and sigh of waves breaking on his beachfront in Malibu. Sometimes dogs barked. He began playing that old Rolling Stones song over and over. The one with the line about not getting what you want but what you need. Yeah. Quiet was what he needed. No mockery. No condescending jokes. No singsong repetitions of his name. No sniggers. Nothing.

Only quiet.

Beautiful, restful, peaceful quiet.

* * *

On the eighty-first day he realized that it was *oddly* quiet. Like a little too quiet.

One day ninety-four the quiet was kind of weird. Maybe a little disturbing.

On day one-hundred-and-eleven it was *way* too fucking quiet.

It was somewhere around day one-hundred-and-thirty – give or take – that he realized that he really did not like all that damned quiet.

He yelled about it to his five cats. He yelled about it out on the lawn of his big, empty mansion. He drove up and down the Pacific Coast Highway, yelling it at the ocean and the bodies rotting in the Southern California sun.

He yelled about it in the shower. Being very specific about how he was right and the goddam son-of-a-bitching quiet was wrong.

Then one day he woke up and said, "*Oh god, what have I done?*"

* * *

There was a run of about four months where he went absolutely out of his mind. Not just wailing in remorse. Not only screaming to God to let him take it back.

No, we're talking weird.

Seeing ghosts kind of weird.

At first it was his parents, whose ghosts somehow made it from Westwood Village Memorial Park Cemetery in LA to his living room in Malibu. They stood there, staring with reproach at him. Screaming and screaming at him.

Screaming in silence.

After that, he started seeing his snotty Malibu neighbors. The actor from that sitcom. The director who made those dumb superhero movies. The singer with the big plastic boobs and no hips. All of them.

Shouting and shouting.

So quietly.

Goodie went out, went driving, and nearly wrecked his car when he turned to his right and the waitress from the oyster house on Topanga was seated right there in the shotgun seat, turned toward him, yelling. Without a sound.

He could see her trying, though. The veins in her neck stood out, and there was a really big vein on her forehead that looked ready to pop. But not a sound. Not even a whisper.

Everywhere he went, he saw ghosts.

A few at first, then more each day. Goodie wasn't sure if there was a pattern to it. One day there would be six, the next thirty-four, then over a hundred.

Ghosts, ghosts, ghosts.

Most of them just stood around, or followed him wherever he went. Bathroom time was the worst, though all of it was bad. Then, about a month into the comprehensive haunting, the poltergeists showed up. Goodie had no idea they were even much of a thing except in 1980s horror movies. But yeah. Real. A couple of them moved into his house and started messing with him. Moving his slippers. Putting cat shit *in* his slippers. Throwing stuff. Turning his flatscreen TV on and off, and swapping the DVDs he wanted to watch with stuff he'd already watched. The poltergeists had a thing for Hallmark movies, and Goodie didn't even own any. Yet stacks of those DVDs kept showing up.

All of the ghosts seemed to know who he was. All of them, regular spirits and poltergeists, yelled at him with that incessant silent shrieking.

So, sure…he lost his mind for a few days.

Okay, weeks. Let's be honest.

* * *

Then Goodie had a great idea that cleared his mind.

It was a moment like when the Grinch had an awful idea. A wonderful, awful idea.

* * *

Better still, it was a very *mad* scientist kind of idea. He was proud of it and wished the damn ghosts could applaud. Maybe they were unable to hear as well as speak. He filed that away for future experimentation.

Goodie was well aware that his new idea was as much weird science as it was maybe closer to twilight zone science.

"What's the mechanical equivalent of alchemy?" he asked his oldest cat, who was – like all five felines in his house – named Cat. He thought this was a smart name since they were only dumb animals.

Cat, being only a cat, just looked at him for a long moment, then turned and eloquently began to lick his anus.

Goodie sniffed and stalked downstairs to his lab. He'd had the former owner's lap pool and bowling alley ripped out and the huge basement converted into a truly magnificent lab. All the trimmings. Chem lab with a hot room. Electronics and robotics labs, complete with oversized 3D printers. He even had big rooms for raw materials and premade drone parts.

He also had one hell of a library. It had been big when he bought the place, but since his campaign of extermination he had tripled it, bringing in tons of books on every conceivably useful topic. He felt very smug and savvy for finding print copies of so many critical texts, because there was no internet anymore. No wifi, no streaming. Yet print endured.

The next eleven months were his research time. He often wore blinders to block out his peripheral vision so he couldn't see the silent, screaming ghosts, who now filled every room of his mansion. At night he wore a blackout visor.

He played music very loud because any bloody fool knew that the best muses for really *mad scientists* were classic metal. His favorite playlist included key cuts by Crowbar, Machine Head, Helmet, Anthrax, AC/DC, Soundgarden, and others. In his darker or drunker moments he regretted that they were all dead, too. In his really drunk moments he imagined their ghosts, dressed in leather and chains, singing at the top of their empty voices. His ideal version of Hell would be filled with metal bands with all the amps dialed to 11.

When Goodie was so drunk that he thought he was brilliant – a state even stupid drunks are familiar with – in that state he wondered if the ghosts could only hear *each other*. If so, then somewhere there was a metal concert with fifty bands and a few hundred thousand ghosts trying to cheer louder than the ghostly speakers.

He knew that his psychological and physical survival depended on being able to hear some of the ghosts. He wanted – *needed* – to hear those voices to make the world less quiet.

Oddly, the poltergeists tended to leave him alone when he was working. He wondered if they were not so much prankish as actually evil, and the concept of evil spirits somehow pleased him. He knew that if he had died before killing all those credit card asshats he'd have been happy to come back as a poltergeist and spend eternity driving them to suicide. So, the delinquent sprites seldom bothered him while he was trying to solve his ghost problem.

Mind you, Goodie did not want to bring the dead back to life. Not as zombies, though that would be kind of cool. And certainly not to fully aware life. Not after going to such painstaking trouble to kill them. Nope. His plan was so much smarter. He was sure of that. He wanted to *let* the ghosts speak or, granted, sing, but only when *he* wanted it. Voices that had an off switch. Voices with, maybe, a rheostat for volume control. And a dedicated remote that would only work with his thumb print.

Not that there was anyone else left with a thumb, but – tolerant of what Goodie did in the lab or not – he didn't trust the poltergeists to keep their ectoplasmic mitts off the remote.

Goodie spent nearly as much time with his stash of metaphysical books as he did with his hard science. And bit by bit, he figured out how to make the dead speak. In any other version of the world, that would have been perhaps the most significant feat in the whole history of science. That, he was absolutely sure of.

"I'm the smartest person *in the world*," he told Cat. And Cat, Cat, Cat, and also Cat. He wanted all five of them to know how smart their master was.

It was not until later that he realized his statement was both true and totally irrational. He called all of the cats into the kitchen and yelled again, clarifying what he meant to say.

"I'm the smartest person who *ever lived*."

The cats meowed because he was withholding their supper in order to focus their attention. He fed them and went back to his secret lab and began building the voices for the dead.

* * *

They were drones.

Bright, happy red ones. Technically, the paint was listed as 'scarlet.' He liked all intense shades of red, because it would make the drones easy to see from a distance. And they were pretty.

Each drone had little crystals inside – celestine, selenite, carnelian, moonstone, rose quartz, amethyst, and tourmaline – and these had been cut with great precision based on writings from Aleister Crowley. He attuned the drones using frequency theories from one of Tesla's untried experiments. He tucked a tiny pouch filled with Rose of Jericho, a plant that symbolized resurrection, along with pieces of lavender, thyme, myrrh, mugwort, chervil, and frankincense into each.

Writing the software code was almost a relief, because that, at least, wasn't sticking a big fat toe over the line into woo-woo territory.

"And who is going to say either jack or shit about it?" he asked himself in one of his more reasonable moments.

"Possibly the ghosts?" he replied, aware that several cats were giving him looks. "They might...y'know... resent what happened."

"First, don't be a pussy," he countered. "Second, don't be a dick. Third, if you don't like what they say, you can always turn them off."

To which he replied, "Wow...that's really smart."

He said, "I know, right?"

* * *

Goodie Poppleton walked past the dozen or so ghosts in the hall, and the crowd of them in the living room, and turned to squeeze past the two in the foyer. He knew they were incorporeal, but it felt weirdly rude to just walk straight through them. After all, he may have been a mass murderer, but he was polite about it. He ignored the poltergeists who were watching a Hallmark movie about a dog bringing total strangers together in time for the big Christmas concert at the town hall. He didn't recognize the actors, but the plot seemed familiar.

He carried two big plastic trash bags filled with what he had come to call his *scarlet angel* drones. Yeah, yeah, red is a color more commonly associated with demons and all, but as he saw things, it wasn't like the Devil held the trademark on red.

When he got outside, the street was filled with ghosts. He stopped counting at two hundred, and those were just the ones on the front lawn. When he walked to the corners, he saw that the side yards and backyard were crowded with ghosts. He set the bags down and waited until the ghosts had more or less formed a circle around him, then he knelt and opened them and began laying the scarlet angels on the grass. Each bag held fifty of them, and he spent some time unfolding the wings and making sure the special self-charging miniature solar panels were secure.

The ghosts watched him, and with a jolt he realized that their mouths were still. No speaking or shouting. No screaming. Odd how he could tell the difference even without sound.

He looked around at the translucent faces. "It's too quiet around here," he said reasonably. "I think we can all agree about that."

No response, just watchful eyes.

Goodie picked up a scarlet angel and held it out for inspection. "This is a special kind of drone.

Nothing like it has ever existed. If there was still a patent office, I'd...well...okay, that's not relevant. Might even be crass. Sorry."

The ghosts watched.

"What I mean," explained Goodie, "is that these are really unique. A lot of bleeding-edge science, which is kind of my thing. Some of you know that. I mean I *was* famous. Remember the Evil Anthrax Child-Killer guy? Yeah, that was me."

They watched, eyes unblinking.

"Okay, tough crowd. Point is the science is in there along with something that I really hate to call magic but it's...y'know...magic. I actually proved that magic exists and that it's really science. Kind of. That's a big thing. You guys have no idea how many people tried to prove that it even exists. But hey, check it out."

The eyes never blinked. He sighed.

"Right. Well, let's just say if this works – and it should work because I invented it – then you'll be able to speak again. Or...be heard. Not all of you, there's just too many. But as many as I can handle. I made a hundred of these and I'll make more."

No reaction. They weren't even moving.

He flicked the switch on the scarlet angel he held, and the tiny rotor instantly began whirling. The gathered ghosts leaned in a bit, apparently fascinated. Then Goodie looked around and spotted someone he recognized. It amused him that it was an actress who was in at least five of those Hallmark Christmas movies. Blond, skinny, pretty. Someone who wouldn't have spit on him if he was on fire back in the day.

He tossed the scarlet angel at her and watched it zoom over, pause for a moment in front of her, and then move forward slowly until it was inside her body. In her throat.

The actress looked alarmed. Then surprised, briefly angry, very confused, and scared. She turned to one of the other ghosts and spoke.

Not screamed. Just spoke.

"What's going on?" she demanded.

The other ghost looked confused. He held a cupped hand up near his ear and shook his head. With dawning wonder, Goodie realized two things. First, *he* could hear the actress speak. Second, the ghosts around her could not.

The actress turned toward him, startled to hear him speak. "You...you..."

"Yes," he said, interrupting. "I can hear you."

"Did not see that coming," he said aloud. Smiling, he took a whole bunch of the scarlet angels out, switched them on and sent them out into the crowd. "Party favors!"

Her look of consternation turned into something else. Darker. Stormy.

"You...you...fucking *asshole*," she screamed.

Goodie blinked.

Another ghost directly behind him roared, "You killed my entire family, you worthless, ugly piece of shit."

Before Goodie could reply, another ghost yelled. And another, and another.

Not really *yelled,* though.

They screamed.

They screamed bloody murder. Really loud. After all that quiet, it was like thunder. Goodie reeled, clapping his hands to his ears. The ghosts shrieked louder than any heavy metal amplifier. Everyone with a drone inside screamed at him.

They all knew him. They all knew who he was and what he'd done.

All of them.

As he turned in his panic, Goodie saw three of the most annoying poltergeists pulling scarlet angels out of the bags, turning them on and tossing them randomly into the crowd. Every drone found a throat, and every throat found its voice.

The screaming was horrendous.

Goodie staggered through the crowd toward the front door, but as he did so he dug furiously in his bathrobe pocket for the remote. It had the rheostat for volume control. He'd show them.

He dug and fished and scrabbled. Then he checked his other pocket, cringing as the screams grew louder.

Then Goodie froze.

The remote was not in any of his pockets.

"Over here, dickhead," said a voice and he whirled to see one of the poltergeists holding it and grinning like a ghoul.

"Give me that," Goodie snarled as he lunged toward the sprite. He blundered through many of the ghosts, and in one case even succeeded in knocking loose the drone, stilling that one voice.

Only that one.

The poltergeist danced away, laughing a high, shrill, piercing laugh.

Goodie chased him.

They went across the lawn, over hedges, through yards, out onto the highway, back to his property, back out to the street. By then Goodie was screaming, too. The hundred ghosts with scarlet angels were all in full voice now. They chased him.

Relentlessly.

All day. Everywhere he went.

When Goodie tried to go back inside, he found his door locked, and a familiar mocking laugh coming from the other side.

He pounded on the door until his hands were bruised and bloody. Then he picked up a rock and hurled it through a plate glass window, knocking a hole big enough to let him crawl very, very carefully through.

Almost through.

The screams muffled the sound of the rest of that heavy glass snapping loose from the frame. It fell silently. Like an axe. Like a guillotine.

When he woke, he was on his own floor. In a red lake that was as bright as the paint on the drones. He got up and looked around. Saw the ghosts. Saw the poltergeists.

Saw Goodie Poppleton laying in a lake of blood.

He said, "No."

One hundred ghosts screamed *yes.*

He heard their voices.

Their screams.

So loud.

So loud.

Going on and on and on.

Eternity, he discovered, is a very long time. And he was going to spend it listening to the screams of those ghosts. Those solar panels would keep the scarlet angels charged for years.

Many, many years.

When he screamed, none of the other ghosts seemed to mind.

Or care.

The cats cared, though. They were very emotionally involved in the large amount of cooling meat sprawled in the nicely open window. Dinner and a stroll?

Cat suggested that to Cat, Cat, Cat, and Cat.

They were all delighted.

Author Note

So much harm is done on any given day when worldviews collide. Worse still, when someone feels that their worldview is the only valid one, and is compelled to enforce that vision. We know about Hitler and Genghis Khan and Napoleon, but there are many more less famous people who acted on their need to rewrite the world to fit what they believed.

My father was one such.

For him, a differing worldview was proof that anyone in opposition was wrong. He tolerated no objection, would allow no contrary opinions. He acted without hesitation to set the world in balance.

His intractability manifested quite often as violence.

He hated people of color and therefore not only joined the Ku Klux Klan, but rose to run the local chapter. He openly said that Black people were not human, as he saw humanity. If Black families moved into our neighborhood, he was one of the first to hurl a Molotov cocktail through their front window. Sadly, that's not an exaggeration.

His hatred of Jews – he felt – justified his wish that the Nazis had completed their Final Solution. And he said this openly and often.

His hatred of the growing autonomy of his children was such an insult to his sense of ownership of them that he oppressed us all with violence and sexual abuse, justifying it as only his right. If he'd had the power, he would have reached out to reshape the world into his skewed image of what was true and right.

If he read this story, he would think Goodie was admirable and justified, and would judge the ghosts – and those five cats – as the villains.

Bangs

Emily Ruth Verona

SIX TEETH. That is how many teeth should be visible when I smile. Fewer and my lips look flat and uneven. More and it draws the skin too taut, adds a wild glint to my eyes and makes the skin beneath my chin bunch up. It's hard to look pretty. The kind of pretty that people call pretty.

I've had years of practice staring into the bathroom mirror and cataloguing every minute detail for deeper study. Figuring out how to best accentuate even the most hopeless of flaws. I know tilting my head to the left enlarges the shape of my nose. Makes my face look bloated. When I turn right, however, the line of my nose is more bearable – not perfect by any means, but the best I can do with what I have. That angle also highlights what little there is to highlight of my cheekbones. So, whenever anyone tries to take a picture, I make sure to tilt right. Smile a six-teeth smile. Look pretty.

My hair has never been an ally. The deep, natural copper-based red of it is good enough, but it's stubborn and thick and falls in jagged little waves around my face. Not cute curls or gentle beach waves. Angry Medusa snakes pointed every which way. Like they're pissed about something. I haven't found the trick to it yet, but it's not for lack of trying. I've changed my shampoo. My conditioner. I've tested creams. Mousses. Sprays. They all either turn my hair greasy or leave it unbearably crunchy and stiff. Finally, I just decided to get it all chopped off. Keep it nice and bobbed, so the waves don't have enough room to get too reckless. I can brush the mess as best I can and hope for a decent-hair day. My face, though – my face I can fix. With time. With care.

The bathroom has the brightest lighting in the apartment, even if the space is small. I lean in over the sink and examine every curve in the mirror. Every blemish. The chapped skin of my lower lip and the way my right eyebrow has more of a natural arch in its shape than the left. I take out the magnifying mirror, the little one that can be propped against the soap dispenser, and proceed to tweeze. That's always the first step. Tweezing. Pulling those few rogue hairs from my chin and then tackling all the strays that crop up like weeds around my eyebrows. I have nice, thick eyebrows. They don't need shaping, but there are plenty of outliers to pluck.

I've waited till today to tweeze. My sister's birthday party is in a little over an hour and if I'd gone and tweezed sooner, I would have run the risk of the hairs growing back in enough to be seen but not quite substantially enough to be gripped and yanked out with the tweezers. Tweezing does turn my skin a little red – on rare occasions a follicle is rooted so deeply the removal of it draws blood – but I have a decent foundation and concealer at my disposal. My skin could be nice, has a natural tone to it which I've always liked, but my nose and cheeks are sensitive and redden quickly. It doesn't take much. A rush of crisp morning air. A moment of mild embarrassment. The slightest irritation of a plucked hair. They say a little rosiness in the cheeks is good, but on me it just looks wrong. So, I blend that rosiness away with a smooth seamless foundation. It makes me paler than I usually intend to look, but pale looks prettier in pictures than fire engine red. Red cheeks make you seem drunk. Or worse, sweaty. I sweat too much, I know. It's a problem. One I'm hoping the foundation will hide at the restaurant as it's likely to be crowded and stuffy and packed with people who adore Lettie like she's a goddess dropped from heaven. My sister Lettie inherited all the best features from both of our parents. Our father's delicate nose and our mother's big, beautiful eyes. Lettie's cheekbones are flawless, and her face is the same shape as Audrey Hepburn's.

She's tall and thin to the point where everything, even ugly clothes, look elegant and beautiful on her. Imagine being pretty enough to dress ugly whenever you want.

After the plucking and the foundation, I move on to the eyeliner. I don't use eye shadow. I wish I could. But my hands don't possess the artistry for it, and my eyes are shaped in such a way that eyeshadow once it smears looks extra messy and unforgiving. It's easier to just forgo it altogether. My hand is hardly steadier for the eyeliner, but I can't exactly go without that. I have chestnut brown eyes that really need to be framed by a good liner to pop. It takes a few tries. Three, to be exact. With every mistake I have to start from scratch, rubbing the penciling out with a wet makeup wipe and then drying the patch of skin before beginning again. I can't afford too many mistakes because all the rubbing will turn the whites of my eyes red and the last thing I need is bloodshot eyes with my blotchy cheeks all teetering on my hopelessly weak chin.

The chin is really what carries a person's face – not anatomically, of course, but in terms of serving as a base for all your other features. It's the fine point to which we are all drawn. Or, in my case, the weak lump on which I try to balance.

When I finally get the eyeliner just right, wispy with a firm sense of dimension, I apply some extra foundation where the wipe took a little off and lean back to examine myself in the big mirror over the sink. Looking at your face half-done is like looking at a drawing done by a five-year-old. There's definitely something there, but you have no idea what it is or if it's what the artist had originally intended. You want to ask – to open your mouth and say "why?" but you can't. You're afraid to admit you don't know. Afraid to hurt the five-year-old's feelings.

Lipstick will save me. Lipstick is always my favorite. My lips look good with a little color. I have a pretty pout of a bottom lip and, while the top is somewhat thinner, it's got a nice shape to it. When it's filled in with a little lip liner and Crimson Passion, it's almost even sexy. That's my biggest problem too, though. I'm sure of it. Sexy and pretty can coexist, but one does not necessarily guarantee the other. It's not hard to look sexy if you know your features, know what to flaunt and how to flaunt it, but pretty – pretty is different. Temperamental. Like a plant that won't grow.

They say if redheads are going to wear red lipstick it should match their hair, but with how pale this foundation makes me, I can't really afford to look too washed out. So, I go bright. Not too bright, but bold. Crimson Passion is the perfect shade between a bright scarlet and deep carmine. It adds an element of vitality, I think. After applying it using the magnifying mirror, I glance up again at the sink mirror, tilt my head to the right as if posing for a picture. Decent.

Not great, but not bad. It would help if I had a steadier hand. I can't draw or blend as sophisticatedly as I'd like, but we have to work with what we've got.

I tilt my chin up, eliminating that little pouch of flabbiness under my neck and accentuating the line of my jaw. Sometimes I like my jaw. Sometimes I hate it. I guess it's just one of those things. It would be nice if I could take a piece of sandpaper to it – even out the shape a little. Not that my clumsy hands would be fit for the task.

Occasionally, I think I'm almost naturally pretty. And it's worse than being ugly, because the potential is there. Pieces of my face can look really nice individually, but together – together they're not cohesive. It's like mixing up a few pieces from two very similar but ultimately different puzzles. The full picture will never be flawless. It will hardly be a picture at all.

I am far from flawless, but I can strive to look at least less flawed and that's what really matters. They say it doesn't, but what they mean is it *shouldn't* and that's not the same thing at all. And it's not that beautiful is inherently better than not beautiful, but we ascribe value to it and in doing so solidify beautiful's place as a highly prized commodity. We think it's important. And that makes it important.

I frown in the mirror, but only for a second. Because frown lines are no good. But I wish there was something I could do. You know, there are days when I'm certain bangs could fix my face. In practice they'd probably just make it worse, but we like to believe there's something we can do to transform ourselves – something that is simple and affordable and within our power – and for me it's bangs. Every so often I'm struck by the overwhelming impulse to try them. Just take the scissors one day and *snip, snip, snip*. Like they do in movies. When a girl is ready to change her life.

I check my face in the small mirror again, then the big one – *again*. I pull up a pleat of hair from the back of my head and fold it over the front to imagine what bangs would do. My forehead is small and that is worrisome, but bangs might make my face, overall, look a little less long. A little more Audrey Hepburn.

Opening the drawer, I drop the lipstick and the lip liner inside and flash a longing look at the scissors. At least, the look was meant to be quick, but now that I've got my eyes on those scissors it's even harder to look away. What if I did it? What if I threw out all sense and restraint and just gave myself some bangs? Lettie would be shocked. I just know it. She never thought I could pull off bangs. It would surprise her. And if someone is never going to be impressed by anything you do, then surprised is the next best thing.

I take the scissors out of the drawer, just to feel them in my hand, the firm but easy weight, and hold them up so I can see them in the mirror behind the sink.

There's a smile on my Crimson Passion lips. A small, subtle smile. The kind you always *want* the camera to capture but it isn't noticeable enough and you just end up looking mad instead. Or bored.

I have neither the talent nor the skill to cut my own bangs. But, just for fun, I pull out a single strand of hair – not a top strand that might frizz but one from a layer close to the neck – and cut the end off. *Snip.* It's immensely satisfying. Shedding a piece of yourself. I take another strand from the same place, cut the tip of that one too. *Snip*. It's such a crisp, concise sound.

Setting the scissors down on the counter, I lean in over the sink and consider my features line by line. Forehead. Brow. Nose. Upper lip. Lower lip. Chin. Neck. I wish I had a delicate deer neck like Lettie. Mine more resembles the stump of a tree. If only I could shave a little off. Like with my jawline. Or cut a new silhouette for it like hair.

Those two loose little flecks of cut hair lie dormant on the bathroom counter. I go to sweep them into the sink, but they get stuck on my fingers and I have to turn the faucet on to rinse them loose. That's the mistake, because I do it quickly and dry my hands hastily and without thinking – before I can even realize what is happening – I scratch at an itch in the corner of my left eye with a not-quite-dry finger.

A gasp spits out of my mouth like bile, and I turn to the mirror, horrified. The eyeliner. I smudged the eyeliner. *Damn it*. I have to start over. There's no way to fix the cascade of charcoal black that now stretches like a melancholy rainbow across my eyeline. That's the side I show for pictures. *Double damn it*.

Without a moment to lose I've got another makeup wipe and am trying to wipe the eye perfectly clean so I can start over, but I'm frazzled and my hands are shaky. Just like the first time around, it takes a few tries and then, even when it's finally bearable, it still doesn't look as good as it had before. I could do it again, but what if it turns out worse? Besides, it's getting late and I'm already starting to sweat – that gross, dewiness surfacing from beneath the foundation. Fresh and vivacious on most but disgusting on me. Plus, my eye is all watery from the rubbing to remove and reapply the liner. If only I had bangs, then at least they'd help to distract from my eyes if not shield them entirely.

The idea courses through me again like a rush of adrenaline. I could cut them. Don't some girls cut their own bangs? Yeah. Sure. Pretty girls. Naturally pretty girls. Girls like Lettie. They can get away with a thing like that. But my watch says I have to leave in twenty minutes and I don't know what to do about the eye or the sweating and it's just a mess.

I fluff at my hair, unruly as always, fussing with the front. Maybe bangs will help. And if not, well, I could call and make an excuse. Say I have a migraine or something. Lettie would understand. In fact, I could probably just skip the whole thing without a word and she wouldn't even notice. Lettie has friends – good friends. Everyone loves her. She doesn't need her sweaty, awkward sister with the big nose getting in the way. Ruining all the pictures with my innate mediocrity.

My fingers press to the countertop, feeling for the scissors. I slip my fingers into the loops of the handle and stare at the mirror over the sink into my not quite big enough, always a little sad-looking, chestnut eyes. Catharsis hums in the tips of those fingers. All my fingers. I can feel it fizzing in my brain. That urge to do something impulsive. Daring. Un-take-back-able. What if it's the sort of thing you can't know for sure won't work until you try it? Yes. Surely. Like a dress that looks bad on the rack but good on the body. *A* body. Not mine.

I drop the scissors again, find a hairbrush and carve out a little section between the part of my hair with my forefinger. I fold the hair in half, but it's not quite right so I add a little more. They need to be fluffy. Effortless-looking. Isn't that funny, how 'effortless' always requires the most effort. The most consideration and care. Pulling in a deep, deep breath, I let the air fill my chest. Hold it. Pick up the scissors and – *snip!*

Snip, snip, snip! The hair falls into the sink. My lips part. It's uneven but almost in a shabby chic way. I trim and shape it a little, pressing my face closer to the mirror. Curls of red lay scattered across the inside of the sink like little drops of blood. My stomach drops.

Not shabby chic. Just shabby. I should have known. I should have known I couldn't do it. I want to cry. My lips part to do so, but that just worsens the effect. Now I have bad hair and look like I'm going to puke. Maybe I will. Maybe if I throw up enough, I can sound more believable when I tell Lettie I can't make it. Not now. *Look at me*. The bangs cover my eyebrows, my actually nice eyebrows, and that just puts unwanted emphasis on my big, bumpy nose. This damn nose that has led more than one person to ask if I'd somehow broken it as a child. Because apparently that's a perfectly suitable thing to ask someone. Especially when they've got a big nose and a forgettable face.

Placing the scissors on the counter, I use my palms to pull back the skin of my neck. Because maybe that will help. If I could only look more delicate then maybe my rougher features won't matter so much. Only, there's nothing to do about my neck. Unless I tape it. Could I tape it back? The skin? No. No, that wouldn't work because my hair is too short and you'd see the tape on the back of my neck. Possibly my cheeks, but I haven't found a good direction to pull the skin of my cheeks in. Up is unflattering and down deepens those awful lines that angle out from the sides of my nose to the corners of my lips.

Grabbing the scissors, I place the flat edge up against the skin of my jawbone and pull to see what it would look like if I had less skin there. Not too bad. If only there were a way to trim it. Pull it back and add a stitch to keep it in place. Sure, that's what facelifts are for, but you never want to say you 'had work done' especially when you're young. No. You want it to be natural. Feel natural. An authentic evolution of features. Effortless.

The stainless steel of the closed scissors feels good against my skin. I shut my eyes and imagine myself with Lettie's attributes. The elegant easiness of them. My eyes open again. I suck my cheeks in, just a smidge, and there it is. A solution. The inside. If I can't get rid of the outward excess maybe I could lose some of the indoor fat, so to speak. Cut a little of it out of the inside of my cheeks. Put greater emphasis on the cheekbones. No one would even see the cuts because they'd be on the inside of my mouth, and I don't have to talk much at this thing.

It could work. I know it could. Only my mouth is small and it's hard to open wide enough. Figure out how much I need to remove from each side to keep both cheeks even. And the blood. I will need to account for that. I can put gauze in for now, but leaving it in all night would defeat the purpose of removing all that excess in the first place.

I stretch my jaw as wide as it can go, put the partially opened scissors in my mouth, and press the blade up against the inside of my left cheek. Not too deep. Too deep would pierce the outside and I can't have that. I close my eyes. Hold my breath.

Snip!

The pain is immediate and ongoing mostly because the scissors are too dull to completely cut away a clump of fat in one go. A little piece of loose cheek is still clinging to the inside of my mouth. I can feel it pulling. And so, I cut and cut and cut until I am sure it is loose and spit the freed flesh into the sink.

If I hesitate now, I won't have the courage to do the other side and so I quickly repeat all the steps with the inside of my right cheek, this time pressing harder with the scissors so that it only takes three squeezes instead of five. More blood and tissue are spit into the sink. It's all loose hair and discarded flesh in there now. Pieces of my former self. But I think this is helping. The pain burns, but it's a pure burn – a defining one. There's so much blood pooling in my mouth and I didn't bother to take the gauze out ahead of time, so I stuff some toilet paper in there to stop the bleeding and return to the mirror.

Only, with my cheeks stuffed full like this, you can really see now how small and wrinkly my chin can be. Especially when I frown. It wouldn't be so bad if not for the skin that connects my jaw and my neck. There's just so much of it. Too much. How I would love to take some off.

The bloody scissors are still in my one hand. Maybe I could take away a little skin – a centimeter from that plump part just below the ear before the jaw. I could put Band-Aids on afterwards and style my hair over my ears, so no one sees. Yes. That might do it.

I lift the scissors to my jawline. It needs to be done right or else I won't be able to hide it with my hair. I get as close as I can to the earlobe without coming up against the bone. I can trim some of the skin and pull it back. Not the whole side. Just enough to show some definition.

Snip!

The burn as the scissors pierce the flesh is different here. It has more of a bite to it and, as the skin joins the rest of the garbage in the sink, a shaky breath slithers out from between my toilet-papered cheeks. Quick. The other side. Then the band aids.

I work fast – I have to – and it hurts more than anything has ever hurt before. But pain is temporary. It doesn't feel like it will be, but it is. If I can get beyond the pain then I can reap the reward. Look effortless. Pretty.

I apply the band aids, but they aren't as strong as I'd imagined they'd be and there's more blood than I'd anticipated. It's streaming down my neck like tears, slippery and stubborn. The collar of the little black dress I had taken such pains to choose as it's less unflattering than most of my dresses, is stained with it. I should have put a towel around my shoulders. *Fuck*.

It takes three band aids on each side to get the bleeding under control, only now you can definitely see the bandages no matter how I wear my hair. It's useless. Completely useless. Everything burns. The inside of my face. The outside. A searing pain. And the tears in my eyes have smudged the eyeliner and the color has gone all blotchy again in my cheeks. At least my lips still look all right. If anything, the blood from the inside of my mouth has only added a deeper stain to the Crimson Passion.

The buzz – the adrenaline – is still swirling in my brain but less so than it had been initially and the shock of it is making me dizzy. There's nowhere to sit except the toilet and it feels too far away. Instead, I brace both palms on the counter to steady myself. Look up into the mirror.

Something doesn't look right. In fact, all of it looks wrong. I've cut too much from too many places and now the parts that I didn't touch don't seem to fit to scale. The skin on either side of my nose, under my eyes, for instance, isn't right. I'm not sure how exactly, but I can tell. Maybe there's something I can do. Maybe I can fix this too.

I grab the scissors and stare at my face in the mirror, smile a six-tooth smile so I know just how much needs to come off to keep my face from looking wrong in the pictures. Just a little more trimming and then I will have it. Then I will be pretty enough. Or close to enough. I know it. There isn't that much hair and blood and skin in the sink. There's still room for more. Just a few more cuts and my face will be perfect. The kind of pretty people call pretty. Like it's supposed to be. Perfect. Easy. Effortless.

Snip! Snip! Snip!

Author Note

When I was maybe five or six years old, I became convinced that I'd grow up to be pretty. It felt inevitable. I had a cute little face and beautiful eyes and a lovable smile. How could I not turn out pretty? It felt exciting to get older. I couldn't wait to grow into myself. Then, puberty hit. I developed curves I didn't want, and my nose became longer and less smooth than I had expected. It felt devastating, as if my body had betrayed me. Everyone else in my life, my friends and my family, were all so beautiful and I was...not. Or, so I believed. It is easy to believe such a thing at such an age. Society breeds specific and unrealistic expectations, especially in young girls. It breeds insecurity, which is its own kind of rot. Over time, insecurity can poison your self-esteem until you believe yourself to be a failure as a person – a disappointment to everyone who has ever pretended to love you (because, yes, my insecurity manipulated me into thinking they were only pretending). We see in ourselves what we believe to be true, regardless of what the truth actually might be. It took me a long time to realize this, perhaps longer than I'd even like to admit. I wrote 'Bangs' because I now understand that the insecurity I experienced as a teenager and young adult was predatory. Something like that can do terrible things when left unchecked. I wish I hadn't spent so many years punishing myself for misconceived shortcomings. I wish I had believed others when they told me that the terrible things I thought about myself were not the sum of my parts. They weren't even real. They were rot.

Sawn Wife

Stephen Volk

I HATED HIM before he killed me, and, of course, I loved him before that. Every marriage has its ups and downs, I know. But ours was blessed by many more ups than downs, even if the 'down' that ended it was a pretty big one.

I had thought him a great man. He was called The Great Kavalyov, so that was a hint. The most famous magician in Petersburg. Perhaps the whole of Russia. A girl can't fail to be impressed by a man who can produce a coin from behind your ear or the Queen of Spades from your cleavage. You couldn't help wondering what other secrets he had up his sleeve, besides doves. Or, at least, I couldn't.

His biggest trick, looking back on it, was to convince himself he adored me. I think I gave him reassurance. Said I believed in his talent when he needed it most, and provided the attention he craved more than food and drink. In return he showered me with gifts and set me on a pedestal marked 'do not touch', superior to all examples of the female sex, except when he plummeted and, in bereft darkness, he would demean me in front of my friends and make me shrink to a quivering nothing. I was nineteen and I'd come from nothing, so it didn't take much. Sometimes, on his arm, I'd feel like the sparkling duchess at the most beautiful ball in a romance by Pushkin. On other occasions like a cur he would gladly put down, and he did put me down, when jealousy and vodka turned love to poison.

He must have been planning it for a while, how to bump off the saint turned adulterer. I imagine he gave as much thought to his method of ridding the world of me as he did to the design of a fantastic new illusion. Dreaming about it. Stroking his chin as he pondered the practical problems. Weighing up the pros and cons. Something suitably apt. Something that would teach her a lesson. The idea must've occurred to him during one of his performances, as the teeth of the shining-sharp blade cut down into that slot between the two boxes. Sighing-shimmering as it pulled and pushed, pulled and pushed…

Sawing a woman in half! His most acclaimed showstopper.

What could be better?

"Tonight I shall cut my wife in half," Kavalyov must've thought gleefully in his gleeful moments.

"That'll teach her for messing around with other men, that wanton hussy. And if half of Petersburg is in the audience, who cares? They will see what I have done. And if the police cart me off to prison, I shan't complain. Everyone will know what a witch she has been and how badly she treated her husband, who did nothing but love her and dote on her for years and give her a luxurious lifestyle. When did she last beg for a loaf of bread?"

I knew nothing of this. I was donning my spangly outfit with all the pearls and feathers, coating my eyelids with lapis lazuli makeup and my lips with a scorching red that would dazzle in the limelight. I knew the routine of the sawn-in-half-lady by heart after having done it a hundred times, and knew what was required of me (not that I am going to share it here: the confidentiality of the Magician's Code is paramount!). Having said that, I had no notion of his evil intent as he escorted me into the familiar contraption and closed the lid.

I lay with my stupid grinning head sticking out of one end of the coffin-sized box and my feet protruding through the holes at the other. Kavalyov tweaked my big toe, and I giggled as I always did. The audience laughed. His patter continued as he tweaked his moustache. I gazed up at his face as his jaw moved and a trickle of sweat navigated his cheek. The dye in his eyebrows was running. He grimaced with horse teeth as he leant over, lining up the blade of the saw using an extended index finger for precision, pausing to give me a wink before he started going in.

The wooden box moved under me on its trestle, but not a lot more than usual, though Kavalyov was applying more than his usual gusto. He seemed almost frantic with concentration and a curl of black hair fell onto his forehead.

My smile was intact when I felt the fangs of the tool ripping across my garment, but it was gone when it ripped across my skin. The music of its motion became hypnotic, and I was sure I would pass out. I mean, die. I realised dispassionately I didn't have the breath to cry out. Probably shock. I didn't even consider the strangeness of this method of execution. I was busy wondering how long it would take to slice through my internal meat and get to my spine – hello! That's it, sounds like! Something cracked me open like an egg.

From my odd vantage point, I watched him pull apart the two halves of the box, passing between them to be drenched in the thunderous applause that was forthcoming. He took a bow and stepped through the red curtain to take another. The crowd were giving him a standing ovation.

(Bravo, you bastard! I thought.)

Needless to say, I was surprised to find I was still alive, as, no doubt, you are too.

* * *

"Good show tonight," I said as Kavalyov returned to the dressing room after a night out with his friend Vasily. He always got half-cut with Vasily after a show. His head swivelled so sharply it almost dislocated his neck. He couldn't believe I was sitting at the mirror removing my makeup. And he couldn't believe that I sat there severed at the waist, everything below my belly button non-existent.

The scream that came from him was roughly equivalent to that which might have occurred had a rat been inserted up his rear passage. His feet left the floor and his back flattened against the wall.

I wiped away the scarlet of my lipstick. In the mirror I saw him shrink away, trembling, then turn to grab the door handle. Another scream even more appalling than the first escaped his lungs.

He had seen the bottom half of me propped against the table under the framed poster of an old, dead clown. My legs, hips, and pelvis – shapely, if I do say so myself – rested there as nonchalantly as a drunk leaning against a lamp post.

"Do cover yourself up, my dear," I said. "You're showing all you've got." I tossed a towel in her direction. It floated down to cover her like a skirt. She crossed one leg over the other with a sort of insouciance.

I thought Kavalyov would faint.

"It'll be all right." I turned to him and opened my arms wide. "Cuddle up, the two of us."

Having dropped to his knees, he waddled to me and I took him to my bosom. The reek of vodka rolled off him like mist from the sea, making my eyes water.

"There, there." I petted his cheek and tried my best to soothe him. I told him to light a candle if it would make him feel better. Say a prayer, perhaps. To Serapion of Novgorod, perhaps. That's what my mother always did. But he was in a right old state, was Kavalyov. Couldn't relax at all. I encouraged him to sleep. Sleep it off, in a way, but no.

"I can't. It's her. Watching."

"She can't watch, petal," I said, pointing out the obvious. "She has no eyes."

My bottom half was tapping her bare feet. He was staring at her small toes. My small toes.

"No. It's no good. I can't bear it." Sobbing, Kavalyov broke away from me and used the handles of the drawers of the desk to climb to his feet. He wiped green snot from his nose – all the more lurid in the glare of the light bulbs that surrounded my mirror – and looked at my other half with terrible, hateful disdain. "I have to…I have to…"

"Do what you have to do," I said.

He whispered into my ear in a tremulous voice that he had decided to dispose of the bottom half of the corpse.

"Don't call me a corpse," I murmured. "That's not very nice, is it?"

* * *

Kavalyov wrapped her in sailcloth he stole from the prop store. It wasn't hard to hail a cab near the theatre district and it didn't look suspicious because he was only carrying half a dead body, not a whole one. There were probably lots of people carrying half-corpses around Petersburg, for all he knew. If pressed, he could say he was transporting rifles, or part of a cannon. Or food. Keep it vague is probably best. Tools is another one. Tools is good. Definitely not legs. Definitely not the naked legs and hips and generative organs of a formerly alive female. Definitely not that.

After the cab dropped him off, Kavalyov carried my bottom half to the Catherine canal, which starts at the River Moyka at the Field of Mars and flows into the Fontanka. At that point, under cover of darkness, he couldn't resist his urges and unwrapped her like a long loaf, made an A of her legs, and inserted himself. It was his way, and she couldn't stop him – being minus her arms – and he, poor thing, poor man, could not stop himself.

This I know because she knows, and she is me.

* * *

"The cause of all our troubles is gone at last." He shook raindrops off his cloth cap and hung it up on a peg. I saw a patch of wetness around his groin.

"There, there…" I said as we lay on the small bed in the dressing room, and he pulled up the blanket to cover my raggedly severed stump of a midriff. I wondered if a small part of him wanted to pull the blanket away and – hey presto! – I'd be revealed to be whole again. But no. Shivering, he kissed my cheeks and forehead. It was almost like old times, but his mouth was icy.

"You're not going to dispose of me, are you?"

"Don't be silly, Ma-ma," said Kavalyov, using his pet name for me. "I love you. More than anything."

We drifted asleep in each other's arms. I daresay his legs would have entwined mine if I had any.

His nose was almost touching my own when, in the middle of the night, I saw his eyes flash wide open. I heard the same gentle pitter-pattering as he did. With a grunt he heaved himself up on his elbows, then groaned deep in his chest as if someone was extracting his lungs with a spoon.

My lower half stood in the middle of the room, actually squatting to be exact, a golden rope of piss running from her front hole to the carpet. Tinkle, tinkle, tinkle. A spreading pool forming under her. I'd forgotten I'd drunk three or four glasses of water while my husband had been out.

"No." He rubbed his eyes, but the vision wasn't eradicated.

He sobbed as the flow of urine stopped and she straightened her knees. I liked those knees. My papa always said that when the rest of me went, I'd always have good knees.

"No… How did she get here?"

"Well, she has legs, my darling," I said. Though the legs in question were wet and streaked with the weeds and moss she'd accrued from being dumped in the canal.

His nostrils flared. I could see he was disgusted.

"I don't want her here." He covered his head with the moth-eaten blanket. "She smells."

"Only of you, my sweet."

"This time I'll cut her up in tiny pieces. I'll…I'll burn her!"

"It's your desire that's burning," I told him calmly. "You can't put that out."

I touched his earlobe but he shrugged me off, whimpering. He looked like a little boy lost, bless him.

"What am I supposed to do?"

"Have you heard the expression ménage à trois? We can live in harmony together, the three of us."

"You must be joking. How would that work?"

"Free love. That means you can make love to her and I won't mind." I could see he was less than convinced. "Go on." He tried to look away, but I turned his cheek to face her nakedness. She rocked her hips from side to side, making her dancing patch of hair all the more alluring. "Don't knock it till you try it, big boy."

I sensed saliva on his lips and hunger in his eyes. Dog and steak hunger. Peasant and potato hunger. But he shut it off. The dungeon door clanged.

"I can't. I can't! Not with you watching."

"I'll close my eyes. Pretend you're kissing my lips when you kiss hers."

He sat up. He tore off his nightshirt – an action I remembered usually prefigured a night of passion in those bygone years of affection and mutual longing. He stood. He put on his trousers. He took them off. His arse was white as cotton. His cock was red as rhubarb.

He dropped to his kneecaps on the pee-sodden carpet. Squidged. Teetered dwarflike forward. His hair tousled, the flames of a half-dead fire. His two hands, fat fingered, went to her two hips, steadying them from their figure-of-eight gyrations, and he brought the cup of her towards him, that verdant valley, that palace, faltering only at the last lip-curling hurdle.

"I can't. It's no good, I can't."

"Why? You like her, don't you? You've always liked her more than you like me."

"No! Yes. No! I mean, yes. I mean…"

"You mean?"

"I mean…I love you and I hate her."

"But she makes you happy."

"Don't say that. Don't!"

"Does she make you happy?"

He shuddered. Chin to churning chest. Strings of his head cut. "I don't know."

"Why?"

"Who wouldn't?" said the magician. "She doesn't answer back. She does what I say without question. She never says no."

"She can't say no. She has no tongue. Leg, calf, though, yes. Pudenda, yes. Tongue, no."

"That's why I hate myself."

I said: "Interesting." Hmm… "Perhaps you need to get to know her after all these years. You know what they say. A stranger is just a friend you haven't met yet."

He eyed my legs as if I'd asked him to mate with a sow. And an ugly one at that.

"She won't talk to me, will she?"

Not with that mouth, billy-o. Not even in a story like this.

I gave a rolling gesture with one hand, an invitation to the dance. Proceed. Take your partner. Fill your face. Meanwhile I shall turn up the whale oil. I plumped the pillow and planted my thorax on it.

He made love to my other half while I watched,

eating bonbons to the sound of the pumping and rutting. Let's be honest, it's what men want, the bottom half. When all is said and done, they're quite relieved not to have the talking half attached. The half with the brain. It suits them just fine to have the fanny with a pair of dangly legs they can shove behind their ears or part with their cold, rough-as-cardboard hands before getting stuck in.

I felt him shrink. Poor magician, made it disappear. What a pity. Making a squirrelling, chirruping sound as he folds his pork dumpling away.

"Oh, little baby," I said. "No abra in your cadabra?"

"Shut up, shut up, shut up!"

I felt his hand across my throat. My head cracked against the wall. His face filled my eyes. My arms cartwheeled uselessly. My wedding ring tinked against the glass of the lamp, sounding like the fork tapping the glass for speeches. My papa rising with a piece of paper in his hand, monocle wedged in his eye socket, stains of hope on his cravat. Holy Anthony, save us. I poked out my tongue. It wasn't a decision. My breath wasn't having it. Both hands now, both thumbs pressing. Not a trick. Not an illusion. Not an act. Not a show. The private show. The behind-closed-doors act. The husbandry voilà. The vodka hornpipe.

He raised me off the pillow. Inches. Then, feeling the lightness of me, or seeing how little of me remained hovering over the white cotton sheets, his resolve evaporated. Withered, as his ardour had, on seeing the shadow on the wall – thinking, perhaps, I cannot hit half a woman, for I am a gentleman. I cannot kill her. Not her! (Mainly because I already have.)

He dropped me. I toppled, not having sufficient limbs for the purpose of stability, falling on my hands like an acrobat, seeing him, upside-down, exit through the open and shut door.

"Trousers!"

"I know, I know."

He could not be seen. Not in that state. Shirt. Belt. Buckle. Cravat. Quick look in the mirror. A surly frown tossed in my direction. Me, still upside-down. He sidesteps the inverted torso like I'm a bucket. I sink to one elbow then both. Scratch my chin.

My foot is next to me. I whack it with my knuckles. And now she's hopping. The canal stench is nasty. Plus the other. She could have gone before she got home. But is she sorry? I doubt it. And without a hand to rub it better, serve her right. Let me tell you this for nothing: it isn't easy being bisected, and don't let anyone convince you otherwise.

* * *

Anyway, I think it's safe to say we thought we'd never see him again. Kavalyov. You tend to think that when someone literally runs away from you and you hear their footsteps echoing on the cobbles. He had a point in a way. Life's too short to endure one woman, let alone two halves that seemed intent on plaguing his mind. We thought he might take to the canal himself – goodbye, cruel world! – or the Neva, if it wasn't frozen solid, or hand himself over to an asylum keeper to be measured up for a strait waistcoat, but no. Within the hour he was back with his tail between his legs, looking as handsome as a beaten whippet. Top hat askew. The top hat wasn't fooling anyone.

He didn't show any surprise that I was playing a folk song on a squeezebox and chewing on his pipe.

He wasn't even bewildered by the sight of my bottom half dancing the Kalinka, knees up, shaking it all about. Hands on her waist if she had hands. If she had a waist. Heel, toe, heel, toe. The Great Kavalyov didn't so much as twitch an eyebrow, to be fair to him.

He simply laughed hysterically. Shoulders convulsing. Kicked off his boots. Picked me up in a waltz, though I had no legs to dance it. Cavorted around the admittedly tiny room, rotating, spinning, with a grin on his face so fixed it might have been applied by makeup. "Ménage à trois!" he cried repeatedly, and with increasing exuberance. "Ménage à trois!"

It was loud, it was extravagant, it was exciting, and for a fleeting moment it felt like the days when we had been a courting couple. Then, just as quickly, it all came crashing down as he tumbled into his mind's muddy ditch, as his feelings always did – collapsing onto the bed with me, the top of me lolling in his arms.

My legs sat cross-legged on the floor as he wept copiously. I handed him a corner of the bedsheet to soak his tears.

"All I wanted was for you to love me, Ma-ma!"

Pull yourself together, I thought. Ironic, since I was the one who had been pulled apart.

He drew a heart on my shoulder with the tip of his forefinger. He reached into his pocket and took out a jewellery case. He opened it. Inside, against red satin, lay a necklace of shimmering gems. He took it out and fastened it around my neck.

Kissing my hands, he told me he had a wonderful proposal. A fabulous new idea. The greatest magic trick ever performed! The sawn-in-half-lady like no other! "Now you are in two halves, we can truly create a spectacular illusion! In fact, no illusion at all! See, the illusion will be when you come on stage and we pretend you are one whole woman. We can do it by the use of a corset and some straps, I'm sure. Don't you see? It'll bring the house down! Why are you looking at me like that?"

He expected an outpouring of enthusiasm. He expected it all to be put right again, but it wasn't.

It's hard for things to be put right again when you've been sawn in half.

I said: "Look in the mirror and what do you see?"

"Nothing."

I said: "Exactly."

"What do you mean? What is this, a trick?"

"No, you do the tricks, my love. I do the truth," I said as he narrowed his eyes at his reflection, who narrowed his eyes back. "There was no other man. I was not an adulterer. There is no perfection. No saint. No virgin. No fallen woman. Nobody is fallen but you."

"No!" he spat. "No!" he shouted. "No!" he raged. "No! How dare you? This is typical! Why do you say these things? There's nothing wrong with me. Trying to make me feel guilty when I want to feel happy. Why do you always have to attack my happiness? You always undermine my big ideas."

"No, I didn't. You were always The Great Kavalyov, and I was always nothing. We were nothing."

"That's not true!"

"It is true. I opened the vanishing cabinet and there was nothing there."

He beat the sides of his head with his fists.

"No! We can start again. I will change. I will not betray you. You are perfect. You are the love of my life."

"No, I am the love of *my* life," I said. "I wasn't, but I am now. You broke me in two, but here we are. Together. And we are strong because we have no secrets. What she knows, I know."

He sneered at the knotted legs on the floor.

"That bitch, that whore, she knows nothing! She was only good for one thing. Other than that, I never trusted her. I loathed and detested her!"

My lower half stood up and tapped her foot impatiently. Then swiftly kicked him in the groin. He made a noise like a door hinge that hadn't been oiled for a century, then keeled over, curling up like a baby on the floor.

"Well, anyway. Here we are." I turned up the lamp, tapped out the cinders from the pipe.

It was time.

I slid off the bed, unclipped his trunk of props with two loud clunks, and took out the saw. I bent it one way then the other and it sprang back straight, emitting a sonorous musical twang so pleasing I did it again. It was a shame it couldn't accompany our activity with a little ditty, the kind fishermen sing when they haul in the cod.

I crabbed over to the prone shape of my husband and stuffed a handkerchief in his mouth. My lower half put her toe under his knee and flipped him over so he rolled onto his back, then she plonked herself on his chest, winding him. Her pubic beard confronted his goatee, face to face. Knees up, she clasped her ankles firmly against his ears, holding his head in position like a medieval torture device. I scuttled between his legs, wedging myself there, facing his private package, one hand holding a knee flat, his other leg kicking uselessly as I swiftly unbuttoned his trousers and delved into his undergarments.

In his egg-like eyes I might have seen the shimmering reflection of my necklace.

Finding the offending reptile, I took it in one hand, lining up the teeth of the blade against its root, and quickly sawing with the other.

The blade sighing-shimmering as it pulled and pushed, pulled and pushed...

* * *

From the diary of Nikolai Gogol (1849)

An extraordinarily strange occurrence took place in Petersburg in March of that year. A well-dressed woman wearing a crinoline arrived at the municipal police station with a large trunk or travelling case, demanding she be given the ear of the Oberpolitzmeister (a German term for the highest authority under that roof). She was hence escorted to Alexander Andreevich, a cousin of the mayor, who at that time was contemplating the depth of the Neva from his office window, but nevertheless offered the visitor the courtesy her sex deserved, and her disability required, since she was moving upon crutches. Giving her name as Marya Vasilyevna, the woman said she wished to report a murder.

The police chief listened with bemusement bordering on indifference as she explained that Sergei Sergeievich Kavalyov had cut up his wife; cut her in two pieces, to be precise.

At this point Alexander Andreevich rocked back in his chair and gave a hearty laugh. "Of course he has! As the foremost magician in the land, he does it twice nightly! Let me explain, my dear. It is quite a cunning trick, but quite innocent. I've seen it myself. I assure you, no crime has been committed. Now, go home to your bed and rest easy."

The woman did not move from the chair.

"I suggest you open the trunk," she said.

Andreevich gestured to two of his officers to unbuckle the straps and reveal the contents of the luggage. After doing so, the pair backed away, open-mouthed. Exasperated, the Oberpolitzmeister demanded that the simpletons describe what they saw.

"Legs, sir," one of them said in a falsetto, his cheeks visibly pale.

"Legs," the other repeated like a feeble echo.

The woman then whipped off her navy blue and indigo skirt to show a space within the crinoline cage that was completely empty. Not even bloomers on display. Nothing.

Alexander Andreevich's intake of breath was audible.

"Now open this, if you please."

The finely dressed lady placed a jewellery box on his desk. The flat, long kind that is used to contain a necklace. Something that would be adequate to contain something six inches long – but, then again, something smaller.

Alexander Andreevich opened it.

There ensued such a commotion that, it was said, every single person ran out of the building and stared up at the window in horror, so much so that it was first thought there must have been a fire.

Author Note

I have become fascinated by the idea of psychological 'splitting' in relation to people with Borderline Personality Disorder (BPD), whereby a trigger event may spark fears of abandonment, separation, and severe anxiety (possibly a reflection of previous traumas in childhood). The patient with BPD, viewing everything in absolute terms without being able to accommodate paradoxes or allow for grey areas, becomes unable to reconcile the idea that good and bad can co-exist in the same person. 'Splitting' therefore is the psychological defence mechanism that helps them bear, and manage, the intolerable emotions they are feeling. It can lead to a situation where the merest slight can cause a person with BPD to feel betrayed and unloved by someone 'toxic', while an idealised partner can find themselves at the mercy of a co-dependent relationship.[1, 2]

A secondary inspiration for this story is the famous trope of psychoanalytic literature, the Madonna-whore complex, the idea that develops in men who see women either as saintly virgins or debased, sexually active sinners. Such men are drawn to a sexual partner who is degraded, yet they cannot exhibit physical desire for the worshipped object they respect: "Where such men love they have no desire, and where they desire they cannot love," as Freud puts it. According to Marie-Louise von Franz, the complex is a 'negative mother' complex projected into the external world as the 'split anima' – the personification of the inferior function of the personality and the doorway to the unconscious. Notable examples are illustrated in

1 Gould, J. R., Prentice, N. M. and Ainslie, R. C. (1996). 'The Splitting Index: Construction of a Scale Measuring the Defense Mechanism of Splitting.' *Journal of Personality Assessment*. 66 (2): 414–430. doi:10.1207/s15327752jpa6602_18. PMID 8869581.

2 Pec, O., Bob, P. and Raboch, J. (2014) 'Splitting in Schizophrenia and Borderline Personality Disorder.' PLoS One. 6; 9(3): e91228. doi: 10.1371/journal.pone.0091228. PMID: 24603990; PMCID: PMC3946324.

Alfred Hitchcock's *Vertigo*, where Kim Novak plays a virtuous Madonna and a fallen woman, in *Taxi Driver*, via the two contrasting female characters played by Cybill Shepherd and Jodie Foster, and in David Cronenberg's *Spider*, based on the novel by Patrick McGrath.

Self-Portrait

Cynthia Pelayo

I THOUGHT she loved me. I loved her.

I remember the very first time I saw her; it was in my studio. I was painting. Searching, for something deep within the canvas to appear, to speak to me, to tell me that this loneliness was not all that existed for me.

I didn't hear the door chime, but still, she was there.

Sleek. Perfect. Eternal.

I knew with just one look into her sparkling obsidian eyes that she was mine and I was hers. I would do anything and everything to be with her.

However, I didn't realize loving her meant watching my life deteriorate, like a painting flaking and fading, beneath the beating of scorching sunlight.

She was beautiful: dark hair, dark eyes, a fairy tale in a wood.

"What's this?" she asked me as I stood there, paint splatters across my face and hands, a canvas coming to life before me.

"The very deepest parts of me," I said.

She was tall and slender, wearing a long black wool coat with black buttons. Her dark hair was long and straight. She wore black leather gloves. Her hands clasped in front of her, and I, I stood there perhaps gawking at her perfection, her sleek features and radiant skin.

I myself felt heavy, run down, my hair a mess, in a white t-shirt and faded jeans and white sneakers, all of me splattered in red and blue and yellow and green acrylic paint, and all of me unsure when it was the last time I'd changed clothes or slept or ate.

This painting was not yet complete, and if it was not yet complete, then I was not yet completed and so I needed to remain here until it was done, until she was done.

"Van Gogh painted himself," she said. "Over and over. I think we're mesmerized by his self-portraits, thinking that looking at them will provide us with some sort of insight into his personality and his thoughts. His life was extraordinary. His art amazing."

I wiped the sweat that beaded on my forehead with my forearm.

"Van Gogh painted *The Starry Night* from the room of his mental asylum," I said.

She smiled. "He spent a year there, but even in isolation, even in madness, he had his art."

And that was truth. That even in my isolation, even in my loneliness and confusion, my frustration, I had my art, and no one could take that away from me. Because of my art, I could still stand, I was still whole in some way.

We spoke more, much more. She understood me like no one has ever, and will ever, understand me again. We had one of those marathon dates that first day, lunch at the Gage, her seated against one of their crimson tufted booths. Whiskey-braised pork poutine. A prawn cocktail. A bottle of Blanc de Noirs Champagne – Vadin-Plateau Chêne la Butte.

She raised her glass, and I touched mine to hers.

"What are we celebrating?" I asked.

"It's my birthday." She smiled, her bright red lips pressing against her champagne glass, bubbles kissing the top of her lip.

We walked along Millennium Park, on that December day, cradled among sparkling silver and steel skyscrapers. Snow began to fall, and I felt the world secure all around me, the city sounds silenced, and all went muffled for a moment as we stood in front of the Jay Pritzker Pavilion, an otherworldly shell structure that looks like a headdress. Attached to the bandshell, beginning as frames against the stage and swooping above us, were stainless steel crisscrossing pipe ribbons connected to giant speakers.

She hooked her arm into mine. "We'll come here in summer and listen to bands play jazz and blues, and we'll dance and we'll sing and we'll drink champagne."

On our first date, she was already planning a future with me, and I longed for it all to be true. I longed for her to be real.

I asked her what she did for a living, and she said she created things, and from all of the knowledge she told me about the buildings that painted the city skyline I assumed that to mean architect.

We walked through the modern wing at the Art Institute of Chicago, past galleries and a sleepy wintery garden. We stood in front of large windows that looked out at the cityscape, beams and lines, and mist and snow.

"Every window is a shifting canvas," she said to me and then held my hand.

"It is," I agreed.

"That painting, in your gallery, the one you were working on today, what do you hope for it to accomplish?" she asked, but I was unsure how to answer that.

How does an artist answer that each piece of work is a slice of them, meant to exist as part of us but separate.

I thought about the essence of what I'd hoped for all of my art to accomplish, and I said finally: "I want to be eternal, through my art…but I also hope that it allows me to feel…"

"But…" she said, as there is always a condition, a fear.

"I fear in this splintering of me, that all of these creations are fragmenting and reshaping what and who I am," I answered.

"And is that so bad?" she questioned.

* * *

For months, years, she consumed me, my thoughts, my dreams, my waking hours.

Her. Her. Her.

She came home with me that first night and in many ways she never left.

I wanted her. Not in a sexual way. Not in a monogamous way. Not as partners. Not in any way that I think any known relationship structure could shape or define. I felt like our connection transcended labels, terms, because we were more.

We were so much more.

In the morning, she would be there, while she was at work, she was there via text messages and phone calls and pictures and videos she would send me throughout the day of her walks, her musings, things she had spotted that she found beautiful and profound. A stitch of pink streaked across the sky as the sun rose. A new pair of patent leather shoes she came across in a department store on Michigan Avenue. She would send me pictures of her window, how the scene shifted throughout the day. She would message me more than "I love you." She would message me: "You are mine, and I am yours and we are forever."

She was another voice in my head, and from the moment I awoke to the moment I closed my eyes at night I longed for her. Her voice, a balm on my heart and the electricity that charged my painting, her words in my phone, typing away her deepest thoughts, all parts of her fueled me, and consumed me with this creative blaze that I knew if I continued this path, she would set me on fire, and I would hand her the match. I'd forgive her if she did, because my darling could do no wrong. If I were set ablaze, I only hoped that she'd be there to watch me turn to ash.

"Why a self-portrait?" she asked me of the painting that I was still working and reworking, years after our initial meeting in front of it. Colors were layered onto each other, building up to thicker ones. Shadows and highlights, and still, it was not yet ready. The picture was not yet fully formed.

"It's said that Vincent van Gogh painted over thirty-five self-portraits, and he created so many because he wanted to practice painting people. Sometimes I wonder if he created so many because he was lonely and wanted to be surrounded by something, even the likeness of himself. X-ray examinations also uncovered self-portraits Van Gogh had painted of himself that existed beneath other paintings."

She kissed me on my neck. "Are you lonely now?"

I closed my eyes and felt the tears stream down my face. "No, I have you. I need you. Don't ever leave me."

"I promise I won't," she said.

* * *

For our third-year anniversary she took me to the Art Institute once again, and this time it was to see him.

Vincent van Gogh
Self-portrait, 1887
Oil on artist's board, mounted on cradled panel
41 x 32.5 cm

With her delicate finger she pointed to Van Gogh's beard. "You see here, the vivid color palette."

It was as if his eyes were piercing right into my core. I felt something unraveling within me. Something was wrong. I knew what it was, but I did not want to admit it to myself, that I was losing a grasp on things.

I felt her hand take mine. I don't know how long I'd been standing there staring when she asked, "Have you slept?"

"I…" I started but couldn't recall when I last did.

She brought my hand to her lips and kissed the back of it, but I could not feel anything. "But you finally finished your self-portrait?"

"I did," I said, "because of you. I can't ever imagine creating anything without you in my life. That self-portrait: it exists because of you, and in a way, this incarnation of me now is because you entered my life, and if you left it, I'd be broken."

She smiled and I felt my heart sink, because that was not her normal smile; there was deceit within the lines around her mouth. I searched her eyes and found infinity within her pupils, and I felt right then that I should slip inside of her, because if I did then she would forever be mine, and if we were one, she would never leave me. Yet, if we were one, I would find myself all alone again, in ways. There was no escaping me.

I turned back to Van Gogh's self-portrait. "This took him time, but he was able to perfect this technique, the brightness, through the overlay of small and even brushstrokes. This was his response to the Pointillist-style technique used by Georges Seurat. Seurat used it in his famous *A Sunday on La Grande Jatte* in 1884. It's just people in a park enjoying a lovely, bright Sunday afternoon, but when you get close to the painting, inches from it, you can see the millions of small, distinct dots of color applied to the canvas in a pattern to form the image."

"So, what you're saying is, sometimes you need to zoom in on something to determine what are the parts that make up that whole?" she asked.

"In a way, I suppose. We are all made up of many things. Maybe there's a danger to that, to getting too close, inspecting something too precisely."

* * *

By the time I arrived back at my gallery she was gone. All of her clothes. All mention of her. It was like she had disappeared completely. I tried her phone number over and over, but the line was dead.

For months, getting out of bed was a challenge. No amount of coffee could give me a jolt of energy. I was richly and deeply exhausted and lost without her. There was no one to talk to as I painted. There was no one to message me in the morning or to wish me well at night. There was no one to embrace. I missed her smell. I missed her voice. I missed all the parts of her, and I wondered each and every second of my waking hour if she missed me, too.

My life was a mirror shattered into pieces without her. I could no longer see myself. I could no longer think clearly. My dreams were thick white mist. How could I move on without her inspiring me, motivating me, loving me?

Sleep came to me at all hours, and in time day became night and night became day. It didn't matter what planet or star was setting or rising. My body, my mind, my thoughts, they all failed me. I'd look to the paints, oils, acrylics, pastels and charcoals scattered on the floor in front of me, my great studio and bedroom and home, all morphed into one, and no matter how hard I tried to paint I could not.

She had ripped my ability to create from me. She took my greatest prize with her when she left: my gift of art, of creation. It was the cruelest thing that she could have ever done to me, but still, I loved her. I loved her no matter how much she had destroyed me. No matter how much I suffered, no matter how many times I'd cry in front of a blank canvas, unable to start, struggling to pick up a paintbrush or choose a color, I still called out to her: "You promised me something greater than love. You promised me eternity."

* * *

Months passed, and I made it somehow to the doctor's office.

"You have a show today?" he asked.

I nodded, looking at the scale which told me how many pounds I had lost.

"You need to eat," he said.

"I'll try," I said, thinking about how she loved the truffles, and beets tostada at Smyth, and how she'd delicately dab her red lips after drinking the Heart of Stone, a cocktail with bourbon, tea, Fresno chili pistachio and peach at the Aviary.

"I'm just so tired all the time," I added.

My doctor called it something greater than fatigue.

"Myalgic encephalomyelitis/chronic fatigue syndrome," he said.

When I asked him how it happened – was it a virus, something else that caused this? – he said: "It could be that your brain is now attacking your body after all that you have been through."

All that I've been through? I didn't know what to call it, exactly, but I explained it to him as best as I could.

Was it a breakup? Or was it abandonment?

Perhaps it was a great artistic performance, manipulation by way of love: enter my life, make me dependent on you to create, make me love you, and then leave me crushed after I'd completed my greatest piece of work to ensure I could never create again.

Perhaps it was a way to break me as Van Gogh had been broken.

Was she somewhere now? Delighted in how she had crushed the artist?

I asked him when I would get better.

"It's difficult to tell for certain, but what I do recommend is rest."

My doctor began tapping away at the keyboard, updating my medical record.

"Is there medication that I should be prescribed for this?"

Without turning away from the screen he said: "No, that would dull your creativity."

He must have sensed my shock because he paused and turned to me. "There are many different types of medications we can turn to, but let's try rest most importantly. I will also leave you with a list of some recommended therapists who specialize in a variety of modalities, such as Cognitive Behavioral Therapy, which may offer some relief."

"Will I paint again?"

"Yes," he said. "You will, but you need rest. You've been through a lot. You painted so much in the past three years. Thousands of paintings. It's astonishing. Genius. But the schedule you kept, sleeping so few hours. So much work in so little time. Get some rest, please."

My doctor stood up, extended his hand, and we shook. "I hope you feel better, and good luck on your gallery opening this evening. I heard it's a very private audience. Hopefully, I can make the next one if you open it to the public."

* * *

I approached the red brick building, and none of the lights were on, as I'd expected. Inside, I turned on the light, and there it hung, that single self-portrait, that painting I had meticulously painted, so carefully, painstakingly, detail by detail, stitch by stitch, each layer a thought, each layer a prayer of some sort to perfection, to understanding, to connection, to easing loneliness.

I approached it, that self-portrait of me, but it wasn't really me. It never really was just me, in all of that time, and in all of those years. There she was and there I was. One person on that canvas. Her and me, all the same. Our dark obsidian eyes. Our long dark hair. Our dark wool coat with black buttons worn on that day.

It was her. It was me. We were always one. Maybe she was never there. Maybe I was never here.

Author Note

What is creativity? What is madness? Is there a point in which the act of creation can cause the human spirit to spiral beyond themselves? In 'Self-Portrait', an unnamed artist challenges the mental and spiritual boundaries of these limits.

The Mark

Grace Chan

THINGS HAVEN'T BEEN RIGHT for a few months.

I can't describe it exactly. The air is spongy, each molecule bloated with turgid energy. We've had three lightning storms this summer: dry, pounding storms without rain, purple branches crackling across a cloud-dark sky.

Several times, I've woken before sunrise, convinced that something has changed in the middle of the night. As though some god has reached down, and, with a colossal finger, nudged the Earth, and now everything is sitting two degrees off-kilter.

On these not-quite-mornings, I pad into the street in my pyjamas. I stand beneath the linked steeples of fluorescent streetlights and power lines. I scan above for the subtle movement of the clouds, to assure myself that the sky is not a two-dimensional poster glued onto a false backdrop.

One day at the end of summer, James returns from his morning run. He barrels into the bedroom, a whirlwind of breathlessness and heat, and ploughs through the drawers to find a fresh pair of jocks.

I watch him from where I lie, tangled in the too-warm sheets.

"Did you do a round of washing last night?"

"Yes," I say. "It's hanging in the laundry."

He strides out of the room, returns a minute later, clutching his favourite jocks. He pulls off his sweat-soaked singlet.

"What's that?"

"What?"

"On your chest." I point. At the base of his sternum, where bone turns to soft fleshy abdomen, his skin bears a mark like a stamp. It seems to have the muted redness of an old scar. But then it catches the light coming through the crack of the curtains, and it gleams silver.

"This?" James touches the spot absently. "It's nothing. An old birthmark."

"Can I see?" I sit up, but he swats me aside.

"I have to rush. It's nothing. I've had it forever. Shouldn't you be getting up too?"

He disappears into the ensuite. A few seconds later, the shower starts with a torrential roar. The pipes clatter in feeble protest. There'll be water all over the tiles, which I'll have to wipe before I go to work, or else damp will settle into the floor and we'll have mushrooms sprouting from the skirting again. Also, I need to call the plumber to check our water pressure.

James emerges and dresses in his usual uniform (tailored grey suit, white shirt, no tie) with a steadfast frenzy that characterises most of his waking hours. Somehow, in every vector of movement, he conveys to me a subtle disdain – as though, in rising an hour before me despite the lack of a fixed work schedule, he possesses a more exquisite moral fibre.

I lie in bed for another thirty minutes after he's gone. There's a strange smell in the air – sort of like bleach, and sort of like burning metal, but not quite like either. I sniff for a while, trying to figure it out but having no success. I'm starting to get cold. I run my hands over my body, feeling the hard shape of my hips, the stagnant putty of my lower belly, which is scarred inside.

My phone buzzes. It's a message from Michelle, the other PA.

Emma – you in yet? James is here. Wants you to fix up his PM list.

In a wry coincidence, my boss's name is also James. To most of his colleagues, he goes by Jim or Jimmy. In my head I refer to him as Dr. Entmore, to distinguish better his separateness, his seniority. He's a gastroenterologist. He spends four hours every afternoon negotiating the serpentine twists of the large intestine with the grim determination of a kid navigating the final level of Super Mario World. Dr. Entmore refers to me as Em, or, tongue-in-cheek, the queen of his office.

I check the time: 7:51 a.m. It'll take me twenty minutes to get ready and half an hour to drive to the hospital in traffic. Parking will add another five minutes, and walking in another…ten?

I stall in a mire of numbers and possibilities. My mind is as sluggish as the air. I toss the phone onto the bedside table and drag myself from my stale cocoon to face the day.

* * *

That night, I'm lying in bed. James is next to me, on his back, breathing the heavy, sonorous breaths of someone in deep sleep. Moonlight comes through the crack in the curtains and falls in a grey bar across the pillows, splitting James's face in two. My husband of ten years is a stranger. I study the straight lines of his nose, which my parents always admired, and the rough plane of his cheek, which has begun to soften with age.

Gingerly, I pull back the sheets.

He doesn't stir. The mark is still there. Triangular and somehow iridescent. How could I have never noticed it before? After a decade of intimacy, his body is an extension of mine.

I peer at it closely. It's not flat, as I'd first thought, but raised around the edges, and silver as the skin of a fish. I touch it.

It's a zip.

Holding my breath, I grasp it between the pads of my thumb and forefinger. Then I pull. There is next to no resistance. The skin of my husband's torso divides soundlessly, like the front of a hoodie, revealing a black, gaping gash. I lean closer to examine what lies within, but I'm jolted by the pipes' loud banging.

I blink into the oppressive thickness of waking. I'm alone in the bed. On James's side, the quilt is flung back. His pillow is cold.

I wait for my heart to stop pounding. Gradually, sounds come to me. I hear him pacing through the house, treading a figure-eight loop from kitchen to dining room to lounge to dining room and round and round again. There's a curious rhythm to his steps.

Then I hear the tapping. Musical, light, like someone tapping a beat on the rim of a drum with a pair of chopsticks. It goes on for what feels like half an hour.

James's voice is an undercurrent to the rhythm. His murmuring ebbs and flows. I can't make out any words through the tapping noise and the buzz of electrified air. I climb out of bed and creep to the door.

I hear my name – once, then a few sentences later, again.

I step around the doorframe. James glances at me immediately. He's silhouetted by the street light pouring through the lounge room window – a lean, dark figure with no face.

"Emma," he says.

"What's going on?" I ask. "It's 4 a.m."

"Business call," he says. "I've got a new client in the UK."

"I thought I heard you talking about me."

"No," he says. "Business call. Sorry to wake you. Go back to sleep."

I return to bed, dream-James and real-James swirling in my head. I roll myself so tight in the sheets I can hardly breathe, and pull the quilt over my nose. It's only as I'm drifting off to sleep that I realise my husband wasn't holding a phone.

* * *

March is a difficult month, but that's to be expected. The 8th falls on a Sunday. James is out playing tennis with his university friends. I close all the curtains and go to the second bedroom. We've converted it into a library of sorts – plush armchair with matching footstool, arranged in front of shelves of James's finance and history books. To me, though, it's still the nursery.

I still find it eerie that their deaths fell on consecutive days. That even though they were separated by three years, they tried to be close together in some way. For me, it was a double-punch to the gut – the first blow rendering me immobile for the second, the second intensifying the first. It was the ripping of a half-dried scab to expose a festering wound.

I stand in front of the chestnut dresser and open the top drawer. I take out a green shoebox. Should I light a candle? Play some meditative music? No, that seems stupid. Meaningless. They can't hear it anyway.

I lift the lid. The first item is a delicate gold anklet. My mother gave it to me, her eldest daughter. I wore it until I was twelve years old and my ankle grew too wide for it. I would have given it to Jade, if I'd kept her.

The second item is a little book of baby names. Bought on impulse from a two-dollar store, when I still wasn't sure if I'd keep her. Before James convinced me that we were too young, and it wasn't the right time.

The third item is my hospital wristband, with my name and birthdate and a seven-digit number beneath a barcode. The numbers are burned onto the inside of my skull. I muttered them over and over again as they scraped Jade out of me.

The next two items are Jasmine's. A pair of canary-yellow socks, exquisitely tiny, crocheted by my maid of honour when she found out I was pregnant. Never used.

And an ultrasound still from the twelve-week scan, crumpled from that day I threw it out. I'd hunted frantically through the garbage to retrieve it.

Jasmine, the wanted one, planned once James and Nish had got their firm up and running, hadn't made it to seventeen weeks. We'd lost the wanted one, you see, because we killed the unwanted one. James grieves, but not as I do. For him, the losses are cognitive, and sometimes emotional. For me, they are visceral – bloody with rage and regret.

Through penance we make amends.

I take the final item out of the green shoebox. It's an old torch, the bulb fried, with a thick corrugated cylinder for a handle. The curtains are closed. I remove my jeans and my underpants. I press the end of the torch to my vulva. Cold and dense. Through penance we heal. I make no sound as I push, even though the pain is monstrous.

* * *

On an unseasonably cold night in April, I wake in the soundless hours to discover that my husband has climbed on top of me. His weight imprints my body into the mattress. My wrists and hips ache.

His fingers fumble at my waistband.

"James," I say, but he doesn't reply. In the wan light, I see that his eyes are glassy.

I make myself still, burrow into the recesses of my mind. The air congeals with unspent energy. As James moves over me, the mark shifts in and out of my vision. A triangle, beautiful in its symmetry. Raised around the edges and silvery-red.

* * *

Nish and his wife come for dinner, and a man I don't know, called Paul Andreski, a new business client. Paul's wife, Tara, also comes. I make roast beef with rosemary, and a grain salad. Nish and his wife bring a potato curry, which doesn't complement the meat. Paul and Tara bring a bottle of shiraz.

James tells me the day before: "Please do your best, Emma."

I know I haven't been myself lately. Getting through March left me exhausted. The air is so thick it's difficult to string my thoughts together. And I can't help feeling that there's something horribly wrong with my husband.

The evening gets off to a rocky start. I put the roast into the oven too late, so everyone's hungry. I cobble together a platter of sesame crackers, salmon dip, green olives that are only a little slimy. James finds a bottle of Prosecco, and the conversation starts flowing.

They talk about the cryptocurrency tumble ("only a matter of time"), the Me Too movement ("its breadth is its weakness"), and Paul and Tara's recent tour of Southern Italy ("splendid in the middle of spring"). James laughs uproariously at Paul's jokes and lavishes Tara with compliments about her knowledge of classical history. I stare at where my husband's left hand rests on the table, flat and waxy, next to his plate, creasing his napkin. It flops there like a pale fish. My own hand rests three inches away, small and dark and neat.

I move my hand, close the three inches, press our pinkies together. His skin is as cold as dead meat. James moves his hand away, unconsciously, still talking.

After dinner, I load the dishes into the dishwasher while they go to the lounge room to work on the bottle of red and a wheel of Camembert. I drift to the back door. The sun has long descended behind the melaleuca trees that divide our property from the neighbour to our rear. A sweep of vivid orange holds out against the descent of the starry night. I push my toe against the fly screen, nudge it open, and step onto the back porch.

The night is cold and smells like burning fuel. At this time of year, the trees have mostly turned. Brown and yellow leaves pool across our backyard. The geraniums are drowning in weeds. The neighbour's creeper spills over the fence in a dense tangle. Usually, James would have pruned it long before it got so wild. He would have raked the leaves, too, and weeded the flower beds. I frown. He has always been an avid gardener.

I think about skin, cold as dead meat, and glassy eyes, and a triangular scar in the exact centre of the torso. The dark sky presses down on my head.

* * *

As soon as I realise the truth of it, everything falls into place. That's why, despite the utter bizarreness of the situation, I know there can be no other explanation. The electrified air, which lifts baby hairs vertically from my scalp, is charged with radio waves transmitting messages to his system. The mysterious 4 a.m. phone calls: check-ins with whichever intelligence agency has commissioned him. The triangular mark: the final stitch in his fabrication.

The house has become my territory. I clean the kitchen with a specific fierceness; I am a guard holding the outermost frontier. As I sponge the counters in firm, circular strokes, I glance through the window to the backyard. The trees are grey and bare. Rotting leaves pile up in banks against the fence, releasing a sickly-sweet scent.

He comes into the kitchen, in search of breakfast. Of course, I haven't said anything to him about my thoughts. I haven't breathed a word to anyone. I've decided to pretend that everything is normal until I figure out a sensible course of action.

I watch as he gets the box of rolled oats from the pantry, pours half a cup into a bowl, adds milk, and puts it in the microwave. As he waits for the oats to cook, he leans against the counter, tapping the spoon against his chin.

His face is not even right. That's why everything felt off-kilter. His eyebrows are dark, like they've been tattooed on. His eyes are too far apart; the contour of his hairline uniform and lacking the patches at the temples where it had begun to thin. And the two little moles beside his left nostril – completely gone.

He takes the bowl from the microwave, plunges his spoon in, and lifts it to his mouth. James would have added a carefully measured tablespoon of ironbark honey and stirred it to achieve an even distribution of sweetness.

My blood is as cold as ice. I lick my lips.

"Do you remember when we went to the hospital for Jasmine's first scan?"

He stiffens, but I push on. The memory is an ocean wave: once it has attained enough momentum, it can't be stopped. It must rise, swell, peak, crash, and be endured.

"Remember how excited the sonographer looked when she called my name – and then, when she saw me, how her smile disappeared? She was so confused."

With a surname like Kavanagh, she'd thought she was meeting an Irish sister. She hadn't expected black hair, chestnut skin, single-lidded eyes.

He says nothing.

"Then you stood up, and the world made sense again. She adored you. Kept asking where your parents and grandparents were from. Kept saying you've got the same eyes as one of her cousins, from a town south of Cork – Bandon? Baltimore?"

"I don't remember," he said.

His expression is blank. There is no recollection.

"How could you forget? She started implying that you'd bought me from some third-world slum. Remember?"

"No, I don't. You always read too much into these little things. She was probably just trying to be nice."

He takes his oats to the lounge, to eat in front of the television. Even his voice sounds different. Hollow. Alien. A sensation of prickling needles rises all over my skin.

* * *

That night, I watch it sleep.

It lies flat on its back, arms by its side, like a corpse laid out on a morgue table. Eyes closed in repose, face still. Only the susurration of air moving through its nostrils, lifting the chest in gentle undulations. The fingernails look like plastic discs, glued on.

In my right hand, I clutch a metal spoon. This will confirm my suspicions once and for all.

I step closer to the bed. The silver-red mark gleams at me, tempting me to touch it and tug it and watch everything unravel.

I press the hard edge of the spoon to the soft part beneath the left eye. It sinks as easily as a knife through wax. It's as I suspected. Wires, wires, everywhere. I push on, following the contour of the eye socket.

Conducting fluid, cold and oozing, wets my fingers. In the back of my mind, I wonder where the real James has gone.

⁂

Author Note

'The Mark' is one of my darkest stories, touching on heavy themes like domestic violence, self-harm, racism, miscarriage, and psychosis. Although it's an unsettling read, I'd like to think it's not entirely grim. My story claims power for the protagonist by embracing madness, monstrousness, and abjection.

At the start of 'The Mark', Emma is in a powerless position. As a woman of colour married to an abusive white man and a personal assistant to a white male doctor, she is constantly objectified. We notice how her husband expects her to manage the domestic mundanities (laundry, cleaning, hosting a social gathering) without a word of complaint; we cringe at the patronising nickname that her boss bestows upon her. We have a glimpse into Emma's psyche, but it seems those around her have no curiosity about her complex internal world.

Emma is on the verge of vanishing beneath the weight of her husband's oppression and her accumulated grief. Her loss of self extends to her culture and ethnicity. She has given up her surname, left her family behind, assimilated into Western society – but she can't hide her 'black hair, chestnut skin, single-lidded eyes'.

How does Emma resist erasure? One can only bear so much transgression before one crumbles into annihilation – or, conversely, transforms it into a righteous fury. The central question in 'The Mark' isn't whether Emma is suffering from the Capgras delusion (the belief that an identical imposter has taken the place of a loved one) or whether James has really been replaced by a robot. Through violence, secrecy and so-called madness – domains of the feared, feminine Other – we see our protagonist discover truth, strength, and a reclamation of selfhood.

Poppet

Freddie Bonfanti

THE MORNING SHIFT LOOMS, five minutes away. By now, you should be scrubbed and ready for work. Instead, you have been sitting in the viewing room of the mortuary for almost an hour, staring at a four-foot-tall plastic Christmas tree nestled between the sofa and the fridge, its tiny lights throwing splashes of red and green up the walls.

Memories of snow drift unbidden through your mind. Pristine white blanketing the world, muffling all sound, transforming even the grimiest corners of London into something magical. It's been years since you've seen real snow, since before everything changed. You swallow hard, tasting the bitterness of a thought you can't shake: will you ever build a snowman with your daughter again?

Nostalgia is a scalpel, you think, dissecting memories with surgical precision. But even the sharpest blade can't cut through the calcified horror of this new reality.

You badge into the gallery as Sammy, the night security guard, nods as he leaves. Exhaustion etches deep lines around his eyes, yet he smiles. It's small, it's meaningless, but it's human.

The first body arrives at 8 a.m. A woman, mid-thirties. Cause of death: exsanguination. The irony isn't lost on you. Her family has requested a viewing before cremation, so you work methodically, prepping her for the service. Your colleagues orbit around you, their chatter a distant hum as you focus on the task at hand. They sign off, leaving you alone with her. The LED lights overhead cast an almost otherworldly glow on the body. The woman's skin is pale and waxy. Your gloved hands move with practiced efficiency as you begin the embalming process.

First, the disinfection. You clean the body with an antiseptic solution. The chemical smell mingles with the faint, metallic tang of death – a combination you've long since grown accustomed to. You know this will be a challenging case; exsanguination has left her circulatory system almost empty. Using multiple injection points, you carefully introduce the formaldehyde solution, watching as the tissues firm slightly under the flow. Blood drainage isn't necessary here – there's barely any left – but you still insert the cannula into the jugular vein to relieve any pooled fluids. A pitiful amount. Not worth your time.

The third body arrives at 11 a.m. A man in his fifties, victim of a car accident. His family has requested a viewing, so blood drainage is necessary this time. Your pulse hums with anticipation. Standard procedure dictates the full amount must be collected for testing. You insert the cannula into the carotid artery for injection and another into the jugular vein for drainage. A pinkish fluid courses through the arteries, pushing the blood out through the jugular vein. Dark liquid flows down the stainless steel table, a thin river seeking the drain at the foot. The quiet gurgle as it disappears into the collection container below is barely audible over the hum of machinery.

You work quickly, efficiently. When the initial rush of blood slows, you glance at the door, ears straining for any sound of approaching footsteps. Nothing. Just the steady pump of the embalming machine and the soft splash of liquid.

With practised movements, you retrieve a one-litre flask from your hidden stash. You've done this before, many times. Always just a little, never enough to raise suspicion. You slide the flask under the drain, just above the collection container. The dark liquid flows into it, beginning its journey to the brim. You watch the flask closely, carefully gauging the amount and then pull it away, replacing it with the standard collection container.

Once the blood drainage is complete, you prepare for cavity embalming. You pick up the trocar, ready to aspirate the remaining fluids from the body cavities.

Lunch break comes. A group of nurses huddled in front of a TV screen in the break room, another government announcement. The Prime Minister's face fills the screen, his expression grave but his eyes alight with that charismatic gleam that won him the last election. His words are carefully chosen, speaking of breakthroughs and cooperation, of trials and hope. You've heard such promises before and wonder how much of that oratory is truth, and how much is carefully constructed illusion. You keep moving, not stopping to listen. The less you know, the better. But you can't help wondering – if everyone speaks in half-truths and whispers, what reality are they constructing? A reality where children disappear behind closed doors and adults pretend not to notice the emptiness of playgrounds?

The day drags on, a grim parade of bodies. With each one, you perform your duties. And with each one, a little more blood finds its way into the flask. It's dangerous, you know. If you're caught…but you push the thought away. You have no choice.

As your shift nears its end, your trolley holds the full flask, carefully hidden. A new body arrives. A child, no more than ten years old. Your stomach clenches as you begin your work. Children are always the hardest, but their blood is the purest. Your hands move with cold precision as you prepare for the drainage.

Without hesitation, you retrieve the flask and empty its contents into the drainage container. The child's blood, you decide, is worth the risk. As the cannula slides into place, you're taken aback by what surges forth. The boy's blood is brighter than you've ever seen, almost luminescent under the lights. It races down the table faster than any adult's, as if eager to escape its small vessel. You scramble to position your flask, nearly fumbling it in your haste.

The rich red liquid splashes into it, filling it rapidly. You watch, mesmerised, as it reaches the top. The drain gurgles hungrily, devouring what you can't capture. You tilt the flask, determined to salvage every precious drop. The child's face blurs, becoming just another in the endless procession.

Suddenly, your ears prick. Footsteps. Your heart racing, you quickly drain the flask into the container and conceal it. Just as you straighten up, the door swings open. You don't startle, don't give any sign that anything is amiss. It's Dr. Ghaznavi, but he's not alone. A stern-looking man in a crisp suit follows him in.

"DCI Rogers, this is Mrs. Hawkins, our mortuary technician. Mrs. Hawkins, this is DCI Rogers. He's here about the new directive."

Your stomach drops, but your hands remain steady. You nod in greeting.

DCI Rogers steps forward, his eyes scanning the room before settling on you.

"I'm here to discuss the new blood drainage accountability measures," he says, his tone businesslike. "We're implementing stricter controls starting Monday. I'll be overseeing the transition." You force yourself to meet his gaze.

"Of course," you say, your voice steady despite the panic rising in your chest.

Rogers' gaze shifts to the container, his brow furrowing.

"Tell me," he continues, "how much blood would you typically expect to drain from a body of this size?"

Your mind races, calculating quickly.

"It depends on various factors," you reply, "but for someone of this build, typically around two litres."

Rogers nods, then gestures to the drainage container. "And how much would you say is in there?"

You glance at the container, your heart pounding. "It looks to be about three and a half," you say, knowing the exact extra amount.

Rogers raises an eyebrow. "That's quite a discrepancy, wouldn't you say?"

You don't flinch, even as your palms are sweating inside your gloves. "The container has been there for a while," you reply calmly, the lie slipping easily from your lips. "It hasn't been emptied since my last break."

Rogers stares at you, his pupils constricting to pinpricks, unblinking and reptilian. The stillness in his gaze makes your skin crawl. He looks around the room again, his gaze lingering on your trolley. After a long moment, he turns to Dr. Ghaznavi. "Doctor, would you mind taking that blood container away? I'd like to start with a clean slate for our new procedures."

"Certainly," Dr. Ghaznavi responds, moving to comply.

You keep your face carefully neutral as your day's work – and your secrets – are carried away.

Rogers turns back to you. "Well, I look forward to working with you all starting Monday. We'll get this place running like clockwork."

As he and Dr. Ghaznavi leave, you let out a breath you didn't realise you were holding. Your hands shake as you wheel the body to cold storage. How will you manage now? The thought repeats endlessly in your mind as you scrub down in the staff room, now aware of every glance, every murmured conversation around you.

When you finally leave the morgue, the setting sun feels like a countdown. You drive through the hospital grounds, past makeshift barricades and through a small gate. The roads are empty save for three soldiers at the first roadblock, their daylight-powered spotlights cutting through the gathering dusk. They gesture at your neck, a silent reminder. You click the bite shield into place. The Kevlar is cold and rubbery against your skin, an unwelcome embrace.

The drive home is quick and tense. There are no seasonal decorations around. Government slogans flicker on LED billboards along the dual carriageway.

SAFE AFTER SUNSET.

STAY ALERT, STAY ALIVE.

NO REFLECTION? TAKE ACTION.

IF YOU SPOT THEM, REPORT THEM.

COMMUNITY SAFETY STARTS WITH YOU.

You pull into your driveway just as the last rays of light disappear, the new curfew looming over the silent street.

Inside, the house is quiet. Too quiet. You pause at the foot of the stairs, listening for any sound from above. Nothing. Relief and dread war in your chest as you climb, your rucksack light without its usual illicit cargo.

In the bathroom, you stare at your reflection in the mirror. The face of a stranger looks back at you. Pale, drawn, looking nowhere near your thirty-two years. You open the cabinet and grab a medical kit you've prepared for emergencies. Inside is a collection of syringes, tourniquets, and stacks of empty blood bags.

You tie off your arm and insert the needle. You've done this before, in desperate times, but never as your only option. The first bag grows heavy in your hand. One isn't enough. You fill another, and another, until your head spins and spots dance at the edges of your vision.

Your legs tremble, betraying your exhaustion. When you stumble against the door frame, the familiar scratching above you begins, faint, insistent. With shaking hands, you reach for the bite shield, adjusting its position on your neck.

As you climb the ladder to the loft, the scratching intensifies. She knows you're coming. You push open the hatch, and the smell hits you – metallic, like old pennies.

"Shh, it's okay," you whisper, though you're not sure if it's to her or yourself. "I brought food," you say softly, your voice weak from the blood loss.

She's huddled in the corner, eyes gleaming in the dim light filtering through the hatch. Your daughter, but not your daughter. Her skin is pale, almost translucent. Dark veins map her face like cracks in porcelain.

You toss her a blood bag. And another. And another. She catches each one with inhuman speed, tearing into them with her teeth. The sound of her feeding fills the small space – wet, desperate gulps. It's not enough. It will never be enough.

As she takes the last gulp, she looks at you, really looks at you, for the first time in weeks. There's recognition in her eyes, and something else. Concern? Guilt? You're not sure if you're imagining it, your vision blurry from exhaustion and blood loss. You collect the empty bag. Evidence to be disposed of, like so much else in your life now.

"Poppet," you whisper, reaching out slowly. "Do you remember the song we used to sing? The one about the little star?"

She doesn't speak – she hasn't in weeks – but her head tilts slightly. You begin to hum softly, the familiar melody filling the attic. To your amazement, she sways gently, almost imperceptibly. Her lips move, not forming words, but mimicking the rhythm of the song.

Tears spring to your eyes, from emotion or weakness, you're not sure.

"That's right," you encourage, your voice thick. "You remember."

You stay like that for a long time, humming lullabies in the darkness. When you finally descend the ladder, closing the hatch behind you, your cheeks are wet, and your body feels impossibly heavy.

In your bedroom, you collapse onto the bed, your mind racing despite your exhaustion. The sheets are cold against your skin. You close your eyes, knowing sleep won't come. Instead, you listen for the scratching above, both dreading and longing for the sound that tells you your daughter is still there, still alive.

You wake to silence. Absolute, unearthly. The world has gone quiet in a way that makes you wonder, for a heartbeat, if you're still breathing. There's a chill in the air that seeps into your bones, familiar yet strange.

When you pull back the bedroom curtains, the whole world outside is blanketed in white.

Author Note

I wrote the first draft of 'Poppet' as I often do with short stories – fast and raw, without much thought for themes. The idea came to me quickly, and I didn't dwell on its meaning or symbolism, just the unsettling image of a mother stealing blood for her vampire daughter. It was a visceral snapshot that landed on the page before I had time to consider what it might represent.

It was only during later drafts and revisions that I began to see the story's connections to my own life. When I was seven, my family moved to a small village, where I was bullied for my accent, background, and the way I looked. I carried undiagnosed mental health challenges that had no name at the time. In those days, children who might now be recognised as neurodivergent were expected to keep up with everyone else, to fit in without complaint. I knew I was different, but there was no framework to help me understand why. Instead, I was compelled to perform 'normality' as though following a script I could never quite memorise, all the while feeling like I'd landed on an alien planet where I didn't speak the local language.

Much like the protagonist's secretive efforts, my mother found her own ways to comfort and contain my anxiety – small rituals that helped ease my fear, subtle strategies to calm me down when my outbursts upset the delicate balance of our family life. She had no guidebook, no diagnosis to consult, and no community of understanding parents. All she had was an unwavering instinct to protect me, even if it meant improvising in the dark.

Looking back, I see how this story, though supernatural in nature, reflects the quiet determination of parents helping children who don't quite fit in. 'Poppet' is not only an unsettling tale – it's also an acknowledgement of the invisible labour and fierce love that shape these private struggles. With hindsight, the piece becomes a nod to all the strange, anxious, or misunderstood kids out there, and to the parents who craft their own gentle, secret remedies to hold them close – no matter how unconventional those remedies may be.

Dissolution of the Self on the Altar of Your Dreams: A Case Study

Sayan J. Soselisa

YOU'VE COME UP with the ridiculously bad idea of watching Cronenberg's *The Fly* while your experiments run. Those minutes of downtime are better spent on something less anxiety-inducing. Graduation is coming up; close, but ever out of reach, and YOU NEED DATA. Data takes time. Data means setting up crosses, waiting for the maggots to crawl up the vial walls, to pupate, to fly. To sort out the females that still have red eyes, whose wings are straight-not-curled, and set them aside for exactly four days, before the real work begins.

You drag yourself to the lab on a Saturday evening, because mornings and evenings are when the flies fly best, and you are not a morning person. The lab is deserted, because even though your colleagues come in on the weekend, at this hour they've retired to the pub around the corner and are already drunk.

The flies from Wednesday sit in the fly-room at 25 degrees centigrade, and you take the vial, tap it down, and quickly funnel the flies into a tube. You stick it into a bucket of ice, only for a little while. Enough for the flies to become sluggish, so that you can take one out with your brush and sweep it onto your cooled holder. You have to be quick now. With the micro-manipulators of the station, you center the fly in the holder, glue it in place with a wire so thin, your hair seems a cable next to it. Then you take out the needles. You need needles, because a scalpel is too coarse a tool for something so fine. Only insulin needles have the edge you need to cut through the exoskeleton covering the fly's head, without damaging its faceted eyes, its extended proboscis. To cut through the fat body and the trachea. To sweep them aside and expose the soft white tissue of the brain.

You let the fly recover from surgery as you boot your stimulus in the imaging room. It needs to be ready to fly when you place it in the virtual reality chamber below the microscope. The cylindrical screen will immerse your fly in a new world, ready to explore. You will show it predators, looming left and right, and measure the responses in its brain. Predict its turns as it tries to escape. The screen flickers on as your fly starts to shake off the sluggishness of the cold. You align the fly's brain with the laser scanning of the microscope. You shut down all the other lights in the imaging room and close the curtains around your setup. Then you press 'start' to let the stimulus play as you set the microscope to record the cresting of brain activity inside the fly's head.

You take a few moments to relax before you have to start preparing your next animal, and put on your headset to continue watching *The Fly*. It disturbs you, seeing that fictional scientist's experiments take effect, while yours come up blank, but you continue watching. The microscope can do this task without you, its laser scanning over the brain, the green fluorescence bouncing back through the objective, passing the filter into the photomultiplier while the fly navigates its virtual world.

You must have been too slow with your dissection after all. When you take it out of your setup, the fly is dead. Your recording shows only noise. Again. You ask yourself why. Why are you still not able to run this experiment? Why does your setup not register the fly's brain activity? You peer through the oculars. Is something happening in there? Do you see the faintest flash of fluorescent green? Probably just the reflection of its trachea, poorly dissected. You curse the microscope. You hate it. The loud cooling of the sapphire-diamond laser. The sensitivity to ambient light that makes you sit in the dark. Mostly how the microscope doesn't give you the data you need. Maybe it has cursed you. Perhaps there is something wrong with the microscope despite your obsessive checking. You think on the movie you've been watching. Could something about the microscope be interfering with your work? Something you haven't thought of? An unobserved force that dooms you to fail? You imagine something hungry, that kills your flies and drains their life away before you can record them. Perhaps, if you were to give it something else, would it leave your flies be?

After five flies, painstakingly prepared, all dead in the head, you pack up. You glare at the microscope resentfully as you shut down your setup, one machine after the other. But the glow of the screen, the glow of the simulator, it doesn't shut off. A light shines from between the blackout curtains. It flickers. You check the power switch. The screen should be off. The laser has shut down for the day. A deathly silence settles over the imaging room as the cooling system stops. But the light remains; an eerie green glow, a beam coming back down from the photomultiplier tube, through the filters and the objective, shining through the empty holder onto the VR display. You hesitate. Is the microscope trying to tell you something? Is it…offering you something?

You shake your head and push back your chair. You need some fresh air. The oppressive darkness of the microscope room is getting to you, and the lack of sleep is giving you strange fancies. You should not have watched *The Fly*. Some non-insectoid company will fix you right up. You grab your bag and your coat, and you head out into the fresh air, walking straight to the pub around the corner. You order your drink at the bar, and the tender nods to a table in the corner, where you see your fellow PhD students playing a card game. You raise your glass in acknowledgement and join them, but the game sits uneasy with you. The chatter of your fellows feels empty. They are all real scientists. When your friend turns to you and asks how your experiments are going, you shrug noncommittally. What are you going to tell them? That you still can't manage a proper dissection? That the microscope is 'acting up'? You might as well admit your own incompetence. Your unsuitability for this career. They should never have admitted you to this program. You furtively finish your drink and leave the pub shortly after.

The screen has stopped flickering when you return to the microscope the next day, but an eerie glow illuminates the inside of the blackout curtains. Against your better judgement, you scramble around for the headset that is connected to your setup. The one that lets you check your stimulus when you're not watching movies. You put it on. A few of the more disturbing images of *The Fly* still play, but then the screen conjures images of neurons you can only dream of. The ebb and rise of fluorescent signals pulsing through them. The clarity of the brain's responses to your virtual predator. You think of your thesis. The hopes and dreams you pin on it. The empty pages where your data should go. The flies, dead and discarded in the alcohol, their recordings trash. The tantalizing images of the microscope. You remember the movie you watched. You would pay any price. To belong. To succeed. Your own brain cells project the only possible answer at the microscope: "YES."

The display dims. The glow dissipates from the microscope and, as you lift the headset off your head, you see *The Fly*'s credits roll. Nothing has happened. Nothing except for the invisible chain that now runs from your soul to the microscope, each link heavy against your conscience.

When you leave the institute, the sun is rising in the east. You are bleary-eyed as you trudge home to get some sleep after a long night of recordings. At last, you have something to show when your adviser asks about your progress. Something other than excuses. And when your mother calls, again, to ask about your graduation, you will be able to answer. Soon. Isn't that worth some discomfort?

You work hard that week, spending more time in the imaging room than ever before. While you feel the chain rattle against your peace of mind, you record fly after fly. They are reacting to your virtual predator. Your adviser is impressed with your results, and you see some relief in his eyes. Perhaps you will graduate before your funding runs out after all. Your data looks good. Promising. You just need more of it. Enough to sink P below 0.05. Who cares about anything else at this point? Certainly not you. Night after night, you continue dragging yourself to the lab, until your fingers are covered in scratches from mishandling your dissection tools and the glare of the sun hurts your eyes when you emerge. During the day you write – words of your thesis, or code to run your analysis, until it all blurs together and you nearly fall over. You cannot abide the taste of energy drink anymore, but it fuels you while your reserves diminish. Sleep is for those without better things to do, and besides, the clinking of the chain keeps you awake. Keeps you working.

Your professor's attitude has changed significantly in the past weeks. All of a sudden, you are the golden child. The journals *Nature* and *Science* are being mentioned. A glow has lit up in your hollow eyes that wasn't there before. You see it when you look in the mirror, faintly green. You work and work away in the dark until that day finally comes.

You write the last word of your thesis, assemble the final figure, and submit your manuscript.

You had expected relief. Expected that you could rest now, take a break, but the chain keeps pulling you back to the laboratory. Before, you thought you'd have to leave science after graduation. Now, you're not so sure. Perhaps, with your newfound success, you don't have to be done with science. Never mind the long hours, never mind your student debt. If you could extract enough preliminary data to write that grant proposal, certainly you wouldn't fail. That's what you tell yourself. The thought haunts you while you withdraw to your imaging refuge, where the hum of the microscope is a comforting background noise to your now-favorite movie. What work would you even be fit for, outside science? What skills do you even have? The doubts chase you like a predator on the edge of your field of view. A green flash, there and gone.

Your colleagues are impressed with your dedication as your life outside the lab becomes less and less real, chatting with them in the pub a distant dream. You have taped your fingers so that you can continue to dissect without bleeding, even if it hurts. There is nothing else for you to do but to continue measuring. You have come up with a new experiment for your flies: a virtual target for them to fly to, twisting forever out of reach, left and right, faster than a fly can turn. You longingly follow their flight with your headset, the movies you watched before all but forgotten. Only the words 'experiment ended' give you any release from the dizzying vistas. You vaguely think that perhaps you should be concerned, but the chain pulls you ever forward. Keeps you focused on your goal.

Your professor has come down to the lab to talk to you. You make sure to keep your eyes trained on him as he moves about the room. To hear the words coming from his mouth. He is telling you something important, you are sure, but all you hear is the buzzing of flies, and the restless grinding of the chain against...something. Surely all will be well, you tell yourself. You nod and smile until your professor is satisfied, and leaves.

You have started seeing flies wherever you leave the lab, which is less and less often. They fly out of your garbage just after you've emptied it. They buzz around the open can of Red Bull on your bedside table. They swirl around your head and make you dizzy even though you try to ignore them as you put your presentation together. When your adviser emails you about the thesis acceptance, the flies are there. When you dig through the pile of old laundry that should contain your best shirt, you see the telltale signs of pupating larvae on its sleeves. You scrape them off in a panic and hope nobody will notice the crusty stains during your thesis defense.

When the champagne is popped at your graduation party, the flies swarm you, their tiny brains glowing green. Your fellow scientists look at your swaying with concern, and you scratch your head, assuring them you're not drunk. When you mistake the bubbles rising in your glass for maggots, you stumble out, leaving confused colleagues behind. You crawl to the only place you feel safe: the microscope. Its chain a comforting set of armor around your soul, that keeps the flies at bay.

You have spent many a night and many a day down in the dark since your graduation, with the flickering glow of the screens, gathering more data from your flies, to assemble your grant proposal. Something has changed about the microscope; you can feel it. It was a comfort to you for a while, sitting here in the dark, isolated from the rest of the world with your flies and your dissections and your microscope. But the chain, it has started to chafe, and every time you step away from the microscope you feel…less. Fuzzier at the edges, as if parts of you are being taken out. The buzz of the flies soothed you at some point, able to drown out the demands of life. But your research progresses very slowly, or at least you believe it does, because you can't think clearly anymore. It doesn't matter: you watch the stimulus on your headset now with an intensity that borders on obsession. Your eyes dash left and right as the stripe oscillates, but if you move your eyes quickly enough, you can keep the stripe in front and it seems to stay still. You've made great progress that way. You only half remember why you were doing this in the first place, as you absentmindedly scratch your arm. But if you become fast enough, you can outmaneuver the flies.

When next you lift your headset, you see that your professor has come in. He moves so slowly compared to your target, that you can barely make him out, most of your vision a haze of green. You have been avoiding him. You have been avoiding most everyone. You lose sight of him when he stops, but you hear him speak to a second person, as if through water: "This is our imaging room, where we recorded all the data from our recent paper. Sorry, it seems to be in a bit of a state right now. Why don't you head on to the cafeteria? I'll be right there."

Both you and the microscope have gone still, and you wonder if your professor can see you through the haze of the flies. But then you sense something from the microscope, and it is echoed within you. Something predatory. The chain, wrapped tightly around what remains of your soul, seems to slacken for a moment. You don't know how to feel about it. It might be all that is keeping you going right now.

But perhaps it is the slack in the chain that allows you to hear your adviser more clearly than you have in months:

"…thought we had spoken about this. Listen, you are free to run experiments here, even if I can't employ you, but this is just not acceptable. I am recruiting a new student, and they will need to work here too. How can you train them, if this is the state of the lab? This is a biohazard!"

You ponder for a moment, but with the student out of sight, the rumble of the microscope, the grind of link on link has returned and it makes it hard to think, hard to speak.

"Do I need to leave?" you manage to croak out. You ask yourself the question, as much as your professor. Didn't you have a life out there at some point? Friends? A mother who cared?

"You need to clean up this infestation! How did it even get to this?"

Infestation. He is talking about your flies, the flies that follow your every movement, that are especially thick here, where they crawl out of the dried-up vials that once contained alcohol, that hatch from the pupation shells encrusted on your socks, your shirt, and even your skin. You don't remember washing in some time, and only now do you notice the itch, the crawling under your skin. Your adviser starts moving towards the door, and you fix your gaze on him as he does, following your target as you have practiced so often now on your headset. The flies follow. They are your babies after all. You raised them from maggot to flight. You trained them on your stimulus, to fly on target. And now they follow your unspoken command, the chain an extension of your will. You feel something flow from you to the microscope as you turn away from your adviser's frantic movements, and the new absence within calms you somehow. You have found your purpose here. You belong to something greater now. The microscope hums contentedly. It has taken all it can from you.

The police show up not long after. They wear masks and plastic shields across their faces, and they lead you away, past the horrified faces of your fellow scientists and your recovering professor.

You stare blankly ahead as you sit in the doctor's office, mild contempt on your mind for someone who chose to practice a trade rather than pursue scientific knowledge. You hear the physician explain your 'issues', words jumping out over the singing of your chain: strange head movements, imbalance, exaggerated startle response, reacting to invisible stimuli, and a strong aversion to open spaces. What stands out to you is that there are no flies here. The physician asks you to follow a light with your eyes, and finally there seems to be something normal about the situation: something you can do. The doctor reassures you that everything will be fine. She's wrong.

They disinfect the finest set of forceps for you. Anything larger would leave too many scars. You barely feel the sting as the needle enters the skin of your scalp. Only a few minutes later, you hear a grinding noise as the doctor saws through your skull and exposes the tissue below. You are frustrated by your inability to move, your head fixed to the chair, because the noise is maddening. You can't see or feel it, but you imagine how the doctor cuts through the dura mater, pushes aside the veins to expose the soft tissue of your visual cortex. A tear runs down your cheek as you see the first of the glowing green maggots drop into the doctor's stainless steel bowl. You are a doctor too now. A real scientist. Your final thought before you close your eyes, is of the microscope: how glorious your brain activity must look through it.

Author Note

This piece was me processing a time in my life when I felt I had one singular purpose at which I could either fail or succeed, and I did not consider failure an option. It started when I was in a position not unlike that of the scientist in this story. Fortunately, I could take action to find a way out of that doomed scenario, but the scientist in the story did not. It's a reflection on being so driven by a goal that it consumes all else – to the point that you even forget why you had that goal in the first place, and you lose sight of yourself.

There are a few key points where the scientist in the story could have taken a different path. Perhaps if they had dared open up to their peers in the beginning, they would not be so tempted by the microscope's pictures. Again when they handed in the thesis, or at the graduation party, there is a moment of reflection there; or even still when the professor comes down to the microscope room and finds the infestation. The chain then represents that obsession that leads the scientist to ignore all warning signs and separates them from their community and from reality itself. Their 'YES' signals the willingness to sacrifice their identity and wellbeing to the perceived recognition that achieving their doctorate will bring. The scientist has been watching *The Fly*; they know how horribly wrong it can go, and yet they don't see another way. They become the experiment, rather than the experimenter.

Finally, by mirroring the acts the scientist in the story inflicts upon their test subjects in what they themself undergo at the end, I wanted to reflect on how the way we treat ourselves influences the way we treat others and vice versa, and this ending became inevitable because of it. They have achieved their goal but have also never been further from it.

Calm Springs

C.D. Vázquez

I REMEMBER the town of Calm Springs fondly. Its grassy hills and rolling meadows come to me often, when I find myself overwhelmed by the intoxicating buzz and humdrum of the city. From its scenic hiking trails that wind through the woods, where the pines reach for the sky like hungry, green giants, to the cool waters of its many rivers, coursing towards destinations that, even now, only live in the corners of my imagination. Calm Springs lives in my mind – a small town full of small charms.

I thread the line between consciousness and sleep, fixing my eyes on the passing treeline, when a sudden shake jolts me awake. *Where am I?*

My mind gathers the fragments of the night before in reverse. I boarded the bus at dawn. Judging by the sour taste in my mouth and the smell of cigarettes hanging on to my clothes, I made my way directly from the local pub. There's a small bag tucked under the seat in front of me. It looks like I packed clothes for three days.

Another bump in the road rattles the bus and the red Moleskine journal slips from my bag like blood from a wound. I expect to find its pages blank, but there's a single line inked in blue on the first page.

The words will *come. Find them in Calm Springs. Love, L.*

That's right. My wife, Lucy, had *infected* me with the idea that I was due for a visit – no, an *escape*, she'd said. Maybe in the town where I once fell in love with writing, I would find a cure for the creative slump that had driven a rift between us. While I rode up north, she would take the girls to Florida and visit her parents.

Confusion gives way to understanding in my mind. I'm on a bus, riding I-65 to this old town of mine, seeking the relief of its small comforts. Searching for calm in Calm Springs.

It's hard to describe the bus; it is distinctly liminal – a place of transit designed to be forgettable. The rows stretch in both directions, with two dull, gray seats on each side of the center aisle. They are nearly filled with unfamiliar faces, most of them lost in thought or sleep.

I try to write a few words, but the well is dry. It has been for some time now. While my thoughts are incapable of putting together a single line of good writing, they excel in birthing the mother of all headaches.

I should call Lucy and tell her I'm fine. Tell her I'll be back soon and—

"You headed for Calm Springs?" An old lady with snow-white hair and thick-rimmed glasses interrupts my thoughts. She strolls down the aisle in a flowered dress that drapes over her as elegantly as worn-out curtains.

"Aren't we all?" I reply. "I'm headed there for the weekend."

She smirks like she's been let in on a secret. "Well, it's been too darn long for me," she says. "I'm Susan." The lady offers a wrinkled hand.

I shake it, hoping she won't take the seat next to me. "James."

I let silence fill the space between us, hoping she would leave. But even then she lingers, fishing for words to kindle a conversation.

"Calm Springs," she says, letting the name of my hometown rest on her tongue, an unsolicited reverie. "I haven't been there since my husband, Robert, passed."

I nod. "I'm sorry for your loss."

"It's such a lovely place," she says.

I feel compelled to agree. Because Calm Springs *is* the loveliest place. Especially this time of year, when it is neither too hot nor too cold.

"I grew up there," I say, disarmed by her southern warmth. Inspired by her assessment of this town I love.

The scent of perfume fills the air as she settles into the seat beside me. It reminds me of my great-aunts. It smells of flowers and old age, and Sunday dresses packed away in closets. Equally floral and pungent.

"Is that so? Which street, if you don't mind me asking?"

"Down by Sycamore Road."

Her smile lights up like fireworks. "Robert and I built our first home on that very same street. He always did say the sun rose and set on Sycamore Road. Lovely, *lovely* place."

Her words lull me back into my mind. I smile, thinking of my first home on Sycamore Road. The one my parents built at the end of the street, with its walls painted blue like the sky. The front porch had a set of red windows that faced the driveway where my father kept his mint green Buick Apollo. A pristine white fence guarded my mother's tiny garden.

We talked about Calm Springs for a while, reminiscing about the town that witnessed the early days of my life. Of its single main street that split the town in two, paved with old cobblestones the mayor had flown in from Spain. Of the town hall by the plaza, where Susan's husband had proposed. Of Fred Dunn's cantina, where I had my first beer at the precocious age of sixteen.

Slowly but surely, we find connective tissue – places and people we both met during our respective times at Calm Springs. Susan's sister used to own the bowling alley where I claimed my first kiss. My mother worked with Robert in a small pastry shop by the plaza. Now that I fine-comb through my memories, I realize Susan and I have crossed paths on more than one occasion. Back then, when her hair was not snow-white but gilded blonde, and she smelled of fresh flowers like the ones that grow in the fields of Calm Springs.

"What a lovely coincidence," I say, easing into my seat. "What brings you back to Calm Springs?"

A slight tremble in her lips gives away her grief. Susan produces a white handkerchief and preemptively wipes at unseen tears.

"I'm visiting Robert," she replies. I can tell the wound of his absence must run deep because she is quiet for a long time. She must be so lonely.

Aren't we all?

I think of the girls and Lucy. Realizing in a way that *I'm* lonely too. Too busy and concerned with work and money and words and empty pages, to enjoy my own family. *I should call and tell them I'll be back home soon.*

"Would you mind if I borrow your phone? I need to call my daughter and I'm afraid this clumsy old lady forgot to pack her charger for the trip." Susan smiles with a set of unnaturally white teeth. "Don't want her to call every sheriff station along the way asking about her mama. She's a worrier, that one. Just like my Robert."

I realize the phone is already in my hand. Lucy's number is dialed in and my thumb hovers over the button that would place the call. I hesitate. Then I remind myself this is Susan. *I've known her forever, and she needs my help.*

I instinctively surrender the device. "Of course."

"I'll be in the back," Susan says, as soon as the smartphone is in her hand. "This might take a minute. She'll want to know *everything* about the trip." The old lady rolls her eyes in a way that makes her look younger, and leaves before I can protest. Her perfume lingers behind her like a snail's trail. I make a mental note to call Lucy when Susan returns and divert my thoughts to the other passengers on the bus.

I wonder if I've met any of them before. I scan through their faces, and slowly find, burrowed deep, memories that take me back to days past. A few rows to the back, I spot Maxine, whom I dated once, right before prom. Cruz, my old gym teacher, sits near the front. He caught me and Jimmy Hartsfield by the bleachers once, leafing through an old *Playboy* magazine that Jimmy had snuck out of his father's private collection.

The warmth of familiarity washes over me. We are *all* going home to Calm Springs. Drawn back, inevitably, to its small-town charms. To the memories that had made us – one way or another – members of a very special club.

The bus makes a pit stop at a 7-Eleven off I-65. I stretch my legs and greet the other travelers I know. The driver informs us we'll take twenty minutes before continuing for the second leg of the trip. I decide to grab a snack, maybe a drink.

A tattoo-riddled clerk greets me halfheartedly from behind the counter. I nod politely and venture into the labyrinthine aisles filled with junk food, thinking of the soft drinks that quelled my thirst after school in Calm Springs. The search leads me all the way to the back. Away from the other travelers to a row of old refrigerators that hum in unison, secluded in a dimly lit section of the store. A dark silhouette catches my eye as I scan through an array of soda cans and pick my bounty.

The mumbling man stands in the corner, facing a rusty door labeled EMPLOYEES ONLY on the opposite side of the aisle. I can't make out his face, but his whispers carry towards me like a siren's song. *I shouldn't be here*, my mind whispers.

The mumbling man kneels on the ground, his hands wrapping around his abdomen. He appears to be in pain.

"Sir?" I step towards him. Drawn by concern and curiosity.

When I get closer, I notice a half-empty bottle of Grey Goose, dangling like a lifeline from his hand.

"Do you need help?"

The mumbling man retches a thin stream of vomit on the linoleum floor. The black liquid pools in front of him. Rivulets of malignant, undigested darkness flow from the corners of his mouth. I watch in horror, expecting a rotten stench to make me lurch the contents of *my* stomach, but the air is filled with a sweetness that reminds me of something familiar. It reminds me of Calm Springs.

"I'll go get some help," I say.

The mumbling man waves a hand like it's nothing. He stumbles through the door meant for employees and is gone.

I walk to the front of the store in a daze and notify the clerk of the mess left behind. The young man curses under his breath and says he'll handle it. My appetite is spoiled, but I queue in line anyway.

I want to go home. I could hike a ride to a nearby station and postpone the trip.

"You headed to Calm Springs?" asks a voice behind me.

"Aren't we all?" I answer, turning to face it.

It's a young girl, probably in the latter days of her rebellious teens. She reminds me of my oldest daughter, Kara. Hair streaked with dashes of pink and purple. Nose pierced one too many times and way too much shadow adeptly applied under a set of lovely, if not sad, blue eyes.

She shrugs – the universal response of her generation. It makes me feel old. Makes me long for the young days at Calm Springs even more. "How about you?"

"Yeah…I'm headed home."

"All by yourself?"

She averts her eyes. "I'm old enough."

It's my turn to shrug, which makes her smile.

"Old enough to know these?" I ask, lifting the soda can in my hand. The label features a splash of reds, yellows, and blues blending in a colorful explosion.

"Whatcha got there?"

"This," I say, cracking the can open and taking a long sip of the dark caramel liquid. "This is Classic Cola. It used to be that you could only get these around Calm Springs."

She smiles and cracks a joke that implies I'm old. "I was only three when we moved out." There's a hint of sadness in the way she says it. "I remember one thing about Calm Springs." Her hands wrap around her elbows and for a second it looks like she's going to cry. "It's the last place where I was happy. Like the world went wrong right after I left."

I know exactly the feeling.

"Good thing we'll be back soon," I say, forcing a smile.

I suspect she's a runaway, but it's not my place to ask. Everyone on our bus is running away from something. Even me. Who am I to judge a fellow traveler seeking haven?

On my way to the bus, I can't help but wonder: if there are places made to build us up – like Calm Springs – then the opposite must also be true. The 7-Elevens by the road could very much be Limbos. Places of transit, or worse, for that clerk, places where we remain stuck forever. Places that break us down, that digest us slowly like Venus Flytraps.

I examine our group in transit, imagining the worlds we've left behind for the weekend. The struggles of making a living, the loneliness we carry, the ghosts we run away from, the frustrations of being less – so much less – than we ever hoped ourselves to be. And how none of it would matter, because, at the end of the day, Calm Springs is a bus ride away. With its slow, timeless afternoons and sermon-filled Sundays. With the neighborly gossip and the reassurance that every face is known and every name is household kosher.

I feel like writing again, but I fight against the pull of it. Sometimes the words need to boil until the bubbling tips over. I will write when I get to Calm Springs. I'll go to Miranda's diner and order a vanilla float with fries. Dip them in the ice cream like I used to. I'll look for the coin-operated cabinet in the back, next to the restrooms. Hopefully, it's still there. I'll break a few dollars and play Galaga until I run out. Then I'll stroll down the main road and the countryside will fill my nose with the scents of pinewood and juniper, and everything will be as it once was. Only then will I write. I'm lost in thought when the mumbling man takes a seat next to me.

"We need to get off the bus," he says. I turn to face bloodshot eyes filled with an unmistakable dread. "You're headed to Calm Springs." It isn't a question. *Why would it be?*

"Aren't we all?" I reply.

He shakes his head, trembling underneath his worn-out Nirvana shirt. "Do I know you?" I ask.

"Listen to me." He places a firm hand on my shoulder. "Calm Springs does not exist." Droplets run down his brow, and some gather over his thin upper lip. He looks ill to me. *Desperate*.

I can't help but chuckle while I respond. "I grew up in Calm Springs, buddy. Down by—"

"—Sycamore Road, am I right?" He blurts out the question in one single word – *amirite*.

"That's right. How did you…?"

He looks around, making sure no one can hear him before answering. "Everyone…everyone on this bus says the same thing. They're *all* from Sycamore Road. Where the sun rises and sets? Don't you find that strange? *I'm from Sycamore Road…*" He glances outside the window. "Do you know who I am?" he asks. "Look at me!" His hand pulls my head towards him. I can smell the booze in his breath. "Have you ever met me before?"

"I—"

"Think! Think hard!"

I dig deep into a well of memories. His face feels more familiar by the second. "*Jimmy*? Jimmy Hartsfield?"

"I *think* that's my name." His index finger taps on his sweaty skull. "But I've never set foot in Calm Springs," he says, feverishly. "I mean, I thought I did until…until…"

I want to help him. Jimmy looks ill and lost.

Aren't we all?

There's still some of the boy I'd met so many years ago in his eyes. I knew then and there that life hadn't treated Jimmy Hartsfield kindly. "Jimmy, it's me. You know me."

He shakes his head in disbelief. "That's what it wants us to think," Jimmy says. "We need to leave this bus, by God, James, you need to come with me. I could live with leaving the others behind but not you. NOT YOU." Tears run down his face.

"You have to calm down, Jimmy. We're almost there. We're almost home." I place my hand on *his* shoulder. A plea for reason. A bit patronizing, I know, but it *feels* right. "*Excuse me…*"

I squeeze by my old friend to reach the center aisle. Jimmy doesn't react; his eyes are suddenly transfixed on the passenger window. I rush to the back of the bus feeling sick. The door to the restroom springs open with a gentle pull. Just in time for me to arch my face over the toilet seat. Nothing comes, at first. Then it all comes out at the same time. A black slush that looks like viscous tar sprouts violently from my mouth. Every time I think the retching is over, it returns more viciously until it suddenly stops. There's knocking on the door.

"Are you OK, James?" It's Susan's voice.

I wipe a black tendril of gunk still hanging from the corner of my mouth before responding. "I'll be out in a second. Can I have my phone back?"

A moment of silence. "Of course. Just come outside."

Susan greets me under the arch of the door. "You look terrible. Why don't you take a seat, James?"

I tell her I'm fine. "Just need to call Lucy and the girls."

"You can call her when we get there," she says. "You know there's no signal here, silly." She flashes a genuine smile. Susan escorts me next to Jimmy – who's shivering next to the window. "Look at our beautiful town!" Susan cries. A single tear of devotion rolls down her wrinkled cheeks. "Isn't it beautiful, Jimmy?"

Jimmy nods. Jimmy cries. Jimmy isn't really here. Who the fuck is Jimmy Hartsfield? Where am I?

Home, my mind whispers.

The answer lies in the horizon, beyond the blood skyline, above the trees. Like some ancient outer god lurking in the wilderness, Calm Springs awaits. I wonder how nobody has ever seen it towering as tall as a skyscraper. Long bony arms – hundreds of them – spread in an eternal embrace. Every mouth in its gargantuan body recursively gives way to concentric circles of teeth from whence it feeds. Each crevice is a rose-tinted memory luring us to venture in, blissfully unaware. The buses drive toward them, willingly. I blink in disbelief and the visage of the abomination is replaced by the silhouette of the town that never was: *Calm Springs.*

The other passengers gather around us, a concerned bunch – no – an old group of friends. The old lady who worked at the school cafeteria, the postman who delivered correspondence every morning, classmates from our grade, and even Coach Cruz are here for us. Susan pulls my head back. Other hands force my mouth open until their mouths lean above mine and pour the black tar down my throat. The sweet nectar of nostalgia fills me.

Jimmy is next. When we are done, Jimmy looks serene, lost in thought. Here but not here. I wonder if his mind is soothed by the cozy memories of our collective experiences. Of the times we played hide-and-seek around the neighborhood. Of Sycamore Road sunsets – for the sun did rise and set on

Sycamore Road. Of racing on our bikes toward the ice cream parlor right at the end of Memory Lane. I know my mind drifts to these corners when the living gets rough. When the bills rack up and the going gets hard. Thinking of Jimmy, Susan, and Coach Cruz, soothes me. Thinking of Calm Springs, which I often remember fondly.

I return my eyes to the road. The pine woods stretch around us in every direction, an endless sea of warm greens and grays. A small sign in serif font reads WELCOME TO CALM SPRINGS. When the bus crosses the threshold, I feel it.

I'm finally home.

The bus pulls up to the station and we exit in a single file with our belongings close to our chests. The things we carry in our hands and the burdens we carry in our souls. We can walk from here on out. Calm Springs breathes around us, expanding and contracting with the rustling of the leaves. It rejoices in our arrival, almost as much as we revel in it.

There is so much to write about.

Calm Springs unfolds, as it once did before me. A town full of memories, a cozy place for the mind, a shelter for the lost and the broken like me. The most beautiful place. I finally close my eyes at Sycamore Road, where the sun rises and sets at Calm Springs.

Author Note

Calm Springs isn't a real place, but make no mistake – it exists for us all. It resides in the corners of our minds. For James, it manifests as an idealized version of his hometown. For us, it might take the shape of a place of comfort, a past relationship, or a moment in time in which we seek shelter when reality becomes too much to bear. Should you be tempted to linger for long, a warning: Calm Springs can be a dangerous place.

'Calm Springs' is informed by my struggle with generalized anxiety disorder. The narrative voice is intentionally trancelike and feverish. It tries to capture the erratic cadence of a mind grappling to be present amidst waves of intrusive thoughts. Descriptions of the town are verbose but vague, almost primitive, like they draw from the basic building blocks of a memory of a memory. They elicit a questioning of reality, mirroring the way anxiety distorts our worries and weaponizes our perception against us. The same way our protagonist is manipulated by the sinister entity that infects his mind.

The monster that stalks James is written in the tradition of Lovecraftian horror: a being that escapes comprehension, elusive in its description. To me, anxiety is a gargantuan beast with many faces and no name. Most days, the more I try to understand it, the less likely I am to truly unravel its source. I like to think of Calm Springs, the monster, as a metaphysical Venus Flytrap. A creature that lures its victims and slowly digests them. What better lure than the proverbial good old days?

Escapism is a common coping mechanism for those of us who struggle with anxiety. The rose-tinted memories of youth, a common breakpoint when we reminisce. A moment of respite before 'the world went wrong', like the young runaway in our story points out. Living in 'safe haven' memories – as opposed to confronting the harsh realities of everyday life – can consume us. When we glorify the past, the present always falls short. Fixating on an idyllic future sets us up for disappointment – or worse, digestion by an otherworldly abomination.

Mindfulness is not a cure, but it is a start. To those of us who struggle, rest assured: While our protagonist's journey ends in Calm Springs, the beasts that haunt us can be slain.

The Soup of Life

Callum Rowland

THREE WEEKS since we arrived, and still my brain aches with just how different this planet is. Thinking about Earth, it is like recalling a first draft, a rough sketch, simple and grey by comparison. It is even more mind blowing for Julie, who spent her whole life on Lunar. Grant seems underwhelmed, but that's just Grant.

This morning, we watched three suns rise over the purple sea. The coffee was good – even through the feed-tube – and our suits let in just enough warmth. One of the whale-like creatures we've named a Mobius breached the water, and we witnessed the first murmuration of an avian species.

We keep finding reasons not to return to the ship. Sampling is the sought-after role, but even external maintenance is preferable to analysis; to being shut away from this extraordinary place. We've abandoned rotas for chance. Taken to rock, paper, scissors as a very scientific method of determining who does what each cycle. I lost today, but Julie won. Her smile made the prospect of thirty hours inside seem like less of a hardship.

Speaking of, my samples aren't going to dissect themselves.

* * *

I'm looking forward to sampling today, though we are a little late getting started. Julie wanted to discuss the implications of the planet's tidally locked moon, and it took Grant interrupting for us to realise just how long we'd been sitting together.

Scans show zone nineteen is mostly brush at surface level, sedimentary rock below. It's a long walk, but my most recent analysis session has given me plenty to think about en route. Three different species of invertebrate were dissected, each distinctly different, yet each with an internal make-up too alike to be called coincidence. Most akin to that of a crayfish, but the organs appear fluid, or interchangeable. I don't exactly know yet. All three samples were also riddled with parasites. I incinerated them upon completing the analysis but retained a sample of the parasite for further study.

We're yet to identify anything land-based that could potentially prey on us. No mammals, yet. Grant jokes about sounds he hears in the night. Neither me nor Julie put any stock in what he says, but still, it would be prudent to return before dark.

* * *

There was an undercurrent of tension in the ship last night, and I fear I may have been partly to blame. The suns had set by the time I returned. As I stripped and sterilised, I could hear Grant telling a droll story. Julie occasionally laughed, mostly out of kindness, or to indulge him, I suspect.

Grant asked me about the empty sample in slot three hundred. That was the parasite I had retained. I was halfway into my suit, in quite the panic, when I realised it was a joke. Poor taste, I felt. My reaction was less than adult. I sulked for a time, before Julie pulled me out of my foul mood. She is so good like that.

Zone nineteen was just as fascinating as every other zone thus far; home to a host of strange, small creatures, but it was the plant life that captivated me most. The brush covering the ground was alive in an almost animal way. It reminded me of coral, with polyps that opened and closed. Fine tentacles extruded from them, grasping at the air. There must be a food source of some kind in the chemical make-up of the atmosphere here, and the knowledge made me thankful for our suits.

I checked in on Harold before bunking down. Harold is a reptile, similar in appearance to an axolotl, only larger and with an additional set of legs. We have a handful of live studies in the sealed tanks, but Harold is the most interesting. Inquisitive, and quite adorable really. It would be unwise to get too attached to a specimen; still, I'm enjoying studying him.

* * *

In the last couple of days, Grant's jokes have taken on an edge I'm not sure I like. Julie goes along with them, but she always lays a hand on my arm or offers a smile after, with a look that says, 'let him have his juvenile fun'.

I do, for her sake. Conflict between two parties can have a detrimental effect on team efficiency, and I don't want her to think poorly of me.

We played rock, paper, scissors again. Grant won, though there was some controversy for the first time. Serves us right for gambling with our desires. My turn to be confined to quarters. I can't say I object. The long hikes of the previous days have taken it out of me. I feel depleted, and a little dejected.

Just me and Harold tomorrow.

* * *

It is my third consecutive day on analysis duty. I'm fairly certain Grant is cheating, though how you prove cheating in a game of chance is quite beyond me. Perhaps I have some unidentified tell.

The confinement is making my skin itch. Of course, I can stretch my legs whenever I feel like it, but stepping out under the azure sky to stare at a phenomenally alien landscape only makes me all the more sullen to return inside. I've found myself talking freely to Harold on numerous occasions. I know he can't possibly understand me, but it's more cathartic than stewing in my thoughts.

Julie commented on my pallid appearance this morning. I was too embarrassed to tell her I've suffered mild dysentery for the last twenty-four hours. I ran a scan on myself: all clear. Dirty suit tubes to blame, perhaps. Maintenance has been passed between her and Grant. I don't want Julie to think I'm accusing her of failing to keep things clean, so I plan to speak to Grant in private about it at some point.

On the plus side, I've dissected a selection of amphibians, reptiles, and even a fish Grant managed to spear. What I have now confirmed is fascinating. Every species shares two things and two things only. The fluid nervous system I observed previously, even when this serves to work against their body, and the parasites. I have no theories as yet on the nervous system, but I begin to suspect the parasites are relatively harmless. None of the species collected show any signs of distress or loss of faculty. Perhaps it's some sort of symbiotic relationship. Harold must harbour them, and he is quite the happy reptile. We could really do with a larger animal to study.

Grant is outside the ship now, returned early and making an awful racket. I'd better not leave him out there any longer.

* * *

I didn't need to have that chat with Grant. Turns out the dysentery got him too. He'd been sick in his helmet – horrible smell. Julie had quite the panic that we might have been exposed to something untoward, and I was forced to confess my own ailment. Grant was furious that I hadn't spoken up about it before, and Julie seemed upset for the same reason, which in turn left me quite maudlin.

Twenty-four hours of isolation are almost up, and examinations of our stools and bloods show no sign of anything malevolent. I'm much improved, so we're remaining optimistic that it was just a bad batch of rations, or those dirty tubes Grant vehemently denies.

I think the isolation was probably a good thing. Grant and Julie have been spending more and more time in private conversation. I catch his looks and suspect I might be the butt of a few jokes. He's not good for her, and I miss our own private conversations.

The lack of maintenance has allowed the local flora to encroach on the ship. It consists of mostly weed-like plants, capable of very slow travel. The thin vines that weave across the ground in this zone have started to wrap around the legs of our ship. Speeding up the playback from the ship's external cameras, it almost looks like it's investigating us.

* * *

Things have been busy. Grant's condition relented and he returned to his self-appointed role of sampler. The days of rock, paper, scissors are over. He refers to himself as the explorer of our group, though less than three days ago he was an incontinent mess. Every suggestion of rotating roles is met by what I can only describe as hostility.

Julie spoke with me in private for the first time in a while. It should have been pleasant. It was not. She spent a large portion of the conversation circling around the suggestion that I was causing friction, before trying to convince me she was speaking from concern for me. Apparently, I've not been myself, whatever that means. Too much time cooped up in the ship was her analysis.

As a result, I have been relegated to maintenance. To attempting, in vain, to fend off the encroaching fauna of this planet while also sampling what I can from nearby zones. Each morning, I wake to find vines coiled ever further around the legs of the ship. It is a thankless and relentless task to keep them at bay, and I feel the vines constricting within me also. The lustre of our little team is beginning to wear thin. The pair of them have ostracised me.

But even as I lose my connection to them, I feel as though I am making new ones in other places. Understanding more of this environment, of this world.

I miss my talks with Harold. The absence of judgement or condescension.

* * *

They don't understand this planet. Not like I do. Julie is an adequate analyst, and in another situation could be made to see, but all my suggestions about patterns and behavioural correlations between species are shot down by Grant. He seems to think he is in charge, despite being the least qualified of the three of us. A neanderthal. His sole interest seems to be in how many animals he can kill with his spear.

I have lost the battle against the vines, or else given up, conceding the ship to them. It is entombed, and it is all I can do to hack the door clear each day. Instead, I am utilising my time to observe what I know to be true. This ecosystem is connected in a way ours is not. Or maybe ours is, only it is more readily observable here.

The similarities in species go beyond their nervous systems. I have seen murmurations of birds moving in the same patterns as hordes of tiny insects upon the dunes. Mobius whales in the bay of the purple sea, watching me with the same expression Harold wears within his tank. Shelled beachcombers waving their claws in the air in a mimicry of the brush-plants' polyps.

More than that, I can feel it. It is as if all the creatures, the plants, the sea, they all have a secret language, and I merely lack the vocabulary to understand it. Something has changed within me. I do not feel well, but at the same time I do not feel unwell. Just, different.

I will speak to Julie, and I suppose Grant too, again tonight.

* * *

Grant killed Harold. Said he was just a specimen to study. Said that was always his purpose. To die. His obtuse nature disgusts me. As if anything on this planet is simply here to dismantle, is merely a reptile or insect or plant. It is all so much more.

He has infected Julie with his mindset, twisted her perception of me. I see the way she recoils. How she turns away. I wish he was gone, then maybe she would understand.

The rejection I feel is not only from my crewmates. The vines around our ship are dying, the once pale earth it rests upon turned black and dry. I fear our mission may be in jeopardy if we do not do something. I can smell the purple sea, and it smells…like home.

* * *

I am watching Grant on the ship's external cameras. On the screen he looks small, despite his bulky suit. He bangs on the door with his spear. Julie is crying. I have explained the situation to her as clearly as I can. Grant is a threat to our mission. My insides might feel like they have been replaced with a roiling snake, but the sense in my gut is strong. Grant will kill me if I let him in. The same way he killed Harold. The same way he means to kill everything inside the analysis lab. He is decay. He is death.

Clangs ring out around the ship as he hammers his spear once more. Julie flinches with each echo of metal on metal. When he first returned, she attempted to open the door manually, but I have control now. She will understand, in time.

Something else is approaching the ship, slinking towards Grant. It is dark, so the cameras pick up no movement, but I feel it like I feel all the fine threads of life around this planet. Grant must feel it too, for he flees. He spares one last glance into the camera, and though I can see his expression clearly, I'm not sure what expression it is.

* * *

Julie has been far more pleasant to me since Grant's departure, though she is possessed of a newly developed nervous disposition. She doesn't look particularly well, poor thing. I have quite a pale demeanour myself, though I feel excellent. Peaceful. It's as if my mind has become more focused. Clear. I hardly have to think, simply act.

I feel like going out, and without the cumbersome suit. A few days ago, I might have baulked at the idea. Now it seems obvious. Natural. I said as much to Julie. She nodded along, but I saw the constriction of her pupils, smelled the salt of her perspiration. My senses seem attuned, and her lies of agreement were like a blazing symbol above her head.

I do hope she can come round to my way of thinking. To understanding. The mission has changed. There is no going home for us. I ran my bloods again, out of curiosity. What I found was of little surprise, or consequence.

* * *

Julie screamed as I carried her out. She thrashed in my arms and clung to the ship's door, but this new strength I feel was too much for her. Like a newly married couple, I carried her over the threshold and together we breathed the unfiltered air. She wouldn't stop crying, so I was forced to carry her further, drag her down to the purple sea.

The water was beautiful. I could see every microorganism like the billion stars in the night sky. A soup of algae and writhing cellular life. I made her drink. Taste the rich life of this planet. We must embrace it, or be purged by it.

She was quite violently sick, and upon return to the ship she would not speak, except to call me a murderer. It is not me she is accusing. The person she thinks killed Grant is not a person anymore, not an individual. I think of Harold, and I do not miss him anymore, for what Harold was I now am also.

I released the live samples. Those that were killed I took back into myself, their bodies crunching and popping until my chin was wet with the same liquid I am. I returned myself to myself and myself and myself.

* * *

Julie, the woman, could not be made to understand. Her mind was too small, her fear too strong. Illogical. The man I used to be had cared for her, but those feelings were only confused electrical signals within a nervous system now irrevocably altered.

I had no choice but to purge her, but my attempt was a failure. She surprised me with her tenacity for singular existence, and something within me caused confliction and hesitation.

The injuries I sustained in the process will not heal. Even changed as this one – I am – is, vital organs are failing. My arm, severed by the ship's door, lies useless on the ground next to me. I watch the ship, in which she sealed herself, ascend upon a trail of fire.

I feel myself inside her, where she drank of my life, but her body is rejecting me. If it continues to do so she will die, alone in the ship. Perhaps she will accept the change, as I – this one – did. I can hope. She travels into a place I did not know it was possible to travel; the black sea above. If she accepts, she will show me new wonders. If she does not, she will not. So it goes.

I approach myself on four, taloned feet and examine my – this one's – dying body. A low growl rumbles in my throat as I ingest the severed arm, returning it to myself. I do not make another sound as I consume the rest. From experience, I know this will cause some discomfort to process. The other one did too.

I feel something, some small sensation, as I am consumed. It is something new to me. I do not have a word for it, this feeling, but it makes me want to howl. It is as though I have lost something, some part of myself. This one was different, somehow. Alien, the word comes to me.

I arch my neck, and a hundred different cries fill the sky.

Author Note

I approached this story knowing I wanted to write a 'descent into madness' style story, focusing specifically on the paranoia and anxiety that can warp our realities – something most of us have experienced at one point or another.

Reality as an idea interests me; how one person's reality can be very different to another's, and neither is necessarily right or wrong. Our reality in any given moment is very much based on, or shaped by, our perceptions, and mental state obviously plays a huge part in that.

Taking a group of people and placing them in a confined space for a prolonged period can be a natural catalyst for heightening these thought processes. Using science fiction trappings and an alien lifeform as a physical manifestation allowed me to take this idea to the nth degree.

Many of us will have been in the protagonist of this story's shoes (thankfully, only metaphorically) at some point in our lives – struggling to make or maintain connections with others, perhaps feeling targeted or ostracised, fighting to maintain our own sense of self when faced with the unknown – and I hoped therefore to imbue a level of sympathy, or empathy, for him. His story is a tragedy, as much as it is a horror.

I'm a big fan of bittersweet endings, and despite the horrific events towards the end of this story I like to think there was a glimmer of hope left for at least one of the characters.

Speak

L.E. Daniels

I: Child

A stutter is living in a house haunted by the sea:
Pressurized by gust and tide—panes buckle,
    salt gnaws, trees lean—
Bleached by focus of hungry sun and seabirds
    who cannot fly

Rollers threaten outside-in as the drowned
    gather, washed out,
Muttering in corners—obsessed
with shipwrecks but legless,
Handless in periwinkle rot, waiting to—

Catch hair or hem or heel and send us tumbling
    down cellar stairs
Again, toward sandy seepage and weeping,
    brackish holes
Where ghosts are eager to prove they exist

you stupid
retard
can't you
just speak?

II: Adult

We still don't know when words will—crumble
Slippery as broken clamshells
Underfoot, undertongue

The paintings have always been crooked
In this house—where we slow our breaths,
And walls crawl, and stairs creak by themselves

As paint peels, we learn a stutter
Is just another—witness, another cold ghost
Of ourselves needing to be warmed

we speak best when we sing
from a house galvanized,
anchor-plated, with ghosts in windows
and sirens in repose upon stones

Author Note

Living with a stutter creates a precarious relationship with our internal and external worlds. We learn as children that we can't trust ourselves to *get it right* no matter how much we practice. Repeatedly, we stumble into well-worn traps, our noisy struggle a beacon for bullies and the ignorant. We're told that we'll grow out of it, but instead we grow around it, and while the fear and humiliation of our youth recedes, the lessons remain.

At fifty-three, I discovered with great relief that a stutter is a form of neurodiversity, and that the constant internal parkour of this neurological condition shapes a developing brain. From the speed-searches for synonyms I could say in social situations, I grew to value precision, the cadence of language, and the dovetailing meanings of words. The stutter also gave me lingering insights into humanity's cruelty and subtle gestures of compassion. I learned what it means to have a voice after being without one, and how strong our sense of self becomes when crafted from the bones of our vulnerability.

A Solitary Voice

Ramsey Campbell

WHEN HER PHONE RANG at three in the morning Tina knew only that it couldn't be her mother. The light above the supermarket aisle seemed to flare between her eyes, solidifying into pain. The phone twitched against her hip as she returned both handfuls of razors to the trolley she was unloading. Gordon stopped replenishing a cabinet of frozen meat to watch her disentangle the phone from a handkerchief. She stuffed the shamefully frayed wad into her pocket while she demanded "Hello?"

"Hello, my name is Meryl. How are you today?"

"Awake."

"That's good to hear. We are Compensation For You."

"I didn't know I needed compensating for."

"Have you had an accident in the last two years that wasn't your fault?"

"I don't know how much has been."

"Please hold while I connect you with a supervisor."

Tina winked at Gordon, who gave his head a shake that failed to dislodge a frown from his brows. "Hello, how are you today?" a voice by no means wholly unlike its predecessor said.

"Is this a human being now?"

"I understand you have had an accident that was not your fault."

"I don't think any of them were."

"Can I take some details of the incident so we can arrange the payments you're entitled to?"

"Why don't I just tell you where I bank and all the rest of it and get it over with." The ache between her eyes had begun to reach its spikes for them. "If I had a car I'd take care how I drove," she said. "Maybe I'll be able to afford one with all the money you'll be paying me. Now you really shouldn't use language like that to a lady. You could find yourself in trouble with the police."

The woman left her with a final adjective and terser noun that had a vowel in common. Tina sent Gordon a wry grin, but he only shook his head again, apparently at her. "You oughtn't to play with people like that," he said.

"I don't think I behaved too badly in the circumstances. They deserved worse."

"I mean it's not a good idea to get on the wrong side of their sort."

"I shouldn't think there's any right side."

"I'm saying they're criminals and they can track you down."

"They don't know who I am. You could tell it was a random call."

"Just because they didn't say your name doesn't mean they don't know it. You ought to be careful in case. They can do all sorts of things with technology now."

His suggestions felt like dreams she would rather not have, and didn't help her headache. He fell silent as Lewis appeared in the aisle that separated theirs. "Is there an emergency?" the manager said.

"I think Tina may have got herself into a bit of trouble."

"I can answer for myself, thank you. I was dealing with a scammer."

"You took your time," Lewis said, "if you knew that's what they were."

"If we string them along we're stopping them from calling somebody who might be taken in."

"That's very admirable, but I'll ask you to remember our slogan."

"Whenever you're up we are, you mean."

The motto for the night shift earned a barely patient look. "Customers are our life," Lewis reminded her as though he was reading the slogan on her forehead, "which means they're buying our time as well as their shopping."

"I always give them mine when they ask."

As Lewis left her with a blink that did duty as a caution Gordon said "You weren't telling the truth, were you?"

"What do you mean?"

Her impromptu duet with Lewis failed to make either of them laugh. "You told them you didn't have a car," Gordon said.

"Why would I tell anyone like that the truth? Anyway, I can't afford to run it much."

"I hope you find your salary acceptable." Without awaiting an answer Lewis said "I'll just remind you of store policy on phones. They may be carried on the night shift but only to accept emergency calls."

"Sometimes you don't know what kind of call it is till you answer."

"Are you likely to receive any now you're, you'll excuse me, on your own?"

"It won't make any difference. My mother never would have called. She was scared of using mobiles in case they tricked her somehow."

"Perhaps you shouldn't be too fond of using yours. It could make life harder for everyone if we abuse our privileges."

No doubt his tonelessness was designed to sound professional, but she found it closer to inhuman. When she returned to shelving, the jagged shard of pain between her eyes took quite a time to dull into a persistent pulsing ache. She couldn't risk taking any more tablets yet when she'd begun her shift with two of the strongest the supermarket stocked. She needed a prescription, but it was far too early to make a call.

The Checking You Out self-service lanes began to greet shoppers before dawn. As Tina made for the railway station, she met pedestrians on their way to work if not home to their apartments, in conversation with their phones or intent on them. The lift to the underground platform told her what preceded its descent and then described its progress. "I know they are," her headache provoked her to retort. "I know you are."

Did the train have the same efficient female voice? The security advice it gave at every station ended by assuring passengers "Got a phone, you're not alone." Tina could have felt it was directed at her, since there was nobody else in the carriage. "I know I have," she said more than once. "But I am."

By now the train had climbed into daylight or at least a feeble greyish dawn above her suburb. The voice of a television newsreader passed from front room to front room as she trudged home, but she couldn't distinguish a word. Her own house was quiet until she spoke. At least she could talk freely now that she was by herself – could say things she would never have admitted to her mother. "So that's another night done with. Just hope the day will let me sleep. I'm not complaining, well, not much. They wouldn't let me have my old job back when I'd finished looking after you. I know you'd think I've wasted all those years at university. The supermarket's the best I could get for now. Maybe I'll find something better soon."

Talking helped keep her awake while she waited for the surgery to open. So did a mug of ferocious milkless coffee with her vigorously sugared cereal, though it sharpened her headache. She was rubbing the division of her brows hard enough to ruck the flesh up by the time she was unable to resist making a call. Although the surgery was meant to open at eight, an automatic voice unnecessarily reminiscent of others she'd recently heard insisted for minutes that it was shut. At last it started listing digits for her to poke, and she jabbed the appointments number at once. She was poised to start convincing the receptionist how serious her ailment was when the voice reappeared. "Please tell me in a few words what the problem is."

"I need to see a doctor."

"I'm sorry, I didn't understand that. Please tell me in a few words what the problem is."

"I want to book an appointment."

"I'm sorry, I didn't understand that. Please tell me in a few words—"

"This is just a joke. Are you trying to make sure the doctor won't see any patients?" No doubt it wouldn't comprehend this either. "A. Point," Tina said, and "Meant" as well.

"I'm sorry, I didn't understand that." As Tina took a fierce breath to quiet herself while she searched for language it would grasp, the voice said "Please tell me in a few words what the problem is. You can say you have a cold or—"

"I've a bad headache and it's getting worse."

"You have worms, is that correct?"

"Worse. Worse." To forestall its response Tina cried "Headache."

"You wish to see a medic, is that correct?"

"That isn't what I said. I mean, I do. My head's aching."

"You wish to order medication, is that correct?"

"It's not, but it'll do." To give the voice no chance to claim incomprehension Tina added "Yes."

"You have reached the appointment line. Please redial—"

"No, I want an appointment. I told you. That's why I've rung."

"I'm sorry, I didn't understand that. Please tell me in—"

"Head." The syllable felt like a barb jabbed where her brows met, and so did "Ache."

"You have a headache, is that correct?"

"Yes." Even more savagely Tina said "Yes."

"Please wait while I connect you with an operator."

"I don't want an operator, I want—"

The silence she appeared to have prompted cut her off. How had she managed to lose the little contact she'd achieved? She was about to end the call in a rage and start afresh when a thin tinny phrase on a violin trickled out of the speaker. A few bars of Bach worn ragged kept her company, repeating themselves on a constricted loop until a voice took their place. "Surgery," it said.

"Am I speaking to a real person at last?"

"You will be. How can we help?"

"I need to see a doctor."

"Can I just take your name." She wanted Tina's date of birth as well, together with her postcode, so that Tina could have felt she'd set off a new series of programmed responses, particularly since the questioner didn't sound entirely unlike the automatic voice. At last the receptionist said "What seems to be the problem?"

"It more than seems. I've got an awful headache, and the pills you can buy over the counter don't do anything."

"Have you suffered from headaches before?"

"Since I've been working nights, yes."

Surely it was safe to say yes now. You only had to hold it back when you were talking to a trickster, in case they used it to prove you'd agreed to their scam. Was the woman reading from a script? The interrogation sounded close to automated. Had Tina experienced any loss of vision? Decrease in mobility of any kind? Loss of balance? Did she feel confused? "No," Tina reiterated with increasing force until the receptionist said "I'll arrange for a telephone consultation."

"Can't I come in and talk to a doctor?"

"Your condition isn't on our list for appointments. Is this the best number to reach you on?"

"It's my only one. When will they call?"

"When they find space between appointments. They'll try not to be too long."

Did she mean before they called Tina or that they wouldn't spend much time on her? Tina knew only that she couldn't go to bed in case she missed the call. Surely she could risk resting her eyes, and she sat in her armchair in the front room. Her mother's chair had stayed by the television, where she used to talk about if not just over whichever programme might be on, and Tina did her best not to let the chair suggest a mute rebuke. She'd done all she could for her mother, who wouldn't have anyone else in the house, and now she'd earned the silence.

She hadn't quite. The voice of the newsreader was back, embedded in the wall Tina shared with the right-hand house. It was barely identifiable, if more so than its words. Tina closed her eyes and attempted to relax but felt as though she was trying to retreat from the pain that snagged her forehead whenever she came close to dozing. It failed to stop her nodding deeper into sleep until the phone roused her, hours later. "Unknown caller," it said.

The ringtone felt like a noise the pain it had revived might make. "Hello," Tina said as little like a greeting as she could.

"Am I speaking to Tina Bell?"

This wouldn't trap her into saying yes. "I am."

"This is Dr Driver at the surgery. You were asking for a consultation."

"I don't know you, do I? My phone doesn't either. It's saying you're an unknown caller even though the surgery's on my contacts list."

"I use a different line to call out, otherwise you'd have trouble reaching a receptionist." Before Tina could detail the trouble she'd had the doctor said "Can you tell me what the problem is?"

"Of course I can, only didn't she say? I've still got a dreadful headache."

"Have you suffered from headaches before?"

"I already answered that. All right, it wasn't you, was it? Only why did she ask if you were going to?"

"Our receptionists are trained to judge who needs to speak to us."

Tina could have thought the doctor felt personally insulted. "I've had the headache since I started the night shift."

"Have you experienced any issues with your vision?"

The words weren't quite the same as previously, nor the voice. She could only repeat her answer from the earlier examination, and the rest of them. At considerable last the doctor said "I'll prescribe you something that should help. Please make sure you don't take any other medication. If this doesn't work, come back to us."

Tina refrained from objecting that she hadn't been in the first place. She could collect the prescription from her local pharmacy in half an hour. She felt almost too exhausted to experience the headache – just not quite. At least there were fewer voices in the streets to aggravate it with their muffled observations, or fewer appearances of the same voice. A girl who looked like Tina thought the doctor's receptionist might look asked for her address and then her phone number. "Why do you want that?" Tina protested.

"In case we need to contact you for any reason."

If they were up to no good, surely they would already have the number. Outside the pharmacy Tina managed to swallow two capsules, though the second one lodged in her gullet for an interlude of convulsive gulping that sent up surges of emetic bitterness. She told herself the pills were beginning to exterminate the pain as she made her dogged way home.

She crawled into bed and hugged the quilt as if it might hide her from the ache. She must have sunk out of reach within herself, because the phone eventually returned her to the world. "Time to wake up," the voice she'd selected for companionship persisted in repeating while she clambered back into awareness. Once she silenced it she was afraid to find it had made way for her headache, but the pain was almost gone.

She ignored the occasional dull twinge while she showered and dressed. Cold slices of the Sunday roast her mother had left her in the habit of preparing, together with a salad improvised out of the remains of its accompaniments, did for dinner. A surreptitious voice followed her out of the house and kept reappearing as she headed for the station. Surely only some were the same one, and she hadn't time to distinguish which.

"Got a phone, you're not alone..." She felt compelled to count the stops she'd suffer before she could escape the repetitions, which had started to feel like the threat of a headache. "You don't need to keep telling me," she called and had to laugh, because she hadn't noticed someone else was in the carriage. How had they sneaked in? She could have thought the voice had found itself a body. "Isn't it getting on your nerves as well?" she called, only to see nobody was there – just the reflection of a poster that she'd taken for the face of someone lurking by a window. No wonder she'd made the mistake when the portrait of a standardised commuter looked so much like the kind of person who would own the voice of the train.

"I can see you've shut them," she told the lift. "I know you're going up." How would she feel if a customer spoke to her that way? "I'm sorry, I know you're just doing your job," she said, only to have to explain "And I know you aren't really there. I was teasing." Before she finished making herself clear the doors gaped, revealing a woman who took a step back. "Just talking to my phone," Tina assured her, brandishing a fist she hoped would look as if it hid the item.

Why should the woman stare at her? Most of the people Tina met among the shops were on their phones, and she thought she heard a voice she knew in quite a number of them. She could have fancied it was following her to work, especially since it spoke as she passed the Checking You Out lanes on her way to the staffroom. "Please ask a staff member to authorise the transaction," it said.

A man was scanning the first of a dozen bottles of wine. "I'll do that for you," Tina said.

"It wants someone on the staff."

"It can't want anything. It isn't a real person. I am."

"If you reckon." Not much less warily the man added "Never said you weren't."

"I'm telling you I'm staff."

"Don't sound much like it. What are you really after?"

Tina smelled the wine he must be eager to augment. She didn't speak until she'd typed her staff code on the screen. "Do you believe I'm real now?"

"Nobody said different, so what are you waiting for?"

"Will you be driving? We don't want you having an accident."

"You sound like one of those calls you get about them."

"I don't think I do at all."

"Don't yell at me. You'll be giving me a headache. Wife's outside in the car, so you just need to do like your contraption says."

Tina validated the purchase and headed for the staffroom, only to find Lewis loitering by the checkout exit. How much had he overheard? His gaze suggested a good deal, but all he said was "Is your problem dealt with?"

The question felt too much like a snare. "Which one?"

"Are you feeling better now?"

This could refer to the confrontation she'd just had – might be designed to test her response. "I'm going to be fine."

In the staffroom she downed a pair of capsules with mouthfuls of water to drown any taste. Tonight she was stocktaking, which ought to be dull enough not to cause her pain. People said there were activities you could perform in your sleep, and this felt close. Count the number of an item, write the total by the listing on her clipboard, count the number of an item… If she took her time the job might last her until dawn, and she'd settled into its somnolent pace when the voice of the supermarket spoke overhead. "Helper to Checking You Out, please."

Diane could respond, or Septimus could, or Tran. All the same, Tina felt as if the summons was addressed to her, not least because the amplified voice was so familiar. She left the clipboard on top of a clump of deodorants and hurried to the checkouts, where a customer was peering at the barcode on a box of tampons. "I'm perfectly all right," the woman said. "I just won't be told what to do by a machine."

"You're like my mother."

"Not that old, I hope." Before Tina could establish how her mother's final age had been disseminated the woman said "Can you put these through for me? I'm glad you weren't a man."

Tina fingered the screen to recommence the transaction. "Please scan your first item," the voice that appeared to be everywhere said.

"They aren't mine, they're this lady's," Tina said and felt she had to tell the customer "Only being polite."

The woman gazed at her, even once the checkout said "Please scan your next item."

"I've told you once, they aren't mine." Tina scanned the rest – shower gel in which she roused sluggish bubbles, toothpaste rattling in its packet, perfume from which her haste almost dislodged the cap – so fast the checkout had no chance to prompt her. As the customer loaded a restlessly rustling carrier bag the checkout said "Please scan or insert your card."

"You know that isn't mine either," Tina told whoever needed to hear.

The woman seemed to have acquired Tina's swiftness. "Thank you for the entertainment," she said while she retrieved the carrier, and turned at the checkout exit to add "Sorry about your mother."

Which remark was a sly joke, or were both? Tina might have followed the woman to extract the truth if she hadn't noticed Lewis skulking near the checkouts. She retreated to her section, only to wonder if the customer had genuinely needed help – she'd been adept enough with the card, after all, which entailed interacting with the machine. Before Tina could evict the thought, the frown it prompted pinched an ache into her head.

Surely it would go away if she concentrated on her task. Might counting the stock aloud help? She thought she was keeping her voice to herself until Lewis stared at her as he passed the aisle. She did her best just to mutter, which made her feel her voice was hiding from her, growing less like hers. The impression seemed to probe her skull, opening more of an ache. So did the summons that reappeared overhead. "Helper to Checking You Out, please."

She might have ignored it if she hadn't seen Lewis spying on her from under the roof, where he clung like a lizard in a security mirror. She dumped the clipboard on a stack of bath salts and tramped to the checkout, which greeted her so readily it might have been watching for her. "Please scan your first item."

She didn't intend to be tricked again. "I'm not talking to you," she said and had to tell an abruptly red-faced man "I mean I'm not talking to her."

"Thought you just did."

She'd had her fill of jokes. She clamped her lower lip with its companion while she scanned his purchases, although the gesture squeezed more pain into her head. Back at the shelves she struggled to ignore the voice whenever it returned to harangue her, but she couldn't pretend not to have heard when she suspected Lewis of observing her from beneath the roof. Stifling her own voice dug the ache deeper and wider, and long before she was able to leave the supermarket she knew the prescription didn't work.

This time she wouldn't phone the surgery. She could already hear too many voices of the kind, hiding in the phones of people posted on her route to the station. "I'm not listening," she told the lift, nearly loud enough to blot out its monologue. Anticipating each revival of the message of the train expanded her headache. "I've said I'm not talking to any of you," she kept calling, but failed to elicit a response.

Televisions mumbled at her all the way from the suburban station to her house, but now she realised she wasn't meant to catch their words. At home the voice was waiting in the wall. She slumped in her armchair and shut her eyes, which seemed to invite the blurred commentary closer. By the time she lurched out of the chair her head felt raw with straining to distinguish even a word.

The muffled commentary paced her as she headed for the surgery, so that she could have thought her actions had acquired a descriptive voiceover. She shoved the surgery door aside before it finished dawdling open, and strode to the reception counter. The girl behind it raised her face, which looked smooth enough for plastic and activated with an automatic smile. "I need to see a doctor," Tina said at once. "Don't bother telling me to phone. I've already been through all that nonsense. I want to see a human being for a change."

Did the girl's eyes flicker? They looked too glassy to be altogether real. "Can I just take your name," she said.

"That's what you wanted last time. You're sounding even more like the other thing. Was it you all along?" When the girl didn't blink, although surely she should have by now, Tina said "You found out my name and everything else you were after."

She heard the door idle open behind her, and a woman said "Any trouble, Alex?"

"This lady won't tell me her details, Dr Driver."

Tina swung around to confront the newcomer, a small wide woman apparently determined to reflect the receptionist's expression. "You're who I spoke to. I knew I knew your voice. The stuff you gave me doesn't work."

The doctor performed a slow blink as if miming a decision. "Please come into my office."

She gestured at a straight chair in the largely colourless room and switched on her computer. “Can I just take your name,” she said.

“You’re sounding like her now. You didn’t have to ask last time. How many people need to know?” When she saw the doctor was fixated on the screen Tina conceded “Tina Bell.”

“And your date of birth, Tina.”

Tina gabbled that and appended her postcode without waiting to be prompted. “You say the tablets haven’t been sufficient,” the doctor said.

“Something won’t let my headache go away.” Too late to restrain it Tina heard herself say “Or someone.”

“I’ll let you have a stronger version. Please make sure you return the other one to the pharmacy, and avoid taking any other medication.”

Tina felt several points needed to be raised, but one crowded the rest into the depths of her throbbing head. “Don’t phone my prescription,” she said. “Write it down for me to take.”

The doctor didn’t look away from the screen until Tina heard a surreptitious fumbling behind her. A printer was emitting a prescription slip, which the doctor scribbled on and handed to her. “I hope this will be more effective,” the doctor said.

“Not as much as I do. I hope I won’t have to hope.”

The thoughts she’d neglected to voice followed her to the pharmacy. Why hadn’t the doctor prescribed the strongest remedy in the first place? Surely her name was just a coincidence – surely nobody would be so blatant, however much it reminded Tina of the caller Gordon had warned her against angering. She shouldn't let anybody wonder what she was thinking, and she dashed into the pharmacy with the prescription that had never left her hand.

Yet another smooth-faced mechanically efficient girl took it behind the scenes and transformed it into a sealed bag but kept hold of the medicine until she'd extracted Tina's address from her. Who was she hoping would hear? Outside the chemists Tina tore the box open and scrabbled at the tape that secured the box within. She was gulping down two capsules and the taste they trailed when she saw the girl, whichever one she was, watching her. She oughtn't to have let any of them know how close she'd come to being undermined. Lewis mustn't suspect, and she wished she could have found a way to avoid hinting it to the doctor.

The televisions kept their voice down on her way home. As soon as she was in the house she stumbled up to bed. The ache seemed to have shrunk, and she was lying absolutely still in the hope that it would think she'd gone away when she heard the furtive voice. It was just too audible to ignore or to refrain from wondering who its subject was. "Will you turn that down," she yelled, "somebody's trying to sleep," and sprawled out of bed. The voice was on both sides of her, retreating deeper into whichever wall she ran at. She mustn't careen back and forth across the room like this or she would never sleep, and she forced herself to stop pressing her ears against the walls in search of the elusive microscopic voice.

In bed she clutched the phone in one hand while she buried her head between the pillow and the mattress. She thought she'd hardly slept by the time the phone began to struggle in her grasp. When it spoke she was afraid to hear until she realised it was advising her to waken. Had she forgotten to change the mode of the alarm, or had the criminals manipulated the phone somehow? She didn't need admonishing, because she was finally awake. Her headache had vanished, clearing her mind to think.

The voice was using the televisions to tell her it was everywhere. It surrounded her while she chewed her protracted way through dinner, but she wasn't going to shout and betray it was bothering her. She hummed a tune or a bid to find one that would shut it out as she made for the station. "Got a phone, you're not alone" – at last she heard how the voice delighted in proclaiming that wherever she went she had to take it with her. "I heard you the first time," she retorted. "Can't you say anything else? That's all you can do, read from a script whoever you're pretending to be."

"Doors closing. Lift going up." Now it was telling her that her every action would be watched. "I don't care," she cried. "All you can do is yap yap yap. You can't get to me." She had to shout over the declaration that the lift was opening its doors, only to find she was bellowing into the face of a railway policewoman. "Sorry about that," Tina said and barely stopped short of wiping spittle off the woman's cheek. "All dealt with," she said and snatched her phone out of her bag to prove she hadn't been talking to herself.

She mustn't let people hear. Whenever she encountered anybody on a phone, which was practically everyone in the streets, she clamped her lips shut with a finger and thumb. Surely this made her look pensive, even if they couldn't guess her thoughts, which she wanted to believe nobody could. Above all she needed to keep quiet at work. She mustn't be tricked into losing her job.

A group of late-night shoppers had gathered in the Checking You Out section, setting off a chorus of directions. "Please scan your first item. Plplease ease scscanan youryour firstfirst iteite emem…" Even if the customers weren't involved in the game, they were helping the voice remind her how it had multiplied. She fended off the babble with the Staff Only door and locked her coat and bag up before heading for the stockroom. Tonight she was replenishing her shelves, and at least the merchandise wouldn't talk.

"Here you are, lotions. Here's a new friend for you." She needed to make sure she could hear her own voice solely in her skull, and she kept glancing across the transverse aisle at Gordon until the compulsive scrutiny earned her a troubled look. When the checkouts started calling for help she ignored them. They didn't need hers, even if they weren't feigning helplessness to play another vindictive prank on her, since she wasn't the only member of staff on the floor. She pretended not to notice Lewis hovering high above her while he gestured at her to take a turn, but she couldn't ignore him once he marched into her section. "Helper to Checking You Out, please," he said.

His voice was higher than normal – less concerned to sound unlike the voice that had invaded her life – and his words made the situation even clearer. "It's you," Tina cried. "It's you as well."

"What on earth are you trying to say?"

"I'm not trying. I've said. Did you hear him, Gordon? You were right and I ought to have listened."

Her colleague looked nervously wary, no doubt of admitting the truth. "What do you mean?"

"Those criminals you were warning me about, they can get in everywhere. They've been after me since I showed them up." She felt as if door after locked door were opening in her mind. "I thought the girl at the surgery wanted to sound like a machine, but she was trying not to. The doctor nearly managed, and the girl at the chemists, only why did they give the doctor that name? They must want me to know what they're doing to me." A further realisation made her turn on Lewis. "You wanted me to go to them," she said. "You were asking if I was better. Now I am, and no thanks to any of you."

"I'm sorry if you've got yourself into this state somehow. I think you need to go home and see someone about it as soon as you can."

"I've seen someone. I've seen you. I've seen what's going on."

"Would you like me to ring for a taxi? Maybe you shouldn't be on your own."

"I'm not and you know it. Keep an eye on him, Gordon. You might be next now he knows you know."

Whatever the manager's display of sympathy was manufactured to achieve, Tina wasn't fooled. There was still a last train, and she dashed onto the platform just as it was pulling in, though the lift took its loquacious time to make her think she was too late. At least the carriage was strewn with drunks whose uproar helped to blot out the pronouncements of the train, so that she felt safe in adding her own incoherent clamour. The voice that crowded the suburban streets kept having to be told she wouldn't listen to it, but slamming her car door seemed to cut it off. She barely remembered to switch on the headlights before heading out of the town.

The dim fields beneath a night sky like an invitation to join the dots of stars widened her mind now that it was no longer clamped by her headache. Though the mountains that frayed the horizon were hours distant, she could reach a lofty spot to watch the dawn. When the foothills closed their trees around her she felt the forest fending off the voice she'd left behind, the masses of foliage protecting the car like the contents of a padded box. The narrow woodland road rambled back and forth but always uphill. She'd trusted it for miles when it brought her to a dead end where massive tree-trunks sprawled across the road.

How had she missed her way? There wasn't space to turn the car. By the time she'd backed between a multitude of reddened trees to a hidden unmarked intersection, her hands were clammy on the wheel. She swung the car onto the side road, which distracted her so much with its wanderings that she'd driven a mile before she felt certain it was sloping gradually downwards. She hauled on the handbrake and brought up the map on her phone to locate the closest peak. Was she on the convoluted route the map marked? She sought confirmation from the navigator. "In half a mile…"

"I'm not listening," Tina cried and shut the voice down. How could she have let it find her? She knew only that she mustn't follow the directions it had begun to issue, and she managed to edge the car around without colliding with any trees. She drove as fast as she could risk back to the junction and took the road opposite the one she'd fled from. What might have happened to her if she'd believed the navigator? Yes, the road she'd found was climbing uphill. The headlamp beams fumbled at the trees wherever the road bent, until at last they revealed a straight unobstructed stretch of track. Relief urged her to put on speed, and so she felt the front wheels plunge over the cliff just a moment before the rear wheels did. "No," she cried as the vertical beams brought her only darkness. At any rate, she heard a voice.

Author Note

I've often written about mental illness, as far back as my second novel, written in the 1970s. No doubt the underlying cause of my preoccupation has always been my mother's mental state. She went undiagnosed for most of her life – certainly once I was born, though I believe her family may have suspected but summed her up as simply odd – not least because she indoctrinated me from a very early age not to discuss her with anyone. At three years old I learned to distinguish what she perceived from reality. I'm sure this helped me as a writer to depict – indeed, inhabit – minds besieged from within.

My notebooks swarm with story ideas, quite a few concerning mental problems. When I was asked to contribute to this book I selected one of them. I fear my tale is all too close to reality, which for some people must consist these days of a constant culture shock. We're routinely surrounded by simulations that grow ever more indistinguishable from the real thing, not least artificial voices substituted for human beings, all of which might well prove too much for some minds through no fault of their own. I'd be happier if my story stayed fictitious, but I hope at least it contains some helpful truth.

My Ghosts Have Dreams

Sumiko Saulson

I am haunting myself tonight
Distended voices bickering
Geists populating the edge of sleep
Stretched thin through a taffy machine
Of emotions in endless motion
Caught up in my racing thoughts
Creatures are wearing my face

Graveyard of my past selves
Plotting a future possession
My body preoccupied by vicious
Cyclical reasoning goblins
Have feelings and those needs
Must assert themselves

Stripping me of all reason
They speak to me and I forget
To eat. To bathe.

To clean my house of dreams
That live on the edge
Of my demon-possessed
Bed of nails against chalkboards

My body is a haunted house
Filled with lucid ghosts
Dreaming and scheming to
Keep me up all night again

Author Note

'My Ghosts Have Dreams' is about symptoms I experience as a person with Bipolar Disorder with Psychotic Features and Post-traumatic Stress Disorder, such as racing thoughts that can keep me up at night in a manic or hypomanic state, disassociation, and hallucinations such as hearing voices and arguing with them. I talk to myself sometimes but feel like other people are talking to me, having a conversation.

I have experienced the deaths of several people close to me – such as both of my parents (who died of cancer), a former fiancé, and a best friend, over the last decade or so – and often the racing thoughts and the voices are in the form of loved ones who have passed away. Some voices feel like earlier forms of myself from the past or other defined separate personalities. That's why I used the metaphor of ghosts for this poem, with my body as a haunted house in which they reside.

I have experienced (in 2016/2017) my hand moving on its own, writing notes to me. It felt like I was being possessed and was pretty scary. Voices started to speak out of my mouth, which I did not feel were me. Sometimes I argued with them. Demons and creatures are referenced in this poem as different ways in which the past, and my internal self, seem to haunt me. This, for me, has occurred in ways that are akin to possession by another entity or personality.

Nothing and the Boy

Amanda Cecelia Lang

NOTHING WAITS in the forgotten red house with the chain-link fence and splinter-bone porch. No sunken face peers out the murky windows at an abandoned road and forbidden mossy woods. No crooked feet pace the floorboards, creaking planks beneath a hideous weight. No serrated fingernails scratch the stained yellow wallpaper, and no wheezing lungs exhale against twitching cobwebs. Certainly, Nothing smiles when the family arrives home with their tiny moving van and their nine-year-old boy.

A family of three, not four. The mother and father laugh with desperate joy and hidden bruises as they carry boxes inside the red house, their second house in a year. The boxes marked with black stars go into the old nursery at the end of the darkling hallway, and the boy trails behind. Without tin-can robots and comic books and bunkbeds, the room feels upside-down and strange. While his parents return to the daylight to retrieve his mattress, the boy tiptoes toward the open closet only to choke on a gasp, going wide-eyed.

Nothing crouches in the doorway, wearing shadows for skin and emptiness for eyes.

"Go away," the boy whispers, and Nothing whispers back.

At supper that night, seated around the house's old table, the parents ignore the dust and disrepair and faded wandering footprints. They promise each other this is the new beginning they prayed for. The red house is the same as their old house, but different. Here, they'll find no more nightmares. Here they can forget. Isn't that right? The father nudges the boy, drawing him back from a faraway trance with the sound of his name. The boy blinks, and the father has to repeat his question. And yes, the boy promises, they'll be happy here. Safe here.

Bedtime comes, and the first terrible hours summon shadows into the back nursery. Unused to sleeping alone, the small boy curls up, fetal, on his mattress and clenches his eyes, trying not to breathe. At first, his parents' muffled voices echo like an uneasy lullaby through distant rooms. But too soon, the house wheezes with silence and Nothing stares through the crack in the closet door. Between thin air and the ghost-quiet bell toll of metal hangers, Nothing slips out and scrapes to the edge of the bed. Twitching, popping, crouching low, no smoky fingers tug the blanket, and no spidery invisible tongue wets the boy's bare feet.

Nothing still wants to be friends.

The boy can swallow his shrieks no longer! The red house echoes and the lights snap on. His parents stagger in, and Nothing stands there, slavering and shadow-mouthed.

Nothing at all.

* * *

Nothing belongs to the boy, and the boy belongs to Nothing. This is necessary, this is fate, this is how it's always been. Friends forever. In the wisps of night and corners of daylight, Nothing proves there's no point running, no point hiding. Not from impish hissing voices, not from the gnarled reaching darkness.

It didn't work before, and it won't work now.

Still the family dusts at spiderwebs and unpacks the boy's boxes. Every box except the ones that rattle with broken toys and old family photos. These the father tucks somewhere secret and forgotten. Important to forget.

The first months in the red house, the boy's mother decides homeschooling might be best, might be safest. She mops up old footprints and hangs a chalkboard in the dining room, atop the ghost-grime silhouettes of missing pictures.

The boy tries his best to be quiet and obedient, to relearn how normal children behave so his family can be happy again. Heartsick for that faraway day, heartsick for the family they were before, the boy practices his penmanship and his mathematics and recites the prayers his mother teaches.

But sometimes when his mother steps from their makeshift classroom – to stir the lunch stew or wash the daily stains from his bedsheets – Nothing glooms closer and wheezes crooked promises. And sometimes when his mother returns to continue the lessons, her hopeful smile drains away. Too often the forest-facing window hangs open, whispering with laughter from the forbidden trees. Too often the boy sits shivering before upside-down books, shoelaces untied, a silent sweat upon his forehead, and broken pencils in his hands.

But the boy knows better than to cry about Nothing.

Because Nothing frightens his mother too, because Nothing isn't there. The boy's guts twist when she looks at him so funny, it scares him when she looks so scared. So, the boy pretends his best to be brave. He swallows down his whimpers, burying them deep with the mossy screams and forbidden memories.

Nothing enjoys their game of hush and make-believe.

* * *

The boy's parents try to be decent people. A normal family of three. They pay overdue bills and say grace before meals. They believe in the star-spangled flag and the heavenly father above. They believe in second chances and holy water and sitting in the back pew of their new church, just in case. Sometimes they even attend soup suppers with the other smiling believers and their children. Because despite their hiccups and nightmares and gaunt little boy, his parents believe everything can still be happy in the end.

Because they don't believe in Nothing.

Not out loud, not in the daylight. Though sometimes, somewhere deep down and mossy and hidden, the boy thinks they remember the truth.

Like every Sunday, when Nothing crosses the forbidden forest to leer at the boy through stained-glass windows, slowing time, distorting prayers into backwards infernal hymns. Like when Nothing worms beneath the pews, curling heady fingers of incense and candle smoke around the boy's ankles, unknotting his shoelaces.

Like those awful soup suppers, when the grown-ups gather around tables with lively voices, and the children gather in circles on rugs. The boy needs friends. His mother insists friends his age, *real friends*, will be healthy for the soul. But the other children sit knee-to-knee, exchanging Sunday-school giggles and whispering campfire secrets about poison ivy and caves in the forbidden woods. The boy struggles to keep up. Nothing's voice scratches at the back of his skull, reminding him never to try.

Easy friendships and their dazzling lights have always been an impossible dizzy mystery. And when the other kids turn with glinting curiosity to ask if he has any siblings or any friends, the boy tangles his tongue and loses his phony smile, choking on inside tears. Afraid of himself. Afraid that only Nothing sees him, only Nothing understands.

Because in some terrible upside-down way, Nothing is his only friend.

And after each church prayer, after each empty supper, when the boy slinks away paler and lonelier than ever, he hopes *this time* his parents might finally see. Finally believe. Nothing is real. Nothing always lurks nearby. It doesn't matter where they move or who they meet or who they pretend was never there. It doesn't matter what they believe.

Nothing is forever.

* * *

Prowling the woods between the red house and the church and back again – shadowing the closet to the classroom and back to the closet again. Nothing goes where the boy goes. Always alone and never alone.

Small eternities crawl past, and the baggage beneath his parents' eyes sinks ever deeper.

Because Nothing spiders through unseen rooms and rattles old boxes. Nothing finds the boy's hidden crannies and hisses with sour laughter whenever he begs Nothing to go away. An endless game of seek-and-hide. Of trembling musical chairs. Of wide-eyed midnight staring contests. Nothing knows the boy doesn't mean it. Nothing knows the boy needs tricks and games to help him un-forget. So Nothing unties shoelaces and unhides old toys and scratches at windows while watching the flickering flashlight woods. But as tattered nights wear through neglected seasons, Nothing grows darker with the sky, Nothing grows restless with the boy.

Until one day, Nothing does nothing at all.

The closet door stays closed, and the boy's breath-held silences stretch into infinity. A hush falls across the floorboards, books remain open, shoes stay tied, and the only voices belong to the family of three. Still, the boy braces himself, spine stiff, nerves ragged, for Nothing to appear, grinning and gangly and ghastly, any second, around any corner. And during this first strange peaceful day – when the red house stands hollow and his prayers appear answered – the boy's guts twist worst of all.

Because deep down and worrisome, he aches for the only friend he's never had.

Because who does he have left if he doesn't even have Nothing?

* * *

An empty week later, a message arrives, scratched into the paint of the boy's closet door.

Jagged handwriting forms slantwise shapes and gibberish letters, a language from before. The boy's mother will weep if she sees it, so he tears pages from his coloring book and tapes them across the door.

Still, the message echoes out, shadow-cast and insistent. A clawing, scraping dare, an invitation for midnight.

Come find Nothing in the forbidden forest.

Come discover secrets like a true friend.

Around bedtime, the house trembles, forgotten boxes rattle, and the moonbeam floorboards resume their haunts. But the only thing waiting inside the murky cave of the closet is the boy's autumn jacket. Nothing moans out the back door and Nothing watches from beyond his window, from inside the rustling trees. Will the boy be brave enough to follow? Or will he simply continue to swallow his screams?

He forgets his jacket when midnight arrives. He double knots his shoelaces and slides his window open, and the leaf-blown chill shakes him, wakes him wide. Now, he focuses every movement on escaping without sound. The soft groan of the windowsill beneath his weight, the short drop onto the splintery porch. The sneakiness of it echoes familiar, though never before has the boy snuck outside all alone.

The red house casts a moon-stretched shadow. Cowering in the gloom, the boy counts his quick-pounding heartbeats like before a game of tag. *One-two, three-four…* He promises himself he'll run once he reaches fifty.

The forbidden woods stand ready to catch him.

Beyond the porch and chain-link fence, a graveyard of mossy trees juts from the dirt, branches of knotty skeletal hands clawing up from swirling dead-rot mists. Nothing watches from a thousand hidden hollows with gleeful empty eyes.

The boy loses track of his heartbeats.

Ready or not…

He scurries off the porch, fast as his terror-rigid soul will bend. He unhinges the gate with an awful screech and crashes out between the trees. A maze. An unfair game. Nothing knows these tangled footpaths better than the boy.

Nothing can appear around any jagged turn.

Nothing can end the game with the snap of a branch.

Snap of bones.

The boy shivers forward anyway, wishing for a flashlight…wishing his mother could read the scratches on the closet door…wishing he could've stayed safe in the red house where everything is the same, but different. Wishing for a real friend.

Nothing laughs.

Strange and sinuous and escaping behind faraway trees.

Like well-worn footprints, the twisting laughter lures the boy onward. Leaf rot squelches beneath his sneakers and branches scratch his pajama sleeves. He wonders at the strangeness of Nothing's voice – whooping cries, warbling and wild – and trips over his untied shoelaces.

The laughter snaps to silence.

The boy rights himself as the forest jumbles and the trees turn themselves around.

He holds his breath for Nothing to appear, midnight tendrils, fingers uncurling.

The boy catches the sunken shine of eyes ahead. Except…

No, not eyes. Toys. A glinting trail of tin-can robots and comic books and spyglasses. Forbidden toys nested in the undergrowth, unearthed memories. The boy follows the gifts to a moss-shrouded cave. No bigger than a closet. A low cranny hidden tomblike inside a shallow hill, marked with scratches and ancient dust-scraped footprints.

Nothing's toothy smile winks at the boy from within. Gleaming, waiting.

The boy inches closer and gasps.

Not Nothing grinning at him. A shattered photograph.

Nothing must've brought it here for the boy to discover. Even the midnight shadows of the forest aren't enough to obscure the savage truth. Broken glass circles the picture frame like invisible teeth, jagged memories gnawing the old snapshot inside.

A snapshot of a house.

The forgotten red house with the chain-link fence and splintery porch.

And on that porch, stands the boy – a year or so younger than he is now – a muss of hair and a goofy gap-toothed smile. Strange, seeing himself like that. Happy. Carefree.

Stranger still, seeing himself with one arm arched around the shoulder of a taller boy.

A boy with crooked glasses, crookeder teeth, and wise fidgety eyes. In the snapshot, both boys wear junior toolbelts and hold up the tin-can robots they constructed together. They stand hip-to-hip and betray sparks of laughter, sharing some secret joke. Imaginative, wily, alive.

And Nothing stands between them.

"What're you doing here?" whispers a voice from the forest.

Shaken, the boy whips around and a blazing light dazzles his eyes. That flashlight he wished for earlier. The boy raises a hand, shading his vision.

A silhouette breaks from the murky trees and steps forward, dropping the light-beam toward the cave. "Sorry, didn't mean to blind you."

In the glooming afterimages, the boy blinks at this new kid. "You're not him."

"Not who?" the new kid says.

The boy glances toward the secret cave, but the photograph rattles in his hands now. Secrets rattle in his skull, his ribcage. The tall boy in the picture. He's dead, gone and forgotten.

And this new kid isn't him.

But still, he's someone.

* * *

The boy introduces himself, and for the first time in forever his name feels almost true.

"Yeah, I know..." The new kid shifts from foot to awkward foot, zigzagging his flashlight beam across the lurking trees. "Uh...hi, we've met before. Remember?"

This kid isn't tall and this kid isn't full of fidgety spyglass wisdom, but real blood pumps inside his veins and he reminds the boy where they met. "At the soup supper at church?"

The boy doesn't really recall, but maybe that's good. Maybe that means this kid blends in with the darkness too. Plus, there's something more.

In the ghost-light of his flashlight, the kid's eyes seem to have bruises, the sunken kind that bloom from not enough sleep and too many swallowed screams. As if maybe, just maybe, this kid knows what it takes to have Nothing shadow him through every day.

The boy lowers his voice. "Did the darkness invite you out here?"

"The darkness?" The kid's flashlight skips from the secret cave to the boy's eyes again. "Guess you could say that. You like scary stories?"

The boy's whole life is a scary story. "I don't think so…"

"Well, how about campfires? You look like you need to warm up."

The light betrays the boy's thin pajamas and shivery gooseflesh. He swallows a lump and glances over one shoulder. Is Nothing hiding out there? Between the trees or low inside the mossy cave? Impossible to tell with the flashlight so bright.

Heart rioting, the boy follows the light through the crooked woods and doesn't dare think of this kid as a friend. Not yet, maybe not ever. Flickering firelight burns a hole through the darkness ahead. Voices bubble up, warbling, laughing. Tree branches part like curtains.

Several rowdy silhouettes warm themselves around a campfire, more boys his age, roasting marshmallows. More un-friends than he dares count. It stings when they stand and high-five the new kid, stings when this kid's shadow-bruises vanish in their light. Turns out he's not so new, turns out maybe he fits in somewhere after all.

The boy hides his disappointment and mutters his hellos, stealing a silent seat on a rock around the fire. As with all the gatherings before, he disappears into oblivion, and Nothing echoes inside, hissing, reminding him.

The others take turns passing marshmallows and sharing tales of monsters that go bump. Faces rippling with firelight, the others grin and gasp and pretend to tremble. But each story proves toothless and un-scary. They've never watched shapes take hold from the hollows. They've never been dragged into darkness by smoky twisting fingers.

They've never sat crouching and cowering and slowly dying from the shadows!

When the flashlight finally reaches the boy, he prays this might be his chance – but for what, he isn't quite sure. The others fall hush as he holds the flashlight beneath his chin and turns his frown into a jagged shadow-glow smile.

"Once," he begins, "there lived two brothers, and they were the best of friends."

* * *

The boy holds up the forgotten snapshot for all to see. Around the campfire, shadows elongate as the other kids squirm on their rocks, uneasy, as if they'd heard this story before and couldn't sleep afterwards.

The boy swallows the lump of his breath and keeps going. Raw. Aching to relive it.

"A big brother and a little brother," he says, "born less than a year apart…"

They lived in a red house in the woods and shared a bedroom and a bunkbed and a closet full of creaky homemade toys. Such faithful friends, these brothers, they invented a secret language and whispered the same prayers. Just them against the world. Because the world didn't want them. The townies thought the brothers were spacey and weird, awkward and shabby – and the schoolkids snickered and threw pebbles and kept their distance. But that was okay. All their years in the red house, the brothers didn't need outside friends. They always had each other.

"Until the day they didn't…" the boy says, and the campfire kids chew their lips and exchange flickering glances. Already the misty gloom swirls between the trees, already the campfire burns lower, crackling with somber bloody flames.

"You see," the boy goes on, "the big brother met a friend. Someone almost real…"

And yes, the boy remembers that day. Never did forget. He still feels the gut-punch of his brother coming home, waving the invitation from town. Not written in their secret language, but still painfully clear. His brother had been invited to a private birthday party. A weekend camping trip of cake and balloons and top-secret games that the boy's abnormal anxious heart couldn't even fathom.

Just like he couldn't fathom how his brother, his only friend, could make friends without him. The weekend his brother went away was the second worst nightmare of the boy's life.

How could his brother leave him like that?

At home, alone in their bedroom, the boy lost himself in all the ugly laughter, imagining all the forbidden games and parties and friendships he would never be a part of. A void split open inside him, bigger than forever, impossible to fill. It wasn't fair! What was wrong with him? He swallowed down his first real scream. Alone, alone, alone, he crawled into their toy closet, sobbing and shaking and begging for a new friend. Any friend! His fists pounded and his soul withered and his prayer shrieked out.

And Nothing heard.

Nothing turned a cobweb head.

From inside the boy's cavernous hollows, or from some hideous other world – the boy never did know – Nothing grinned and tendrilled closer, and Nothing filled their cozy lonely closet. The doorknob slowly turned, and Nothing snuck loose. Pacing the floorboards and scratching the walls and staring out the window all throughout that endless weekend. Nothing hissed rancid truths against the boy's spine, promising that the friendship with his big brother stunk of maggots and betrayal, promising that his brother would never be his friend again.

But Nothing would be there. Forever inside.

And once that happened the boy would become Nothing too.

"Except something amazing happened when the big brother returned home," the boy tells the campfire, his eyes faraway inside the shadow-curve of flames. All around, the others lean closer, unsettled to hear what the whole town wonders.

The front door moaned open, and his big brother stood there, lumpy and itchy with poison ivy. The birthday weekend had been a disaster, a cruel rot-hearted prank – the town kids never truly wanted to be friends, only to observe a weirdo in the wild. And now the boy's brother acted sheepish and embarrassed and happy to be home in the red house where he belonged.

Except, it was too late.

Nothing had already crept inside.

When the boy told his brother what lurked inside their closet now, the brother didn't believe. And when the boy begged him in their secret language to open his eyes, his brother insisted Nothing wasn't standing between them. This game wasn't funny. Night after crooked-shadow night, didn't matter how pale or shaken or gut-sick the boy became.

His brother didn't believe – not until the day a new invitation appeared.

Scratched into the wallpaper in their secret language.

Nothing dared the brother to return to the woods. A jagged map. A scavenger hunt.

The big brother believed the boy had left the marks. A trick, a game. He went without question into the trees and murk and laughter. Only after the footpaths faded into moss and a spinning compass did the brother see the shadows for what they were. The trees turned themselves around and the darkness elongated and—

The boy swallows his words.

"Jeez, don't stop there," says the not-so-new kid, leaning forward. The dying firelight unearths more curious bruises around his eyes. Around all their eyes. This dark faith that even the boy's parents keep buried. "What did Nothing do to him?"

"Nothing," the boy says.

When his brother never came home, a search party was formed. They roamed the trees with flashlights and bloodhounds, shouting his name for four days before someone peered inside the low mossy cave. Searchers had walked past it a thousand times. Yet there his brother sat. Eyeglasses crooked, shoelaces untied, cowering, pressed up against the far wall, fetal, hugging himself.

Dead to the bone.

Nothing had touched him, and Nothing kept the dogs from scenting him, and Nothing stood over him while the water evaporated inside his wheezing petrified veins. And only after his organs failed and his heartbeat spasmed to silence did Nothing return to the red house to hiss along the boy's spine, revealing all the slow lonesome secrets of death by Nothing.

They could be friends forever now.

"God, you really are weird," the not-so-new kid says, sitting back. The others snicker and agree and enjoy the last of the light.

"No wonder they shipped him away…" someone whispers, hisses, echoes all their voices.

Shipped away… His home away from home. The boy blinks against blurry shadows. He tried to tell them, had screamed it from his lungs. Nothing killed his brother, his only friend! He told the police and his parents, told his grandparents and his doctors and anyone else who might listen. Nothing lived everywhere, haunted everywhere, hunted everywhere! And everyone agreed. Nothing wasn't real.

Except Nothing *was* real.

Nothing *is* real!

More real than his big brother. More real than his memories.

Nothing snakes between the gloom and the trees and the loneliness.

The shattered photograph falls to the dirt. And as the boy rises to his feet, the campfire hisses and blackens, the screams rise up, and Nothing rises too.

And Nothing darkens the laughter from their unseeing eyes.

* * *

That next empty Sunday, the church pews bustle with believers.

They believe in positive thoughts and buoyant prayers. They believe in the police and the angels watching over them from above.

And they believe the search party will find their missing children.

Even as tendrils of incense and candle smoke twist around the pews, even as the floorboards moan and the stained-glass hollows hiss empty promises of forever. Even as another family creeps inside to join the flickering shadows, taking their seat in the final pew, just in case. A family of three, not four. Two hopeful sunken-eyed parents, they add their choking voices to the prayers and glance ever-sideways from the mossy-dark corners of their eyes.

Nothing sits there.

Nothing and the boy.

Author Note

With 'Nothing and the Boy', I wanted to explore the power of belief and the stories we tell ourselves. Fact or fiction, truths or lies, we weave narratives around our lives for countless reasons. For enlightenment, for comfort, for safety. Stories can be an escape, a refuge, a place to puzzle out the world. And belief can be monumental in ushering us through troubled times and elevating us during the good times. Belief in who we are, belief in our family, friends, and neighbors, belief in something bigger than ourselves.

The ability of the human mind to interpret and shape our world can be a beautiful magic – it's why I enjoy being a writer. Perception can inspire hope, perception can spark imagination and ingenuity, it can give language to love and meaning to grief. The narratives we believe about the world – both around us and inside us – inform our everyday experiences. But what happens when that inner language turns dark and misguided, muddled by isolation or trauma, twisted by fears or misconceptions or countless other personal demons?

What if it tells us we are foolish or unwanted or scary?

What if by indulging such blackhole beliefs we turn nothing into something?

And what happens when those around us don't believe what we do?

As someone who's well-acquainted with racing thoughts and the many anxious shadows they breed, I've fallen into that blackhole before. I understand all too well how old scars and obsessive insecurities can mutate bigger than life. Loneliness, grief, uncertainty. These things can become monsters if I let them, following me outward to steer and manipulate my day.

This is the territory 'Nothing and the Boy' inhabits: the space between the real and the imagined, where belief itself holds a dreamy existential power over us, the ability to enhance or warp our reality. Is Nothing a mere metaphor for the boy's isolation and grief, or is it actually alive? Can both be true? That uncertainty reflects the ways we grapple with our own inner shadows and narratives, sometimes distorting the line where imagination ends and we begin.

The Familiar's Assistant

Alma Katsu

I'M STANDING on the doorstep to the vampire's house.

It's been a couple minutes since my last knock. I've been standing here for twenty minutes, total, been outside this door every night for a week, waiting for hours at a time. It's taken me days to work up the courage to get this far. For weeks, I stood on the other side of the gate, staring at the seemingly lifeless house. Praying for courage. Knowing I had nothing to lose.

There's movement on the other side of the door. It's the vampire's familiar. I can feel her anxiety through the wood. "Go away," she says in a voice taut with anger. "You don't want to be here. It's dangerous."

This is the third time she's spoken. Each time, she'd said the same thing.

Tonight, it's raining. The canopy over the door is tiny and provides no protection. My hair is plastered to my head, my clothes soaked through to the skin.

Nonetheless, I continue to stand, unflinching, in the downpour, as pitiful as a puppy in a shelter.

The old townhouse is somber and foreboding. It's one in a row, all abandoned, each more decrepit than the one before. Once grand, they're the domain of city rats and the homeless now. You'd notice if you watched, however, that someone lives in this one. Lights come on at night from deep within. This woman, the familiar, slips in and out as unobtrusively as a mouse.

My ploy works. The door opens. The familiar is about thirty, maybe younger. She doesn't weigh a hundred pounds soaking wet, so not much of a gatekeeper: I could knock her over and rush inside if I wanted to. What's more shocking, now that I can see her up close, is her appearance. Her clothes are ratty, her hair unkempt.

She appraises me with wary eyes. Once she's determined that I'm not a threat, she asks, "Do you have any idea what you're doing?"

I try to appear humble, sincere. She has to believe me. "I do. I want this."

"That's all I need to hear." She turns, obviously expecting me to follow. "It's your funeral."

She leads me through the house to a little room at the back. It's furnished with two mismatched chairs and a small table, all obviously salvaged on trash day. Heavy drapes are furred with dust. A weak bulb burns overhead. She gives me a rag to dry myself with. "Don't leave this room."

Once she departs, I listen for noises elsewhere in the house. Sunset was a half-hour ago. Is he up? Where is he? My skull buzzes with anticipation. I imagine I can feel his presence lurking in the background, omnipresent. But I only hear one person's movements in the house. Tiptoeing up and down stairs, opening and closing doors. Timid, mousy movements. Hers.

I take off my drenched coat and drape it over the stone-cold radiator, then pull my messenger bag over my head and let it drop to the floor, where it quickly forms a puddle. Next, I tousle my hair and mop my face. As I start to feel more human, the magnitude of what I'm doing hits me like a wave. *I'm going to meet a vampire.* The *vampire.*

The thought is so overwhelming that I have to distract myself. I turn my thoughts to this ramshackle old house instead… How did he get here, why did he choose to live here? From what I can see, the house has been abandoned for some time. It's old and out of fashion. The wallpaper is streaked with water stains, the plaster crumbling. Light fixtures flicker on and off. It's a miracle there's power; I can't imagine someone is paying the electric bill. It's more like an animal's den than a place where humans would choose to live. Is this state of disrepair the familiar's fault? I imagine it would be her job to take care of things, and I immediately like her even less.

After about an hour, the familiar returns. She stands with her arms crossed, saying nothing, giving me a long look of pity and scorn. Assessing me. It's an opportunity for me to get a better look at her, too, and I can see she's not healthy. Her hair is brittle, her skin sallow, her nails chipped and torn.

I see, too, that while she may be small, she's wiry. She's tougher than she looks. I imagine you'd have to be, to be a vampire's familiar. There's got to be a lot of abuse – and yet she stays. She's spotted with hideous bruises on her neck, her wrists, wherever she's not covered by clothing. Purple and that sickly shade of chartreuse. Hidden somewhere within those bruises are little wounds. I wouldn't put up with such abuse – not unless I felt I deserved it, like I do now. But I've walked away from abusers before, so I know I can do it again if I need to.

She fixes me with a glare. "Before we go any further, I want some answers. How did you find out about him?"

She has to cover their tracks, I get it, but I don't think I can tell her the truth. It happened when people I knew began disappearing. Disappearing more than usual, to be honest – we're a pretty transient bunch – and under mysterious circumstances. Then someone started this rumor that a vampire was to blame. I didn't believe it, of course. I figured it was just user talk. Addicts disappear all the time for a variety of reasons – we overdose, yes, but we're also arrested, or kidnapped by family members who want to stage an intervention, or slink out of town because we owe money. We are notorious for making our own problems, so why invent a story about a monster? That's what we do, don't we? We rationalize our addiction. We're always the victim.

But the whispers got more specific. Then, I finally met a guy who claimed to have seen this vampire and there was something about the way he described the encounter that made me believe him. The vampire was impossible to describe, he'd said. Your memory of him faded as soon as you were no longer in his presence. The feeling, though – that had been tattooed into his memory. He thrummed with a million volts of electricity, recalling it.

The experience had been transformative and now all he wanted was to be with the vampire again. Only, he didn't know how: he'd wandered into an alley when the vampire had appeared to him like a vision, then disappeared. And now, this chance encounter had wrecked him. All he had to reassure him that it actually had happened were two neat wounds on the inside crook of his elbow.

This guy said he tried to find the vampire for six months with no luck, but that didn't stop me because, frankly, I'm smarter than him. I made a pest of myself in all the usual haunts, asking if anyone knew of him. There were dozens of false starts (addicts being notorious liars): following people who claimed to know where the vampire was hiding, the delusional who claimed to be the familiar themselves. Finally, however, someone pointed out the vampire's familiar to me. She was good at disappearing in plain sight, though. I had to follow her for three weeks before she led me to this townhouse. And all that time, during the weeks of tailing her, I worked on a way to get inside the door. To meet him.

And now I'm here. It's all going to plan. I can scarcely believe it.

I can hardly admit this to her, though.

I claim to have met someone who told me about the townhouse. Pure dumb luck.

"Have you *seen* him?" I shake my head vigorously. "Then how did you know he was here?"

"I didn't. I just had a feeling."

She rolls her eyes; it's hard to tell if she believes me. "Why are you here? What are you looking to accomplish?"

"I want to meet him."

"No shit. But what do you think will happen if you do?"

This is the important part. The $100,000 question. I've got to sell it. She's got to believe that I'm sincere.

"I don't care. He can do whatever he wants to me." I toss my head, maybe a little too dramatically. "I'm ready to die. I want my life to be over."

She snickers, though she seems relieved. "Death by vampire. Don't think you'd be the first. One last question: it's not painless. Are you prepared for that? It's going to hurt – a lot." She watches, but I stay stoic. I won't give her any excuse to deny me.

"I've already felt pain. I live in pain."

"Stop right there. Not another word. I don't care what happened to bring you to this point, what put this stupid idea into your head," – she looks right, then left, like she thinks someone might be listening – "but there's still time to leave."

She wants to sound tough, but there is a hint of sadness in her voice. Did someone say the same thing to her once? Where is that person now? Does she wish she had listened?

"I've been standing outside your door for a week – and I've wanted to do this for a lot longer. I'm not going to change my mind now."

She chews this over for a minute. "What's your name?"

I consider giving her a fake one, but what the hell. "Eric."

"You're not bringing trouble to our doorstep, are you, Eric? You seem like trouble. Is somebody going to come looking for you? The police?"

Must I respond? In this day and age, it's a rare bird who doesn't have something to hide, who hasn't had a scrape with the law or made a bad decision or two. We're all entitled to our secrets; that's how I see things. It's not like I'm hiding anything terrible, just a few lapses of judgment. One recent lapse in particular.

For the most part, though, those days are behind me.

When I don't answer and try to look repentant, she tries another tack. "What about your family? They're not going to show up to drag you home?"

"No. I burned those bridges a long time ago." Burned them to ash, if you must know. "The reason I'm here is…I'm not a good person. I've done a lot of bad things. Whatever happens to me tonight, you needn't feel responsible. I deserve to die."

If I expected that to melt her stony heart, I am to be disappointed. Her laugh is mean and sharp, like a punch to the face. "Everybody who comes here has a story like yours. Everyone feels sorry for themselves." She's happy enough to help me die.

She pauses, hand on the doorknob. "Just so we're clear, I don't give a shit what you've done and why you're here. I'm here to protect *him*, you got it?"

Where have I heard that before? Never mind. As I listen to her footsteps recede on the other side of the door, I break out in a sweat, my heart accelerating like a jet. *I've passed. She believes me. This is really going to happen. I'm going to meet him.*

* * *

Another hour passes before the familiar returns. By now, I reckon, it's deep into the evening and the sky outside must be like indigo velvet, closed around us like a tent. "If you still want to do this, you can follow me." We go up two flights via a narrow, claustrophobic staircase at the back of the house. The servants' stairs, once upon a time, but today they threaten to collapse with each step. I can't really be afraid to die on the steps, can I, considering that I am on my way to my probable demise? This buzzy, fizzy feeling is familiar, however. It's what you feel as you approach the first big drop on a rollercoaster or pay your ticket to see a horror film. I want to be afraid. I want to be thrilled.

We pass through a door into a huge space – most likely the attic. It's cavernous and dark, with the only light coming from two candles at the back of the room. As she continues toward those candles, she seems to shrink with each step, collapsing into something smaller.

At the other end of the room, there is a presence. He's hidden in darkness, but I can feel him. This feeling is heavy and pulls me forward like a gravitational force. I couldn't run away even if I wanted to.

"Here he is, master," she says, or rather it's what I imagine she says because I can barely hear her. She signals me to stop and goes the rest of the way alone, nothing more than a vague white figure flickering in the gloom. I know that I am not to move. No matter what happens, I must not speak or react in any way.

She takes off her clothes, her body glowing in the darkness. Even from a distance, however, I can isolate clusters of bruises all over her body: buttocks, calves, groin, breasts.

An indistinct figure moves toward her. My heart seizes and I hold my breath. I'm trying to get a good look at him but it's impossible, not just because it's dark but because – just like the other guy told me – he is impossible to take in whole. My vision jumps around, like the ground is shaking. The best I can do is to snatch glimpses of him. How I really know he is there is by *feeling* him. There is terror, yes, but also something more, something thrilling and exciting. His presence triggers something strange and animalistic in me. I want to throw myself at him, and I struggle to remain where I'm standing.

He steps behind her, towering over her like a tree. Eyes closed, she offers him her neck. He blocks my view as he bends his head low, but I know he's bitten her by the sound she makes, more a surrender to pain than pleasure. Then there's a sucking noise, so raw and feral that it turns my stomach.

This goes on for fifteen minutes, maybe more. The entire time, his eyes are fastened on me as surely as the mouth on her throat. The only way to keep from screaming or throwing myself at him is to cast my gaze to the floor, so the two of them are barely in my peripheral vision. When he stops feeding on her, I'm disappointed that it's over – and excited for what comes next.

I wait for it to be my turn, but no. Instead, he positions her on all fours and mounts her. I've had strangers fuck in front of me before (sadly, it's been a recurring theme in my life) but there's something unsettling about this time. Maybe it's her complete joylessness or the sad noises she makes, but there is obviously nothing pleasurable about it. The two of them grind on and on and I'm afraid I'm going to bolt from the room, unable to take any more, when he finally releases her.

She slumps to the floor, but she's not unconscious. After a minute she stirs and starts to dress. Meanwhile, the vampire has drifted back to the darkness. I can no longer see him nor feel his presence.

That's it? I've merely been brought in to witness this – admittedly thrilling – act? I did not expect to be a bystander. My blood starts to roil, but I manage to contain my fury until she's leading me down the stairs. "What was that? What just happened?"

Over her shoulder, she shoots me a look of disgust. "Did you think he would take you the first time, just like that? It doesn't work like that. He always does the choosing. You have to be patient. If you can't be patient, don't bother coming back."

If she thought I'd be so insulted that I'd storm out and vow never to darken the doorway with my presence again, she's wrong. Or that their sado-masochistic performance would frighten me away. There's no question that I'm going to come back. His absence has already left me a wreck. As I am pushed out the front door, in the rain, I'm sweating and trembling.

I used to chase a supreme but elusive high, until I did something terrible and lost it. That's when I tumbled, thinking I'd lost it forever.

Is that why I've come here? To try to find it again?

* * *

I won't experience the vampire's teeth until my third visit.

The second visit goes exactly like the first, except that the sex goes on for much longer. She cries, she whimpers, and once or twice she even begs. She passes out and I carry her to one of the bedrooms, leaving her to wake up on her own, figuring she wouldn't want to be reminded that I am witnessing her humiliation. It's while I'm lugging her downstairs that I realize she reminds me a little of my mother. Something about the eyes, or the way she carries herself.

It's been a long time since I've seen her, my mother, but once I see the resemblance, I can't unsee it.

The third time, however, she escorts me to the attic but stops at the door. Gesturing that I should continue alone, she gives me a look of warning – *are you sure you want this?* Hell yes; I'm so excited that it feels like I'm about to orgasm. Whereas earlier I'd been afraid he was going to kill me, now I know that's not going to happen, so there is no dread – well, maybe not *zero* dread. There's always the possibility. I know that about monsters.

None of that matters. My petty desires, my fears… none of that matters anymore. In a few minutes, I'll only exist to please him. I'm going to freely give myself completely to someone else. I'd given myself to someone before, but it wasn't freely. I was taken. I had no say in the matter, I was young. I didn't understand.

I understand now.

He pulls me toward him through sheer will, his command – not words exactly – booming in my skull. I'm to take off my clothes. I fumble with the zippers and buttons like I've suddenly forgotten how to dress, but finally it all falls to the floor in a puddle. He's closer to me than ever before, standing directly behind. His pull is so strong that it feels like I'm going to be crushed. I can barely think and could slip into unconsciousness at any second.

His hand falls on my shoulder. It reminds me of when I was eight or nine and my father ordered me to hold my palm over an open flame to see how long I could last. My older sister hadn't lasted a minute, earning our father's ridicule. I tried to hold out, tears blooming in my eyes as the heat became unbearable. But this is different. The burning is instantaneous and fierce. It rages all over like I've been set on fire.

I don't think about this for long, however, because he immediately sinks his teeth into my neck. He tears muscle and suddenly everything is red-hot pain, like I've been opened up and lava poured inside. I can't feel where my body ends anymore. I am afloat in an ocean of hurt. I think I'm going to pass out but somehow remain standing. My knees start to buckle as he sucks hard at my throat. I can feel blood sluice through my veins. *This is what it feels like to be consumed*. It's glorious and horrible at the same time. And vaguely familiar.

I struggle for consciousness, willing the rush of pain and panic to pass but only grow weaker and weaker by the second. Suddenly, it occurs to me that this might end differently from the previous two times. He might very well intend to kill me.

And why not? That's why I came here, wasn't it? That's what he thinks I want.

He shows no sign of letting up. His mouth is wetly noisy at my throat, the force of his feeding strong.

With his every draw, I feel I'm being depleted. He holds me up, pressing me against his body, a promise of what I know will come next whether or not I'm awake to experience it.

And yet his touch is the most sublime experience in the world. I thought I'd never feel its like again.

If I die like this, it will have been worth it.

* * *

I am surprised to wake up.

I recognize the bed: it's the same one I carried the familiar to a few days earlier. To call this a bedroom would be a high compliment. I've seen tidier crack houses.

She sits on the edge of the bed watching me. Is that concern I see on her face or is she just worried about getting rid of the body? There is so much *déjà vu* in this moment. By the time I'm fully conscious, however, she's her usual scornful self. "I thought we were going to lose you."

I struggle to my elbows. "Did you pass out the first time?"

She smirks. "Do I look like that much of a wuss?"

Her name is Sarah. She has been with him for two years. Like me, her journey started with rumors. Also like me, she was sick of what her life had become. She tracked him down hoping he would end it for her, but instead she became his familiar.

"Do you hope he'll make you a vampire, too, so you can live forever?" I ask her, once.

"At which point in my story did you stop listening?" She doesn't want eternal life any more than I do. I don't need to ask her why she's stayed: once you've had it, all you want is to keep feeling his touch. You dread it, but you can't live without it, either.

By the end of the first week of nightly visits, Sarah tells me I'm to move into the townhouse. I'm to quit my job. I'm not to tell anyone where I'm going or what I'm doing, not even my family (like that was even a possibility). I'm given a room on the first floor, close to the anteroom where she made me wait the first day, as far from the master's chamber as possible. I'm to earn my way up. Like my older sister, Sarah is the favorite. The master's familiar. I'm only here to assist her.

I'm carrying my possessions to the Uber when I feel eyes on me, but it's a busy city street and there's no telling who's doing the watching. There are a lot of people who would be interested in knowing where I'm going and very few are what you might call friends. I brush the concern away. Trouble always follows me, the way mysterious fires follow an arsonist. I've learned not to obsess over it.

* * *

She begins to tell me about herself in odd moments during the day. She was a lonely child in a large family who acted out for attention. She stole trinkets at the corner shop, pilfered her mother's purse for cigarettes. She graduated to setting things on fire. She was convinced she was unlovable and the notion stuck. We misfits, we're not so different.

By the time she was in her mid-twenties, she had zero friends and her family refused to have anything to do with her. Every time she made a new acquaintance or started a new job, she'd fall into old patterns: stealing from them, lying to them, disappointing them until they left.

I listen – I have no choice, trapped together as we are – but I don't want to hear this. I want her to remain a mystery. Now she's too human. Too much like me. I fight the urge to tell her about myself. It's only natural: everyone wants to be seen, for others to understand how we became the person we are. But I know that in my case, telling Sarah anything would be a mistake. There is no chance for understanding, only revulsion. I destroyed my family, didn't I? Had my father sent to jail even if he was, undeniably, a monster. Left my mother with nothing, with nobody to hide behind. Even my sister hates me for what I did because now everyone knows what she did. What we did.

So, Sarah, reminding me so much of my ungrateful mother – it's no surprise that I start to lose respect for her, that I protest, inwardly, when she gives me orders. I start to question whether she deserves to be the familiar. She is certainly no more deserving than me.

* * *

I ask Sarah about the master. I want to know everything about him I possibly can. I'm curious, it's only natural. What's his name? How old is he? Where has he lived, before? And how did he become a vampire? Is he the only one?

She gives me a sour frown. "It's not my place to tell you these things. If he wants you to know, he'll tell you himself," is her answer. After a few days of suspicious and frightened glances when she thinks I'm not looking, I come to the conclusion that she doesn't tell me because she doesn't know. Just like mom.

This dearth of information only fans my curiosity. I try to imagine what he was like as a human. What could his life have possibly been like before, what unfortunate incident put him on this path? It's hard to picture him human, though, because he is so fundamentally different from us. But if he didn't start out as human, where did he come from? The man he was before this transformation, was he filled with self-loathing, the way I am? Did self-loathing drive a wedge between him and the rest of humanity, turning him into something apart?

The more time I spend with Sarah, the more I see how careless she is. I'd thought at first that she was eagle-eyed, but on closer inspection, I see nothing could be further from the truth. She is slatternly. She is his primary feeding vessel and yet she doesn't take care of herself. She lets her wounds fester and doesn't bathe as frequently as she should. I wouldn't be surprised if she has indiscriminate sex on the outside, or started using drugs again. The house is a sty but when I make the effort to tidy up, it meets with open scorn.

One of our most important jobs as familiars is to find food for the master. This entails enticing strangers to follow us to a desolate area for the master to join us. I quickly see that Sarah is not discerning in her choices. Her victims are obviously unwell or disease-ridden, often weak and half-dead. Surely the master doesn't want to be served dregs, I wonder aloud. "We take what we can get," she snaps when I bring it up. I understand, then, that she wasn't doing me a favor the night she let me come in out of the rain. I was merely an easy meal. She thought he'd drain me dry and that would be the end of me. She didn't expect me to stay on and on.

I don't owe her anything.

She continues to talk about herself. Why not? She has a captive audience. Now, whenever we are together, it's non-stop: memories from childhood, years of regrets, how much she misses her family. She wants to see them – surely all is forgiven by now? She worries they assume she's dead. It's cruel to let them labor under that misconception, don't you think? There is a new gleam in her eye, almost wholesome, as she prattles on all day, every day.

All this prattle annoys me, of course. Her talk of families reminds me of mine, something I've worked so hard to leave behind.

How can she want to go back to all that? I'm afraid she's lost her mind. It's a cry for help.

* * *

Sarah and I are sifting through the debris field that is the dining room, looking for a pair of her earrings that she has allegedly lost, when she tells me a man came to the house looking for me.

"He said you owe his employer money." Her demeanor has changed entirely: one minute she's friendly Sarah who needs my help, and the next she is the familiar. My superior.

I try to blow it off. "Don't worry. It's nothing."

"It doesn't sound like nothing. I asked you about this kind of thing, didn't I? I told you we didn't need you bringing problems to our doorstep." Her voice is shrill, using the tone that makes men's testicles shrivel, as my father used to say. A tone you'd do anything to get away from.

To stop.

But it won't get to that. I have it under control. "I said don't worry. I'll handle it," I say through gritted teeth.

* * *

A few days later, I'm returning from the corner market with cigarettes when I see a car idling in front of the townhouse.

I walk to the driver's side and squint at the glass. It's probably the same guy who spoke to Sarah. I recognize him: he works for Vincent Smalls, an acquaintance of mine for many years, and by acquaintance, I mean someone I've bought drugs from. He is slightly smaller than your average refrigerator and looks like he's gone face-first through plate glass. I think his name is Dan.

It's an overcast day, so dark that it might lead you to think it's later than it actually is. I glance reflexively toward the attic. It's not nightfall, so there's no chance that Dan will serve as tonight's main course. Not that the prospect bothers me; he undoubtedly has blood on his hands and fully deserves a violent end, no matter how that might happen.

I motion for him to lower the window. "Whatcha doing here?" I ask, feigning ignorance.

He looks me up and down with the undisguised amusement he reserves for men he finds totally unthreatening. "Vincent got worried when you disappeared, considering how much you owe him."

Only a fool would advance a lot of drugs to a junkie and expect to be repaid. "You shouldn't show up here unannounced. In the future, call first. It's for your own safety." He's been warned.

Dan answers my obviously genuine concern with a big patronizing smirk. "Refusing to take care of your obligations to Vincent…that's suicide, Eric. Is that what you want? Are you looking to die?"

If I'm honest – yes. Sometimes.

But not today.

I shrug. "I'll have it tonight."

He frowns. "If you have the money, just give it to me now."

"I don't have it at the moment, but I can get it." I give him a location and tell him to meet me there around midnight. "I'll have it then, I promise. And we can put this sordid mess behind us."

"You talk funny, Eric." He starts the car, still wearing his patronizing smile. "It don't bother me but you should know, some people say you're not right in the head."

I know this, of course. It's been said about me my whole life, but by people who had no idea what I'd been through. If he thinks this hurts me or will make me weaker, he's in for a surprise. I've used this pain to make me stronger.

I smile at him as I turn to leave. "See you at midnight."

* * *

Dan is to meet me at an abandoned industrial park outside of town. You can't take an Uber to this kind of rendezvous, so I borrowed the keys to Sarah's old sedan. I hope to be back before she realizes the car is missing, but frankly it's a gamble I have to take.

I lean against the hood, chain smoking, while waiting for Dan to show up. We've used this location about six or seven times for our little operations, Sarah and me, and it's worked like a charm. It's dead deserted. No one comes out here. There's no road traffic and it doesn't overlook a highway. Oh, it might play host to drug deals or other nefarious activity (and I can feel their presence on the periphery like rats, those junkies and prostitutes, curious about Sarah and me but keeping their distance), but they're not the kind to go to the police.

It's half-past midnight when a shiny muscle car comes around the corner of a building. I recognize Dan's bald head but don't recognize the guy at the steering wheel. Of course; Dan wouldn't come alone, even if it's just little ole harmless me. Sweat blooms under my arms; we've never brought two victims for the master at the same time. Will he do it? Can he overpower two men? My mind races, picturing the many ways things could go awry and it goes badly for me in every one of them, shot by whichever one the master doesn't overpower immediately.

The car brakes about eighty feet away and, after a minute, Dan emerges. He seems to sprout taller, taller, taller, like some kind of origami monster folded up to fit inside that car.

He takes his time walking towards me. "Let's get this over with," he says brusquely.

The other man, however, doesn't get out. He remains stolidly behind the steering wheel. This is not good. It will be too easy for him to escape.

I dawdle with my cigarette to buy time. Dan is now twenty feet away from me. I say, "How about asking your friend to come out where I can see him? He's making me nervous."

Dan jerks his head in surprise. "Nobody cares if you're nervous. Stop playing around – I got places to be—"

Then a plan – a possibility – occurs to me. Dan is next to me now, intimately close. I drop my voice to a whisper. "Here's the thing…"

He groans. "I don't like the sound of this, Eric. Don't jerk me around. No excuses…"

"I have the money." I don't have the money. "The thing is I don't have *all* of it. Not quite. I'm shy a hundred. So…how about if I work off the difference in trade?" I give him a simpering look.

He tips his head back, like he's pleading with the heavens. "I'm not into boys, Eric."

The fact is, I couldn't care less what he's into. Boys, girls, or inanimate objects. I'll use anything at my disposal to get him out of sight of the man in the car.

"Is that what you think I'm offering? You should be so lucky. No, no, I'm talking about something else. Could make you some real money. But I don't want to discuss it in front of him," – I nod in the direction of the car, even though there's no way the second guy could hear us. I don't wait for an answer and start walking toward the empty warehouse, looking back at him with my best come-hither smile – and damn me if he isn't following. Though it might be out of frustration, chasing me for the money he thinks I have.

Please, please, master, be out there.

Once around the corner of the building, hidden from the man in the car, I halt and turn to face Dan. He's right behind me, over two hundred pounds of muscle coming right at me like a bull. His face is dangerously red. He's angry. He's not interested in my little offer at all, and if he finds out that I do not, in fact, have Vincent's money, he's probably going to beat me to death right here. "This better not be bullshit, Eric. I don't appreciate having my chain yanked, not by the likes of you…"

He is five strides away from me. I'm trapped. There's nowhere to run. I have finally overplayed my hand and am going to get what I've long deserved. I close my eyes and ready myself for one of Dan's meaty hands to grab the front of my shirt and…

But there's no meaty hand.

Instead, I feel the rush of something go by fast. The force buffets me, the way a truck knocks you around as it passes. The hairs on my arms stand up and the wind quickly drops and then I have the sense – of absence.

I open my eyes. Dan is gone, as completely as though he was never there.

My empty innards fill with happiness. Hallelujah. This is exactly what I'd hoped would happen: the master saved me. *He. Saved. Me*. Dan is strong, a brute and a bully, but the master is stronger. I have been at the mercy of bullies my whole life with no one to protect me. He is exactly what I needed, having been born to a monster, with no uncles to take an interest in me. I had to save myself and look where it got me. But now I have a protector. I never dreamed it was possible, but here he is.

After Dan, the man behind the steering wheel is no problem. When I come around the corner alone, he leaps out of the car like he's spring-loaded. He's pissed and confused and starts coming toward me, getting more worked up with each step. “Hey, where’s—” is all he manages to say before he, too, is gone in a blur, whisked aside by nothing more than a ripple in the darkness. I don’t know how the master is able to move so quickly, or if he bends matter to his will, but it’s just like this when we bring outsiders for him to feed on. Breathtakingly fast, brutally efficient.

He is the perfect protector.

I have seen him feed and it is not pleasant. Not in the least. Tonight, I don’t get to witness what he will do with them. He has taken them away. I will never have to see Dan again. Never fear Vincent again.

Never have to fear anyone.

I am grateful for a second chance. I was ungrateful the last time, an ungrateful child, but this time around, I will be the most loyal of servants. I will keep his secrets. I will be grateful, even when he inflicts pain.

After all, there can be no pleasure without pain, my father always said. No reward without punishment.

I get into Sarah’s sedan and drive home.

* * *

I didn’t think Sarah would find out about what I’d done. It was a private matter between the master and me. But the next day, she pounds furiously on the door to my room, forcing me awake. She doesn't wait for me to answer but throws the door back and barges in. "What the hell did you do last night?" she demands, standing at the foot of the bed.

I pull a tatty old blanket over my head, but she rips it aside. "I don't know what you're talking about," I say.

"Bullshit. You can't hide anything from me. I know everything he does – everything. You had him take care of the guy who came looking for you." I say nothing, unable to think quickly of a way to clear myself. She fills the awkward silence with another roar. "Are you stupid? That guy worked for some criminal, didn't he?"

I roll my eyes and fall back onto the mattress. "Don't be so dramatic. These guys come and go all the time… He won't be missed."

"You're delusional, you know that?" She grabs my shirt and shakes me. "You're bringing trouble right to our door – *big* trouble, things we can't explain. I warned you… We don't need this… What the fuck is *wrong* with you?"

There's nothing wrong with me. I'm perfect.

It happens quickly. I strangle her right there on the bed. I'm so much taller and stronger than her that it's over in no time. She stares at me with bulging eyes and I swear I see acceptance there, if not gratitude. She had to know it would end like this once she'd taken up with the master. You can't accept a monster in your life and think that you're safe. That you'll be able to control him.

I don't feel bad for killing her. At this point, eliminating her is completely logical. She's pathetic. She doesn't deserve to be the master's familiar; she doesn't even enjoy her position anymore. In the few months I've been in this household, she has changed, probably becoming more like the person she was before the master chose her. He wouldn't want that.

Just to be on the safe side – and because I'm feeling a bit squeamish – I put a plastic bag over her head and tape it tight. I wait outside the door, one eye on the darkening sky and at the end of an hour, I go back inside to make sure the deed is done. I nudge her foot, lift an arm and let it drop to the mattress. There is no reaction.

I take the plastic bag off her head. Her eyes are riddled with burst blood vessels. A thin rivulet of red trickles from her nose. Does the smell of blood wake him, I wonder? She said she knows everything that the master does, like there's some connection between them. Up in the rafters, he lies in wait for the night to welcome him. What I did to Sarah – was he jolted awake by her last, dying thoughts? Is he just waiting until it is safe to emerge before I get my reckoning?

The glistening red line running down her face hypnotizes me. It beckons me. What does blood taste like, I wonder. If I taste her blood, will it bring us closer, the master and me?

I dip a finger tentatively, only the very tip wet with red, and then press it to my tongue.

It tastes like family.

* * *

The sun set an hour ago. I stand outside the door to the attic the same as I did the first time, tremulous as a little girl. There are stirrings behind the door, so I know that the master has risen, but I haven't yet felt the familiar tug that lets me know to enter.

He must know that Sarah is dead. He must've felt her consciousness ebb away, even as he was trapped in the box that keeps him safe from day.

How strange it feels to kill another person. I was horrified by what I'd been driven to do, of course, because I am not a monster, but at the same time, there is no denying that it is thrilling. Is this how *he* feels when he kills, I wondered in the immediate aftermath, as I looked at my hands with new wonder. I couldn't help but hope it will bring us closer, make me more worthy of his favor. That it will make me more like him in some small way.

I feel his presence grow stronger, and there's an emotional note I've not felt before that is impossible to interpret. There's nothing to do but wait for his judgment. I'm prepared to accept whatever comes: I'll suffer his wrath, if he's displeased with what I've done, or accept his gratitude for ridding him of the sulky harridan. I came here that first night to let him kill me, after all, so if he were to kill me now it would be no more than what I expected. The end I'd been expecting, come to me at last.

Or he can spare me and – dare I hope – elevate me to Sarah's position? He's going to need a familiar and it's a safe assumption that he intended for that to be me one day, or else why would he have invited me to live here in the first place? That's why I don't think he's going to kill me. Why I don't think this is my last hour on Earth.

There is nothing I can do but wait for his judgment.

And so, I continue to stand outside his door.

Waiting.

Author Note

The funny thing about 'The Familiar's Assistant' is that I didn't know what it was about until after I'd written it. It was the first short story I'd written in a long, long time and I was just grateful for something to come to mind. The words came out in a torrent, scene after scene almost writing themselves, but I didn't know what the story was trying to say. Mainly, I didn't understand why the main character did what he did. Why he was so self-destructive. I saw that he hated himself; that was plain enough. Once I asked myself why someone would want so desperately to enslave himself to a brute who would only abuse him, then I understood.

We Don't Talk About the Sink

Ryan Cole

THE BATHROOM is the only place I've ever seen you walk into, and then never fully leave.

This is how it always is. You've only been home for winter break for three days, locked in your bedroom when you aren't out with your friends, hiding from me – the younger brother you've abandoned – and Mom, who still acts as if you aren't half-dead. Who doesn't hear the catch in your voice when you lie, the groan of the pipes when you leave the shower running for close to an hour, making us believe that you're as clean as you appear. As if you aren't by the sink, your mouth over the drain, feeding the creature you can't live without. Who you've kept at your side ever since you left for college.

Don't try to deny it. You brought it home with you. Again.

Mom hasn't noticed. And yet, why am I not surprised? She can see past anything she doesn't want to acknowledge, that doesn't fit her narrative – a working-class woman with her two teenage sons, doing her best to make it on her own. An honor-roll family, with me in the marching band and you on the wrestling team, no drugs, no drinking, always following the rules.

I bet it's hard for Dad to care now he's half a state away, all settled down with a new wife and kid. Easy to ignore what's in front of my eyes – how your ribs poke out, and your hair has turned to thread, unable to sit without a pillow over your lap, unable to stand without touching your waist, desperate to ensure there's still some give in your jeans.

And yet, we are fine, as Mom likes to say. Everything is fine. If it isn't in our minds, if it isn't on our lips, then it doesn't exist.

But I'm sick of pretending. Sick of appeasing this version of you, all hollowed-out, stripped of the pranks and the popsicle-stick jokes and the weight of your arm as it lay on my shoulders, facing the world with a wide, goofy grin. I want the old you, the one who said everything would be alright on the day that our family of four became three. We don't speak of that person, don't speak of the way that you've wasted away, don't speak of the monster who is eating you alive, one meal at a time.

And do you want to know why?

Because to Mom, it isn't real. To Mom, we are fine.

There is a monster in our sink.

And everything is fine.

* * *

Dinner time. We sit around the kitchen table in silence, staring at the bowtie pasta on our plates, none of us looking at the empty fourth chair and the deafening void from which your monster was born. Your stomach starts to rumble as you pick at your plate. I can hear a soft echo from outside the kitchen, at the end of the hallway. A gurgling of water on old, rusted metal. An echo that started on the day you came home.

"So, Wes," says Mom, as nonchalantly as she can, picking up your name like a fragile piece of glass, "do you still have that…friend?" She says it with a grimace, a plastered-on smile, so close to showing what she still can't admit.

But it isn't enough.

"Phoenix is my *boyfriend*," you say through clenched teeth, so different from the honey-sweet voice I heard while you secretly chatted on the phone the night before.

Mom recoils. That word is unspoken, a piece of her reality she would rather not own. She recovers with a smile, all fake red lipstick and sugar-coated warmth. "Well, please tell him that Sawyer and I said hello."

She winks at me then, as if I'm somehow on her team. As if I haven't accepted you from the moment you told me.

Not that it matters. Not that it offers you much of a shield – from Dad, or the feelings you're eager to purge, the loss of control in an uncontrollable storm.

You poke at your pasta, the pipes growing louder as the three of us pretend. "Excuse me," you say, and you stand up from your chair; you walk out of the room before either of us can stop you. Mom looks at me, looks at you, and she sighs. All of her frustration held in one single breath.

We listen as the light clicks on in the bathroom, and the door slams shut – as violent as the porch door two years ago.

Mom stands and reaches for your plate. She puts on a pair of yellow gloves at the sink, scraping the majority of your meal into the trash can. Neither of us speaks as we hear the shower curtain, and the water starts to run for the third time that day. Mom just stands there, scrubbing your plate with the wrong end of the sponge, her eyes on the wall. Probably lost in what she wished she could do, if she would only just say it.

I, on the other hand, haven't given up.

"I'm going to my room," I say before I leave, tossing my wiped-clean plate into the sink.

When I creep up to the bathroom, all I hear is water – regardless of the fact that your soap-bar will be crusty, your washcloth as dry as the skin around your eyes, which are red-rimmed from crying. It is cruel, where your monster has chosen to hide. First in the shower, then in the toilet, now in the only other place it can survive: in front of the mirror, where you're forced to bear witness to the life that you give it, the life that it demands. No matter how many times I've tried to scare it off, it always comes back, makes its home somewhere else.

But not this time. Not anymore. As I slump to my knees, my ear to the door, I can make out your breath as you push, as you heave, and my heart begins to pinch with the loss of who you were: my world, my best friend, my older, better half.

This time, the monster is going to die. This time, I will win.

* * *

Half past midnight, and the house has gone quiet. Mom is asleep on the couch in the living room, the glow of the TV bright on her face, her fingertips cradling an empty wine glass – her third of the night, though really, who's counting? We all have our own way of burying the past.

You are, as usual, locked in your bedroom. Listening to a playlist of old nineties music, probably a gift from your notorious boyfriend. I wonder if I'll ever get to meet Phoenix, wonder if he likes the same music I like, if he wears the same clothes, tells the same jokes. Maybe that would help me understand your decision – to drop your only brother for a guy you just met, when I needed you the most. When our world started crumbling. Maybe that would bring us back to who we used to be.

But tonight, I need the new you. The one who won't open your door if I knock. Tonight, I have business that you can't be a part of. Too risky, too much of a chance you might stop me.

I walk into the bathroom, and I gently close the door.

Nothing about it looks particularly menacing – baby blue tiles, a white porcelain sink, a shower curtain covered in pink seashell print. There is a circular mirror on the wall over the sink and a faucet that's starting to rust around the handles, but otherwise, the furnishings are minimal, plain. Not many places for a monster to hide.

A whispering gurgle seeps up from the drain – *fat fat fat* – almost too soft to hear. But after so many months, after so many futile attempts to make it leave, I've come to learn its voice. A low-pitched rattling, a clicking of teeth, crawling its way up the miles of pipe. It grows a bit louder as I reach into my pocket – even though it can't see me – and I pull out my weapons: a bottle of vinegar, a pack of baking soda, a newly sharpened kitchen knife, as long as my hand. The former to stun, the latter to kill.

But first, the bait. I have to give it what it wants.

Trembling, I lean into the basin of the sink, my bare stomach pressed against the wet porcelain edge. Hands gone clammy, one finger pressed to my cold, quivering lips. I know what you do, can imagine how light you must be when it's over – emptied of everything you don't want to feel – but still, when the tip of my finger meets my tongue, and I push it all the way to the back of my throat, my muscles contracting, my stomach so tight that I can barely even breathe, my cheeks flush with shame. Knowing deep down that I shouldn't be doing this, it doesn't feel right, it won't give the control you so desperately want.

All of which I stifle. For you. For our family.

Then a voice in the doorway. "Sawyer," you snap, as I cough into the basin, my mouth yawning wide over the open drainpipe. "What are you doing?"

Shaking, my shoulders hunched over the sink, I turn to face you. You look at me then as I had looked at you before, when I caught you in the act for the very first time. Confused, in denial, at a loss for what to say.

Yet, somehow, this is worse. Perhaps you believe that the monster has won. Perhaps you believe it has claimed me too. Perhaps you believe that we are too much alike, destined to walk down the same broken path.

Or, perhaps I am wrong.

"It was *you*," you say, as you pick up my weapons, the knife blade gleaming in the light from the hallway. "You made it run away. First in the shower, and then in the toilet." Cold recognition creeps into your face. "Get out," you hiss, and it melds with the gurgling coming from the drain – the monster I have tempted, and which you want to save.

"Wes, wait," I say, "I was only trying to help. Please, let me help you."

But you don't seem to hear, your green eyes fixed on the rumbling drainpipe. "*Get out*," you say, and you point at the door.

The two of us stand there, neither one willing to admit he was wrong. Then with a sigh, I reach for the knife, re-cork the vinegar, and push past the only other person in this world who I would fight for – even if you don't want me to.

* * *

Somehow, it knows. Maybe you told it. Maybe it learned from the pieces of yourself that you constantly give it, your saliva so rich with your own self-hatred. I can hear its voice clearly now – the drainpipes rattling, growing louder each day. The more we ignore it, the more you indulge it, the stronger it becomes.

What will you do when you meet face-to-face? I imagine it will be as if you're looking in a mirror, faced with the person you don't want to be, the person you've tried to bury deep in the drain. Will *he* be the one that walks out of that door, and you in the sink?

I don't want to find out. But I'm running out of time. I don't have any allies. The only one left is determined to look past the shuddering walls, the insidious whispers, and even though she won't listen, I have to at least try. This might be my very last chance to convince her.

* * *

"Hey, Mom," I say through the flickering TV. "I need to talk to you."

She fumbles with the remote, sets down the half-empty wine glass on the table, and clicks mute. Doesn't take her eyes from the screen. Better to watch someone else's happy life than be reminded of the one she is forced to keep living. "What's wrong, Sawyer?" she says.

"I'm worried about Wes," I say. "I think he's getting worse."

"What is it this time?"

"The mon—" I say, and catch myself. No reason to mention what she doesn't want to hear. "The pressure he's under – it's tearing him up. If you would just talk to him, make him believe that it isn't his fault." Even though it is. Even though Dad couldn't handle your secret, broken by the son he adored and never had, crushed by the grief of unmet expectations.

"Sawyer," says Mom, "we've been over this already. Your brother is fine." He is fine. We are fine. "He's just going through a phase." Everything is fine. "Give him some time, and he'll be alright."

The usual subtext darkens her voice, the empty reassurance. But then, for just a heartbeat, I notice her pause. Notice her dull eyes dart to the bathroom, her lips gone tight with the words she wants to say. The words I imagine I can help break free. "Mom, I don't think—"

But she holds up a hand. "It'll work itself out," she says with a sigh. "These things always do." Then she unmutes the TV.

I stand there in front of her as she looks right through me, lost in a world where she doesn't have to live. Which makes me start to wonder: how much longer can my family pretend?

* * *

We don't see each other much over the next few days. Our house is a fortress of locked doors and silence. There are still two weeks until you return to the dorms, two weeks of skirting the issues we fear. Still enough time for me to come up with a plan.

Until I realize – there isn't.

On the night of the third day, the bathroom door is closed. The scraps of our dinner are cold in the kitchen. That's when I notice the shower has been running for over an hour, no sound aside from the water in the tub. So much longer than it's ever been before. When I lean against the door, I can hear the monster feeding, the *fat fat fat* on its cold hissing lips, tiny teeth scrabbling on old rusted metal, the walls click-clicking with its sharp, eager feet.

"Wes, are you okay?" I yell through the door.

My pulse goes heavy, my heart in my throat. Am I already too late? I jiggle the handle, but the lock keeps me out. An interruption that would normally have brought you outside.

But you don't open the door. You don't say anything.

"Wes, can you hear me?" I ram into the wood, pushing as hard as my thin frame allows. I throw all of my weight at it until the hinges give in, the lock pin snaps, and I nearly fall forward onto the slick tile floor.

You are in front of me, draped over the sink. But this time, you don't look up when I enter, you don't try to tell me you don't need my help. You stand there, slumped with your arms around the faucet, the rest of your dinner still sticky on your chin. Eyes shut tight, breath coming ragged.

And just as I touch you, there is a gurgling *pop*, a releasing of pressure – and a long black fingernail pokes from the drain.

Your monster – for the very first time – shows itself.

I ease you to the floor as it continues to emerge, two solid inches of thick black keratin. "Mom!" I try to yell, but my voice comes out weak. It makes the monster twitch, start to sink back into the drain, retreating from the notice it has evolved to avoid.

"Mom!" I say again. "I need you in the bathroom!"

Thankfully, she listens. She runs to the door, her face gone pale as she sees you on the floor. Limp, unconscious, just barely breathing. She doesn't look at the sink, doesn't look at the tip of the shrinking black fingernail – now that it's been seen, recognized for what it is. She cradles your neck, leans to whisper in your ear. "It's okay, Wes," she says. "It's okay now, I've got you."

And for the first time in over two years, I believe her.

* * *

We sit across from each other at the bare kitchen table. Your chin is wiped clean, your breath comes smoothly, though you still have that hollowed-out look in your eyes. You cringe at the whispers coming over your shoulder – from the monster who is hungry, and still very much alive.

Mom reaches over the table to grab your hand, intertwining your fingers until her knuckles turn white.

She is ready. *We* are ready. But the question is: are you?

You don't need to worry. Just take a deep breath. For however long it takes, I will be here, waiting.

We sit there, together, like we always used to do, back when the world was still unbroken. When everything was fine. And just as the sun creeps in through the windows, just as I start to lose hope…

You speak.

Author Note

Eating disorders are insidious. They can be all-consuming, often go under the radar for long periods of time, and even though they can get better, they never really leave. I don't have one myself. However, over the years, I've realized that I do have unhealthy and deeply ingrained tendencies and thoughts about my own eating and body image, all of which helped to inform this story.

Above all, though, this story was born from a place of me feeling helpless. Someone very close to me has suffered from an eating disorder since they were a kid. It kills me to see their pain, to not know what to do or say, to see the negative impact of my own unhealthy tendencies and habits on them. So, I chose to write a story about a boy who did know what to do, who did know what to say, who wanted to help no matter the cost to himself.

My intention in writing this was to show how deep-rooted and complicated these issues are, as well as to show that, no matter how dark it seems, there is always a light at the end of the tunnel.

Old Friends

Tim Waggoner

PEOPLE AT FUNERALS and viewings always talk about how lifelike the deceased looks. I think that's a crock of shit people say to each other to break the oppressive silence. Once the dead have been favored with the attentions of a mortician, they look like stiff wax figures, features partially melted, makeup troweled on clown-thick. It's one of the reasons I hate funerals, but tonight, looking down at my friend lying in her open casket, I find myself thinking, *Actually, she does look pretty good.*

This is the first time I've seen Aubrey in over twenty years. I can still see the girl I knew in high school, the same narrow face and curly brown hair – although there are threads of white in the latter now. There's plenty of white in my hair as well. Her eyes (closed, of course) are sunken, the sockets of her skull prominent, and her cheek bones jut out sharply. The skin on her face sags a bit, and all of these details put together makes her seem older than forty-one by at least a decade. But death will do that to you, won't it?

When someone joins me at the casket, I don't take my eyes off Aubrey, don't acknowledge my fellow mourner in any way. The last thing I want to do right now is make awkward small talk with a stranger over the corpse of the best friend I've ever had.

The stranger, however, does not share my desire.

"How did you know Aubrey?" she asks. It's the first time I realize the stranger is a woman.

"High school," I say, keeping my response as brief as possible in the hope this person will take the hint and leave me alone. But of course, she doesn't.

"Aubrey and I were friends for years," she says. "All our lives, really. It's such a waste, isn't it? She was so young."

"Yes."

I may not want to have a conversation with this woman, but I agree with her. Aubrey had polycystic kidney disease, and from what I understand, the disease progressed especially fast in her. She needed a kidney transplant, and luckily her aunt turned out to be a match. Aubrey inherited the disease from her father's side of the family, so both of her aunt's kidneys were healthy. But during the transplant operation, Aubrey had a bad reaction to the anesthetic and died. The generous aunt got to keep her kidney, though, so I guess the outcome wasn't all bad.

"It's not fair," the woman said.

"No, it's not."

Be quiet. Go away. Leave me alone.

"She had so many more years ahead of her," the woman said. "She still had so much to give."

I agree, but this time I say nothing, not wishing to engage the woman any further.

Although Aubrey and I kept in touch via social media over the last couple decades, I only knew the most cursory details of her life. Who she married (a guy named Marcus), where she worked (Fuller Elementary School)… But there's one question I wish I could get answered, one detail about her life I'll never know.

Did *it* ever return?

* * *

When I was a teenager, Aubrey Mills was my very best friend. We were both in band, and we played the same instrument – trumpet – so we were in the same section, too. This meant we saw a lot of each other, and we just kind of clicked, the way that some people do. We started eating lunch together and talking on the phone at night, sometimes for hours. Our friends started teasing us, calling us lovebirds and making kissing sounds whenever we walked past. Neither of us were bothered by this, not really, and I suppose it started us wondering if we really were becoming boyfriend and girlfriend. Who am I kidding? Of *course* we wondered that. We were teenagers, after all, and raging hormones was a big part of the deal. We never said anything, neither of us made any specific declaration that we were now 'going together' as the phrase went. But we began holding hands, and we kissed a few times before and after band practice. But it just didn't feel right. It was like kissing your sibling, and just as we began exploring the possibility of a romantic relationship by unspoken agreement, we returned to being just friends the same way. I think we were both relieved that we'd answered that question, and with the issue of sex taken off the table, we could relax around each other again.

Aubrey and I would hang out at my house when we didn't have band practice. I don't know if my parents thought we were dating. They never said anything about it if they did, but they had no problem with Aubrey and me being in my bedroom with the door closed, so I'm fairly confident they understood the true nature of our relationship. Who knows? Maybe they suspected I was gay. And maybe they thought Aubrey was, too. She wasn't exactly a girlie-girl. But who knows what parents think?

We never went over to her house. Her dad didn't like me, always scowled when I was around. I think he saw me as a horny teenage boy sniffing around his daughter in hope of getting into her pants. I couldn't blame him. That's what most of the guys in school were like.

Aubrey had...I'm not sure how to describe it. *Issues*, I guess is the best word. I'd be talking to her, and she'd get this blank expression on her face. She'd stay like that for a while, and if I stopped talking, she didn't look at me, remained silent. Then she'd suddenly look around, startled, as if she'd fallen asleep without realizing it and had abruptly woken. When I asked her about these times, she'd say she was just tired, hadn't been sleeping well, and she'd apologize. She often went home soon after that – we were both driving by this point – but I always had the feeling she left only to make her excuse seem more convincing.

Then one day when we sat down in the cafeteria for lunch – I think it was pizza day, the best day of the week – she asked me a question.

"What did I do the last couple days?'

I looked at her for a moment, trying to understand her question, thinking that I'd missed something.

"What do you mean?"

We sat alone at a table, but Aubrey glanced around to see if anyone might be listening. But the other kids were focused on their own conversations, and, satisfied we wouldn't be overhead, she began talking.

"I don't remember anything about the last two days. I want to know if I did anything...weird."

Aubrey wasn't the sort of person who liked to mess with people's heads, but even so, for a moment I thought she was trying to make some kind of joke. But she'd sounded sincere. More, she'd sounded scared. I thought back over the last two days. Aubrey had been in school, and she'd seemed like her normal self. But she hadn't spent as much time with me as usual, and when I asked if she wanted to come over to my house, she said she couldn't, that she had too much homework to do. I hadn't thought much of it at the time, but now… And there'd been little things. She'd been quieter than usual, and when she did speak, she was brusque. She'd never been the most graceful person, but her movements had been stiff, awkward, as if she'd been having trouble remembering how to work her body. And her eyes… They'd been wider than normal, and they projected an intensity, a scrutiny, that I'd never seen before. I'd noted all these details at the time, but I hadn't put them together and drawn a conclusion from them, other than that she'd probably been overtired. I knew she had trouble sleeping sometimes. But now a new possibility occurred to me.

"Were you on something?"

"You mean like drugs? No." She paused. "At least I don't have any memory of taking anything."

She said this so matter-of-factly that it chilled me. It sounded as if she was used to losing memories.

It also hurt me, too. We were supposed to be best friends, but she'd never mentioned anything like this to me before, had never even hinted at it.

I told her everything I'd observed about her behavior over the last forty-eight hours, what she'd done and said, what it had been like to interact with her. I hadn't been with her the entire time, of course, so I couldn't tell her anything about what she did during the times we weren't together. But when I finished, she seemed reassured.

"Good. Whenever this happens, I'm always so worried that it will do something really embarrassing. Or worse, something that will hurt someone I care for."

There was quite a bit to unpack in that sentence, and I wasn't sure where to start first.

"So this happened to you before. Does it happen a lot?"

She looked down at the slice of pizza on her lunch tray. Neither of us had touched our food.

"Once or twice a week. Sometimes more. An episode can last minutes, hours, or even days. I never know until I return to myself and check the date and time."

I was floored by this revelation. But I was also intrigued.

"How long has this been happening to you?"

"Since I was little. Mom and Dad don't know about it." She smiled. "You're the first person I've ever told."

"I'm honored," I said, and I meant it. "You said you were worried that *it* would do something embarrassing or hurt someone. Do you mean you're not in charge during the times you lose your memory?"

"Like another personality takes over? I don't know. I've done a lot of reading about experiences like mine. Psychological stuff, paranormal stuff. I don't have any answers, though."

"Maybe you should think about seeing a doctor."

She shook her head.

"They'd just give me pills that would make me brain dead. Or worse, they'd put me in a mental hospital and never let me out."

I thought she was exaggerating, but I didn't say so. Besides, maybe that's what would happen.

She went on, "I've handled this okay up to now, and I can keep handling it. But do me a favor. If I start acting strange, keep an eye on me. Just in case."

I wasn't sure I wanted that responsibility, but Aubrey was my friend, and I loved her. And when you love someone, you do things for them, even when it's hard. I smiled.

"You got it."

* * *

Aubrey and I were sitting cross-legged on my bed, facing each other. The door was closed (as usual) and the curtains were drawn. The overhead light was on, but stubborn bits of shadow still clung to the room's corners. Aubrey wore a flannel shirt, untucked, and jeans, and I had on a Misfits t-shirt and jeans. I wasn't a huge fan of the band, but I liked their skull-faced mascot.

"I'm not sure this is a good idea," Aubrey said.

"Don't you want to know more about what's going on with you? Don't you want to understand it?"

Her eyes narrowed, as if she were seeing something in me for the first time.

"Not as much as you do," she said.

A hot flush of shame came over me, and I was certain my face reddened. Aubrey didn't say anything about it, but one corner of her mouth ticked upward in a partial smile.

"You said you've never told anyone but me, right?" I asked.

She nodded.

"So whenever *it* was in the driver's seat, nobody knew. When they spoke to it, they thought they were speaking to you. But I know the truth now. If you can purposely turn over control to *it*, I'll be able to ask it questions. Find out who it is and what it wants. Once we figure that out, we can give it what it wants, then maybe it'll go away and never come back."

Despite my words, I was afraid of what I might find out if *it* – this *Other* – made an appearance. Aubrey had never come out and told me she was being abused at home, but I'd been afraid that was the case for a while. The way her dad acted toward me, as if I was some kind of rival for Aubrey's attention. The mysterious bruises and scratches that would occasionally appear on Aubrey's body which she could never provide an adequate explanation for. And now this Other that took her over sometimes. I'd seen plenty of movies and TV shows where someone dissociated as a result of experiencing trauma. Sexual abuse was one of the most common causes in fiction, the Terrible Secret that Must Not Be Revealed. Was Aubrey's dad sexually abusing her? I didn't know, and Aubrey had never spoken of it. But then she wouldn't if she were repressing the memories, would she?

"I'm not a big fan of maybes," Aubrey said.

"Maybe is the best we've got."

"Okay. What do I do?" She took a deep breath, released it slowly.

Like *I* had any idea. I wasn't a psychologist or a mind reader. I was just a dumbass kid who wanted to help his friend – and in the process get a look at something dark that was sharing space in her head.

"Relax. Try to stay calm. Think about letting go, giving up control, letting *it* come forward and see through your eyes, speak with your mouth. If it really—"

I felt a sudden chill in the air, as if someone had dropped a cold blanket over me.

"Hello."

Aubrey's voice held an edge of cruel mockery, and her eyes were wide and shone with dark amusement. But this wasn't Aubrey. It was *it* – the Other.

"Hey," I said, trying to sound unafraid, casual even, as if I spoke to alternate personalities every day. "How's it going?"

The Other raised an eyebrow, and its mouth stretched into a cold smile.

"I like your bravado. It's charming."

I felt my face flush with anger, and I tried to hold it back. I knew that what I was seeing in Aubrey's eyes was only another part of herself, that this was ultimately a game of pretend. Complicated and serious, no doubt, but it wasn't *real*. And yet...

The room had become so cold I was trembling. I told myself that it was just my nerves, but I'd felt the temperature drop *before* the Other had spoken. I hadn't been afraid then. Anxious and excited, not afraid – not like I was now.

Aubrey's hands had been resting in her lap. Now the Other pressed them down onto the bed, wrists bending backward. Aubrey's shoulders moved back and forth, arms twisting, as if she were trying to grind her hands into and through the mattress. I heard joints pop and crack, and I feared if the Other kept on this way, Aubrey's wrists might break. I reached out and grabbed hold of her wrists, lifted her arms up and away from the bed's surface.

The Other's smile grew wider, and it started moving Aubrey's arms around, slowly, not trying to pull free from me. But there was such strength behind these movements that it took an effort for me to hold on. I kept my gaze fixed on Aubrey's face.

"Who are you?" I asked.

"You know."

Playful, almost teasing.

"No, I don't. What's your name?"

"Puddin' Tain. Ask me again, I'll tell you the same."

"No. You're the Other. That's what I think of you as, anyway."

Our arms continued their slow gyrations as Aubrey shrugged.

"It's as good a name as any."

"What do you want?" I asked.

"Whatever I can get."

I knew that ultimately this was Aubrey that I was talking to, but the Other's taunting evasiveness reminded me of stories where demons who've possessed human bodies attempt to confuse and frustrate those who confront them. And I remembered something about how evil spirits try to break down the resistance of those they wish to possess. Had Aubrey's abuse been part of that process? Had the Other caused it somehow, or merely taken advantage of it?

Stop it, I told myself. *This is no demon or spirit. It's just Aubrey.*

The Other giggled then, as if having read my thoughts and found them funny. Coincidence, that's all.

"Do you know whose body you inhabit?"

The Other's smile faded, and its brow furrowed.

"My own."

It didn't sound certain, though.

"Her name is Aubrey. She's my friend. You have no right to use her like this."

The Other's arm movements sped up a bit, and there was more strength behind them now, so much that it took an effort for me to continue holding onto Aubrey's wrists. Had she always been this strong?

"I do what I want," the Other said.

"You have to stop."

"Why should I?" The smile returned.

"Because you don't belong inside her?"

"All things need a place to be. This is mine."

By now my arms and shoulders were aching, and I didn't know how much longer I could go on doing this. I'd learned enough. Whatever was going on with Aubrey, it wasn't something that the two of us could fix on our own. She needed therapy and doctors who could prescribe her medicine. I vowed to do everything I could to convince her to admit she needed help – *after* I ended this. I didn't know if the Other would really break Aubrey's wrists if I let go, but I didn't want to take the risk. Aubrey was in this situation because I'd wanted to talk to the Other, wanted to experience the full effect of its strangeness. But I'd used my friend to do it, and I knew I'd regret it for the rest of my life – and I'd regret it even more if Aubrey got hurt because of it.

"It's time for you to go," I said.

"But I just got here. I like talking to you. You're so *scared*."

"Aubrey's coming back now." *I hope*. "You're going to go and never bother her again."

I had no idea if my half-assed attempt at hypnotism-slash-exorcism would work, but it was all I could think to do.

"All right," the Other said, "I'll go for now, but I will return, and when I do, you better watch your back."

I went for false bravado one last time. "Take it easy."

The Other raised an eyebrow again, its smile widened, and then – like a taut rubber band that's been released – the tension rushed out of Aubrey's body. Her features became expressionless and her arms went limp. Her head lolled forward, and I quickly let go of her wrists and took hold of her shoulders to keep her from falling onto me. A second later, she sat up and looked around in confusion.

"What happened?"

I gathered her into a hug and started crying.

* * *

We graduated high school and went to college in different states, but we both ended up getting teaching degrees – Aubrey in special ed, me in high school history. I got married; she got married. I had a kid, got divorced, moved into a crappy one-bedroom apartment, and I still live there today. Aubrey never had children, but her marriage seemed solid enough from what I could glean via social media. Time continued flowing, as it will, and we got older, as people do. I never learned whether Aubrey's dad was sexually abusing her or if she ever got therapy. But she'd made a life for herself, and by all appearance, she was doing better than I was, so despite the hard road she'd been forced to travel, she'd turned out all right.

Thank god.

* * *

I suppose I'll never know who or what the Other was, and after all this time, what can it possibly matter? Even if I had an answer, it wouldn't change anything. Answers, like the questions that prompt them, are all meaningless in the end. They all lead here, to a box in a room filled with sad people, soporific music, and the stink of dying flowers.

I forgot about the woman standing next to me, but she's still there – unfortunately.

"Look," I say, "I don't mean to be rude, but—"

I turn toward her as I speak, intending to make an excuse so I can get the hell out of here, go find a bar where I can drink and be alone with my melancholy thoughts. But my voice dies when I see her. See *it.*

"I *told* you to watch your back. But it's good to see you again. I recently got evicted from my home and I'm looking for a new place to live. And Aubrey always *was* so fond of you."

It glides toward me, no longer a woman, no longer human, and as it enters me, I realize that sometimes we *do* get answers, often when we least expect them. But in the last instant before everything that makes me *me* is gone – to be replaced by something else, something cold and dark – I have time for one final thought, one final *question*…

I wonder how long it'll take to settle in?

Author Note

This, as they say, is a true story.

Not the possession part, of course, and my friend 'Aubrey' is still alive and well, and she doesn't have kidney disease. The events in this story occurred sometime in the early 1980s, and back then – at least in my small Ohio town – people weren't open about mental health issues, and they rarely sought professional help. 'Aubrey' was the first person I knew who suffered from the effects of deep trauma. At least, I believe her episodes of missing time were the result of trauma, but I don't know for certain. Back then, I didn't know how to talk to friends and family about mental health issues, and it would've felt like I was violating her privacy and causing her more pain if I had.

I was an imaginative kid, and I lived on a steady diet of science fiction, fantasy, and horror media, so part of me feared that maybe 'Aubrey' was possessed, but most of me knew she wasn't. The conversation I had with her Other had a huge emotional impact on me, and over the years, I've tried to find a way to use it in my fiction, but it wasn't until now that I succeeded. Maybe sufficient time had passed for me to finally get enough distance from the event to write about it. 'Old Friends' is about trauma, of course, but specifically, it's about how trauma can spread, like ripples across water, like disease, like shrapnel in a war zone, like a demonic entity searching for a new home... There's an old question I once read somewhere: Who's the victim of violence (or in this story, abuse)?

Everyone.

A Note for William Cowper

Sara Larner

An excerpt from *The Primary Prospector*, Trade Issue #189:

> On Dec. 3rd, 2047, preeminent deep-sea mining corporation Nautilus experienced extreme setbacks while expanding their Norway operations. Due to a rushed initial evaluation, their two-person mining vessel was hit by an unexpectedly strong plume of superheated minerals, which reached nearer the surface than previously believed possible. One miner died shortly after the incident; the other was recovered with a severe infection. Nautilus's subsequent delay in sending a secondary craft allowed rival company Aronnax to claim the vent, leading some investors to question Nautilus's continued relevancy in today's ever expanding deep-sea market.

* * *

Audio log for mining vehicle #3887632:

3:12:2047 14:02

Oh god. Oh god, oh god, oh god.

I think Mel's dead.

3:12:2047 15:32

This is the crew for mining vehicle number 3-8-8-7-6-3-2. We got hit by, by something, I don't know, the heat of it fried all the computers, and I – Mel was at the control when it hit, but I've got her heart beating again and I think she'll be okay if you just, please, just send help.

3:12:2047 16:08

The emergency lights have come on. I can see outside the sub. The life down here is incredible.

Mel moved a bit, earlier. Just a twitch, but I think she's doing better.

3:12:2047 16:54

I've pulled together a sort of bed for Mel and collected all the food and fresh water rations. We have enough for both of us to survive down here for five full days, though we'll be pretty close to dead when help comes. Not sure how I'll feed her if she remains unconscious.

It must have been the plume from the vent. There's nothing else down here we could hit. I wonder… It must have been something in the lithosphere. It shouldn't have reached that high, but if there was a disturbance… It'd be really great to be able to reach base-hub on the coms.

Well, it'd be really great to not be trapped in a submarine at the bottom of the ocean.

It'd be really great to have medical training.

They should have given us more medical training.

3:12:2047 18:07

Mel twitched again.

3:12:2047 18:29

I think the camera outside the sub is almost certainly broken, so I've decided to catalogue the deep-sea fauna on my own. Earlier there was an eel of some sort, pale white. Maybe four feet long, and as thick as two, no, three fingers. So, two inches thick. I didn't see its face, just the streak of it.

Mostly all I see is this black, with little specks of white eddying about. Could almost be snow on a dark night, if it weren't for the eel.

3:12:2047 18:43

I might die down here. I might die down here with Mel. We'll use up our oxygen in two days. She's breathing less than me, probably, being unconscious while I'm struggling to keep my heart rate below cardiac-arrest levels.

If she…

3:12:2047 19:22

Mel wasn't the first girl I loved, but she was the first girl I knew I loved while I loved her. I think that's important. They send us down in same-sex pairs as though that would stop this sort of thing from happening, but that's – I mean love, stop love from happening, not horrific disaster. Obviously, we didn't crash because we… I'm just saying, I loved her and I want there to be a record of the fact that I loved her, and she never actually said it, but she loved me too. I'm not just making that up. I mean, we were… There should be a record.

3:12:2047 20:01

I saw something red. I think it was a squid, but it's hard to say. It didn't look like it had scales. It wasn't eel-shaped.

3:12:2047 23:22

All the lights inside the sub went out. You should know. I have the light from the camera outside, and that reflects in a bit, but it's pointed away. All I have is darkness in here.

If I were smarter, I'd write poetry. I used to, when I was a kid, but even then I was terrified of improv. I needed so much time to obsess over every terrible line. I'd write it out and mark the stresses like they teach you, and feel like I was a part of something bigger than myself. Then life happened. I was never a part of anything. The grand tradition of literary success has nothing to do with me. I was like a sports fan, dressed up in the jersey and maybe even holding a football or some shit, jumping up and down thinking I was winning the world series because the guys I loved did good.

But if I was smarter, I'd compose something on the spot. Without paper or anything. I have time. I have imminent death.

Oh! Outside! I saw something!

4:12:2047 02:01

I don't know why I lied earlier. I said the life down here is wonderful. I hadn't seen anything at that point. I don't know why I lied.

4:12:2047 03:38

When I first met Mel, I was hideous, sweating and gross from the pit. Heh. That's actually…kind of hilarious. You know, the pit, it's what we call the hold where we train for close quarters confinement, in the event of a crash or an emergency. Funny. Anyway, I was disgusting, and she was beautiful. She was walking towards me, and I wanted to sink into the wall, to hide or run or just *be clean*, and she's walking towards me, and then – she's passed. She didn't even stop, didn't glance my way or wrinkle her nose.

We talked about it later. She thinks the first time she saw me was when we were paired up, three – no, two and a half years ago.

4:12:2047 12:09

Fuck. Stupid idea. Stupid, stupid idea.

4:12:2047 12:23

I found the med kit and took four of what I thought were sleeping pills. Maybe they were sleeping pills. Fuck. I passed out, but I also must have walked or something because…long story short, I've got this gash in my leg and it's not going to kill me but *fuck*.

4:12:2047 13:53

Might as well know. I've been down here twelve hours, you might as well know.

I smothered Mel with the shock blanket when I realized she was breathing my air. I wouldn't have been able to feed her anyway. She was probably brain dead. When we hit the plume, it was with our front end: the front half of the sub actually went *into* the plume. That's around 700°F. Not sure how hot the metal got exactly, but she was touching it and her palms got burnt to hell. She screamed and jumped back, then the sub lurched, she was flung up against the front window. Hit her head, broke an arm. Even as we were falling, I pulled her off the console, but she didn't have a pulse. That's when I left the first message. Made the first log.

I realized as soon as we hit – it was only seconds later, couldn't have been more, so maybe our machine was off about our depth after all – I realized I could try to jumpstart her with the med kit. We have it in case of drowning, which is funny because down here you wouldn't drown; you'd be crushed, and there's no coming back from that. But we have it, so I used it, and she came back. I splinted her arm, applied a local anesthetic to her hands, in case she woke up.

I was trying. I was really trying. I told her stories, told myself stories. Recited some poetry, mostly silly stuff I think she'd like. Then I realized she'd die anyway, so I killed her.

No.

I realized she'd get me killed faster, and every second I waited was another breath I wouldn't have. And—

No. That's it. That's what it was.

4:12:2047 17:41

I slept for a while. It's easy down here. Very dark, very quiet.

I pushed her body into the corner. Disrespectful, but I just…I don't want to fall asleep and wake up spooning her corpse.

Fuck. Fuck.

I…

4:12:2047 19:21

It was many and many a year ago,
In a kingdom by the sea,
That a maiden there lived, whom you may know
By the name of Annabel Lee.
And this maiden she lived with no other thought
Than to love and be loved by me.
I *was a child and* she *was a child,*
In this kingdom by the sea,

But…

Shit. I always…

Coveted her and me…

No, that's later. Shit. I swear, I got it right when I was reciting it for her. I know this.

I know this.

4:12:2047 19:39

There are strange things done in the midnight sun
By the men who moil for gold;
The Arctic trails have their secret tales
That would make your blood run cold;
The northern lights have seen queer sights,

But the queerest they ever did see

Heh. Hehe…

Hahaha, hahahahhahahahaAHAHAHAHHA—

4:12:2047 19:58

Was that night on the marge of Lake Lebarge,
I cremated Sam McGee.

4:12:2047 20:01

Get it? And now I'm stuck here with her corpse, and it's about mining and holy shit how did I recite that whole damn poem to her and *not* get it?

And every day that quiet clay seemed to heavy and heavier grow;
And on I went, though the dogs were spent, and the grub was getting low;
The trail was bad, and I felt half MAD, *but I swore I would not give in;*
I'd often sing to the hateful thing, and it harkened, with a grin.

Heh. With a grin.

4:12:2047 21:10

I'd have to actually touch her face to be sure, but she's grinning. That's what happens, right? Some sort of rictus. But I—

I don't think I can touch her. I can't…

God, she *reeks*.

4:12:2047 23:03

There's no way to get her out of here. I've really thought through every option and there's just no way. Corpses smell because of the buildup of gases, so I seriously considered cutting her up to let the gases out, prevent buildup, but then they'd just *be* here. Not like we have ventilation.

I wonder if you can die from that. From a corpse's fumes.

I wonder if my leg could get infected. I tied up the gash with a strip of my shirt, but it soaked through, so really I'm just pressing a wet, bloody clump of cloth to an open wound and hoping that'll...

4:12:2047 23:23

I saw a squid! It was definitely a squid this time. Red and pale white, it came over to the camera light and was kind of, you know, playing with it. Darting around it, like how dolphins play with the wakes of boats, or like, I don't know. It was small, maybe a foot long, but clever. I could tell. Anyone could tell.

4:12:2047 23:50

I took off the strip, and, I don't even fucking know what I was thinking. I, I guess I was trying...I wanted to see how bad the damage is. So I dug my fingers in there, just...as far as they could go, and I was screaming, really *screaming*. Then I realized I can scream as loud as I want and it won't matter, because no one's coming, so I pushed harder and screamed louder and if it wasn't infected before, it sure as hell is now.

5:12:2047 01:04
Day three. Day three of being down here. Not a full forty-eight hours, but still the third day.

5:12:2047 01:09
I'll kill myself before I run out of air.

5:12:2047 01:39

Merrily did we drop
Below the kirk, below the hill,
Below the lighthouse top.

'The ship was cheered, the harbour cleared…

5:12:2047 02:13

Nor dim nor red, like God's own head,
The glorious sun uprist;
Then all averred, I had killed the bird…

But even there, even there, they say, the poem *itself* says:

'Twas right, said they, such birds to slay,
That bring the fog and mist.

…but then again, can't see for shit down here anyway.

5:12:2047 04:13

No voice divine the storm allay'd,
No light propitious shone;
When, snatch'd from all effectual aid,
We perish'd, each alone:

I never believed. When I was a little girl in temple Rabbi Mendes said God was a feeling. I never felt it.

Mel did. Not often, but sometimes. A rocky patch, turbulence – she'd mutter under her breath, and I know that particular sort of rhythm. All prayers are the same like that, I think. Just a spell, a little noose of words trying to hook around the neck of something divine. Something that might, when you're "snatched from all effectual aid," be there, be...

And I don't even know mine.

I know William god-damned Cowper. Platitudes and *Fiddler on the Roof*. The only thing that felt like magic in temple were the stained-glass windows, stolen from Christ and *their* traditions... ***Crash*** Tradition! HA! Fucking tradition!

5:12:2047 04:22

But I beneath a rougher sea,
And whelm'd in deeper gulfs than he.

Oh, I don't know, Billy boy, you wanna *bet?*

5:12:2047 04:23

Really I'm just in a great place. All things considered.

5:12:2047 06:31

A crab crawled across the window. I didn't notice at first – I'd closed my eyes, because staring at black is just...well, I closed my eyes. It was sitting right there. This pale white, or pale green-white. Long legs. Like, maybe three feet long, each. I screamed when I saw it.

5:12:2047 07:54

AND NEITHER THE ANGELS IN HEAVEN ABOVE
NOR THE DEMONS DOWN UNDER THE SEA
CAN EVER DISEVER MY SOUL FROM THE SOUL OF—

THIS ASSHOLE WHO COULD HAVE JUST LET GO OF THE GODDAMN CONSOLE AND THEN WE'D BOTH BE DEAD OF OXYGEN DEPRIVATION AND EVERYTHING WOULD BE FINE.

5:12:2047 10:14

God...oh god... I don't actually know any Hebrew. I'm down here and I don't know any Hebrew. Please, god, I just...

Baruch, atah Adonai, Elohei, Numelech, shalom... Asher, kidishanu, bamitzvatov, vitzi vanu, la hanuk ner! Shell, ha, nu, ka.

I'm so sorry. I can sing it. I don't know what it means, but it's the best I've got and I can sing it for you again.

Baruch, atah Adonai...

She was a Christian. What do they need?

5:12:2047 10:42

Bless her father for she has sinned. She has been with a loose woman.

I don't know any of the rest.

5:12:2047 13:58

I'm going to kill myself soon. I don't know how much oxygen I have left, but I have been bleeding for a long time and sooner or later I'm not going to have much strength. So I'm going to kill myself soon. I've been hearing voices. I saw my mother. She came down, out of the sea, and touched my face, and told me she was dead. She told me the blessing for the dead, and I said it. The Mourner's Kaddish. There's no blessing for the suicidal, and Mel's God may be merciful, but mine is not. I won't burn, but I will not be among the blessed. So I will kill myself soon, because, God, do I deserve to die.

I have earned it with trying to live.

I have earned it with killing.

I have earned it with every ounce of myself.

I'll be not in the grass, nor in the sky, nor beneath the soil. I'll be here, in this place, full of death and the reek of death. I'll be metal and bone and hard lines. I'll be empty of myself.

Oh. Look at the snow. Outside the window, the light cracks down from far above to strike every floating fragment. Sweeping, almost dancing.

It really is beautiful.

Author Note

This is not a story I ever expected to see in print. I wrote it in college as a one-woman play, shortly after breaking up with my first serious girlfriend. I was interested in deep-sea mining because of a marine biology course. I was interested in guilt because the reason I'd broken up with my partner was that, after three years, I had to finally admit I was not equipped to help her deal with her mental illness while also grappling with my own challenges.

The great thing about writing a one-woman play is that there is almost no chance of it being good. With that in mind, I gave myself permission to focus on something deeply self-indulgent: poetry, and how poetry can interact with being suicidal.

Raised in an aggressively atheist Jewish household, I never had prayers. Flying by myself at eight years old, when we hit turbulence, I didn't pray – I recited poetry. It calmed me down. I felt steadied, reassured by the rhythm of the words. More than a decade later, hospitalized due to insomnia, half-delusional with my grand total of eleven hours of sleep spread over nine days, none of which had been in the past 30 or so hours – I recited poetry.

I wrote this intending to explore how poetry can be both a balm and a companion to madness. I carefully chose Coleridge's *The Rime of the Ancient Mariner*, Service's *The Cremation of Sam McGee*, Poe's *Annabel Lee*, and Cowper's *The Castaway*. I wanted to work with poetry fragments I myself had memorized, while also thinking through which pieces this character might care about as a miner, a queer woman, and a poetry enthusiast with no formal literary education. I also include a phonetic transliteration of the Hanukkah candle-lighting blessing, based on how my family sang the Hebrew; I wanted to include the strange and pervasive disconnect so many American Jews feel with our own traditions.

When life is as hard as life can be, we must all turn to something for support. I recommend therapy, medication, and a support network of more than one person – but barring that (or ideally in conjunction with it), poetry brings the unique solace of recognition without the possibility of judgement, and the comfort that for as long as people have been people, we've tried to tell each other about our struggles.

There's a Ghost in My House

Marie O'Regan

"THERE'S A GHOST in my house."

"What?"

The voice on the other end of the phone sounds shocked. I've taken him by surprise. "There is," I insist. "There really is."

"Alan? Alan White?" Now he sounds almost relieved, as if he's answered his own question.

"Yes," I admit. "Sorry, I should have said."

Silence. Then, "You didn't attend your last appointment, Alan."

"No. I'm sorry." No need to go into detail. Not yet.

There's a pause, as he digests what I've told him. Knowing him as I do, what he's thinking is, what I *claim*. I hear the tapping of keys, no doubt he's calling up my records, checking his calendar.

"I can fit you in this afternoon," he says finally. "There's been a cancellation. Is four o'clock okay for you?"

"I can make four o'clock," I answer, "but I can't come to the office. Can you come here?"

"Why can't you come, Alan?" His voice is soft, soothing, familiar. "Is there a problem?"

"I can't leave the house," I whisper, and I'm surprised to find myself near to tears. "I can't!" I take a deep breath, sigh it out, then ask, "Please?"

"Well..." More tapping, shuffling of papers, then I hear a long, drawn-out sigh. "I suppose I can do that. I'll see you then, Alan." The call is cut off abruptly, and after a moment I put the handset down.

I know I'm lucky. I know if I was reliant on the NHS, I wouldn't be able to get him here. Not unless it was an emergency, and they sent a team to take me away. Section me, or whatever they call it. I don't feel lucky, though, just lonely. Somehow, it's made me feel even lonelier than I did before.

* * *

Five to four. He's banging on the door, impatient now, annoyed I didn't answer the doorbell when it first rang, or at the first knock. I'm waiting to see if all the noise has stirred anything up inside, anything I need to worry about, but the house is still. He's just banging on the door, peering through the glass, misting it with his breath as he calls my name. *Why did I agree to this? Why did I ask him here, of all places?*

The third time he calls me, I give up and let him in.

"I didn't think you were going to answer," he says, glaring at me.

I almost didn't. For the longest time I sat on the bottom stair and waited for him to stop ringing the doorbell and banging on the door as I watched him through the frosted glass. I can't quite figure out why he didn't just give up and go away. I so wanted him to go away. Then I realise. It's not as if his home visit won't come with a hefty fee. I say nothing, just wait. He'll blurt it out eventually, he won't be able to help himself.

"Are you cold?" he asks, looking at me, clearly trying to gauge how I am.

He's shivering as he stands there on the path, bundled up in his wool coat and with a bright red scarf wrapped around his neck, so clearly he must be – it's been so long since I felt the cold, though. Since I felt anything, if I'm honest. Sometimes I almost miss it. Feeling.

"No," I answer, and smile; at least I think I do. "I don't really feel much, these days."

He smiles at me, the lines around his eyes crinkling in encouragement. "Trust me," he says. "It's freezing out here." He pauses, then, "Why didn't you want to let me in?"

He's waiting again. "Come in," I mutter, and open the door wide. "I'm sorry I took a while to answer."

Wait till he realises the heating isn't on in here. I don't need it, after all.

He moves past me through the gloomy hall, eager to get to the living room and warmth, and comes to a sudden stop as he enters that room and realises it's not that much warmer inside.

"You're not cold?" He's staring, dumbfounded, little sparkles in his thinning grey hair from the snowflakes melting one by one.

"No," I say truthfully. "I don't really feel it." There's a pause. He wants more. "I did tell you."

He sighs at that. "That's right, you did." He moves over to the window, stares out as he pulls his gloves off and blows warm air into his cupped hands. I can almost hear him thinking *At least it's not snowing in here*. "And why do you think that is?" he asks.

He's trying so hard not to shiver. "I suppose I've got used to it," I offer. "It's not like I need to be warm."

I can see his breath, pluming in front of him in little bursts like some kind of sleeping dragon, and relent – moving across to the fireplace and turning on the ageing gas fire. It's true I don't really feel the cold. Conversely, I don't really notice the heat, either. But I'm not cruel. Not without reason.

He sighs in relief, and finally undoes the buttons on his coat, takes off the scarf. He stands in front of the fire and holds his hands out to the warm glow now spreading outwards, his muscles visibly loosening as they stop trying to conserve his body heat. "Thank you," he says, and smiles at me once more.

"Of course," I answer. "It's good of you to visit me here. I know you'd be more comfortable in your office."

It's nice, his office. I remember, I used to go there before— Before. Big, comfortable chairs either side of his desk, an equally inviting sofa along one wall, beneath a painting – some kind of abstract. I've never understood those, but I liked the colours. There's a huge window that overlooks a park, and in the park there's a huge willow that sways in the breeze relentlessly. I used to watch it, rapt, wondering if it would eventually uproot itself and start to dance to whatever music the air saved for it alone. I used to wish I could hear that same music, so I could dance, too.

I used to wish…oh, for lots of things. You stop doing that, after a while, when you realise wishes will never come true. Not for you.

"It's certainly warmer there," he agrees, and smiles. I think I'm meant to find that encouraging. "Maybe we could go back to that soon? When you're feeling better?"

"Oh, that won't happen," I answer, and am surprised to find myself laughing. "You know that, don't you? You must do."

"I live in hope," he says, and for just a moment he looks sad. When he realises, he plasters that half-smile back on again, the one that crinkles the corners of his eyes but fails to lift his mouth. It makes me sad, too, when he does that.

"It would be nice to get out of this place for a while, though," I whisper. That's a surprise. I didn't expect to say that.

"It would?" He sounds hopeful. Kind. I wish he'd stop. "Why?"

Can I tell him? Can I *trust* him with this? It's not something most people would believe, but I have to try. I need help, after all. And he knows that.

"Lately I've wondered," I begin, and pause.

"Yes?"

Gazing around, I see the dust dancing in the sunlight, such as can filter in through the permanently closed voile drapes. I see the currents created, and the patterns – the routes – it follows. I try again. "I think – I said this on the phone, didn't I – the house might be haunted."

Now he's nervous, this man of science. This… psychiatrist. He shouldn't give such an idea the time of day, but here he is, glancing over his shoulder into the hallway as if he's heard something behind him. How delicious.

"What makes you think that?" he manages, trying to look unconcerned, and I almost love him for that. To be so strong, even if you're hiding fear behind it.

"Little things, mostly," I offer, thinking back. "At first I thought they were just visitors, come to see me."

"Visitors?"

I nod, enthusiastic. "Yes! There was a woman I recognised from the clinic; I think she was a nurse."

He's gone so pale.

"You probably know her. What was her name?" I ponder for a moment, bringing her face to mind. Her rosy, cheery face. "Sarah, I think." She's not so cheery now. No roses in those cheeks anymore.

"When…when did she visit you?" he asks, this doctor of mine, and I start to wonder if I should turn the heating up more. He doesn't look well. Not at all. His skin's gone grey, all the blood draining from it as I watch. *I do hope I haven't infected him*.

"Oh, I don't know." I gesture, vaguely, though I'm not sure what that's supposed to indicate. "A month ago, maybe? Six weeks?"

"And how did she seem?" he asks, and almost manages to keep the shake out of his voice. "When she came."

"Okay, I suppose," I mutter. "She seemed happy enough, to start with."

"To start with?"

I think back. To that rosy, smiley face as she – *Sarah* – greeted me when I opened the door.

"Alan?" she'd asked. "Alan White?" Then she'd identified herself as one of the nurses at the local psychiatric clinic. "Just a check-in," she'd reassured me, stretching that smile a little bit wider. "Last one of the day! We haven't seen you for a while, have we?"

I'd nodded, smiled, invited her in, standing back as she bustled through the front door so she couldn't smell me. "I've been a bit busy," I explained, "work. You know."

"Very good," she'd insisted, "always good to keep busy." She'd looked at me oddly, for some reason, then she'd bustled down the hall, into the kitchen. "Kitchen through here, is it? Shall we have some tea?" And with that she was gone, swallowed up by the heart of the home. I could hear water running, the kettle filling. I felt sick.

"Not for me," I said. "Just had one." (I hadn't.) "Please," I went on as she paused, her smile falling, "go ahead and have one yourself, won't you?" I looked vaguely in the direction of the cupboard by the door. The big one; a larder unit, I think it's called. "I think there are even biscuits somewhere."

That was all she needed; the smile was back full force as she headed for the cupboard. Larder unit. "Oh lovely," she said. "You're eating okay, then, are you?" I could feel her eyes measuring me, judging, even as she asked.

I made some sort of noncommittal grunt that she took as a yes, and watched as she found an old pack of Garibaldi biscuits and placed them on the table.

"Plates? Cups?"

"I'm sorry?"

She was still smiling, but it looked tired now. Worn. "I need to pour the tea, dear, and lay out some biscuits."

Lay out some biscuits. I smiled, but didn't rise to the bait. "In that one," I said, and gestured towards the cupboard beside the fridge.

I don't remember a lot of the conversation after that. She rambled on about the holiday she was about to take, in an attempt to thaw the atmosphere. Two weeks on the Isle of Wight. How is that a holiday? I'd much rather go somewhere like Paris, or Venice. So much to see! I made the appropriate noises, but didn't take a lot of notice. There were the usual questions, I'm sure. Was I eating, was I sleeping, was I seeing family, friends, taking my tablets… I made encouraging noises, told her what she wanted to hear – *the tablets did nothing. I stopped taking them weeks ago* – but all the time I was looking at her. Really looking. As she nibbled at her biscuit and gulped tea in between sentences, I could see it spreading. Decay. The skin of her fat little hands was growing pale, mottled, as if the veins beneath were congealing further by the minute. Her eyes had taken on that sunken, milky look that told me life was ebbing from them. She was dying, too.

She leaned forward then, concerned. She'd seen something in my expression, I'm sure. She knew what was happening, I'm sure of it.

"Are you all right, dear?" she whispered, and I could smell the rot on her breath.

I had no choice at that point. I had to protect myself.

"Alan," he says, and now his professional psychiatrist's tone is concerned, too.

"Mmm?"

"You were telling me about Sarah," he prompts, his tone kind. It's wary now, though. So there's that.

"Was I?"

He nods, his expression thoughtful, and I notice he's stepped away from the fire, towards the door. He peers out and up the stairs, as he asks, "Was she here long?"

Ah, now there's a question. "Not long," I answer, and smile. "She was just checking in on me."

Boy, was she. "I saw the ghost while she was here, did I tell you that?"

That's pricked his ears up. "No," he says, and turns back to face me. "I don't think you did. Where was that?" I remember it well. I went to look in the mirror in the hall, to see what she was doing without her realising, and there was a figure staring back at me. A man of around my age, thin…reedy, almost, wearing big round glasses and with what was left of his hair falling over one eye. He smiled at me. *Smiled at me!* He shouldn't even have been able to see me!

"Alan?"

I blink, the memory fading. "In there," I answer, and gesture at the mirror in the hall. "He was looking right at me; I could see him in the glass."

"And that scared you, I'm sure." He's moving with purpose now, ready to look for himself as he makes his way into the darkened hall. I stand back and let him pass, flattening myself against the door as he does so.

I nod. "It did, it really did."

"Did you try to talk to him?" he asks, looking at me – then he turns and gazes back towards the kitchen.

For a moment, I can only stare at him, open-mouthed, then I hiss, "*No*! I didn't want to encourage his…presence. I wanted him to go away."

"And did he?"

He had, actually. He started to fade as I stared into the mirror, becoming translucent even as he reached towards me, before fading away so the mirror reflected an empty room and nothing more.

"He did," I whisper. "I don't think he liked being seen."

He's focusing intently on me now, his mouth partly open, lips moving as if he's trying to figure out what to say. He probably is, at that. People don't like to admit ghosts actually exist. Finally, he clears his throat and asks, "Has anyone else seen him, Alan?" He's moving forward, slowly, ushering me back into the living room, towards the fire.

"I don't think so," I answer. "But then it's usually just me here. I live alone."

"There aren't any family members who could visit you?"

He knows this. We've discussed it at length, in his light, airy office that looks down on the park. I like it there. I feel as if I'm above everything; no one can see me or approach me. I'm safe.

"No," I mutter, and now I'm fed up with him being here. I just want him to leave. "You know this. We've talked about it."

"This is difficult," he answers, and he looks almost sad for some reason. "We have talked about your family, I know. Surely one of them – your mother, maybe – could come and see you?"

"It wouldn't work," I insist. "You know that. It's a long way for her to come and she wouldn't be able to see me if she did."

What is there worth seeing?

"I'm sure she'd love to see you."

"Maybe she would have," I whisper, "at one time. But not for months now, not since—"

"Best to look forward," he says, and smiles widely at me. "There's no need to go over all the ins and outs of what happened right now, I don't think."

He still won't admit he knows, but I nod anyway; I don't really have the energy to push things right now.

"How are you doing with the medication? Any problems with it?" he asks, and waits, still with that supposed to be encouraging smile plastered across his stupid, pale, sweating face.

"Not good," I answer, and find I'm backing away from him, towards the hallway. It's cooler there, darker. More to my liking these days. "I stopped taking both – the Olanzapine first, just in case that was the problem."

"And did that help?"

"Not enough," I say. "I gave it a week, to see if maybe it would take a while – but then I stopped the Fluoxetine, too. It made me feel so tired all the time. Barely there. It was even worse when I was taking both."

"Barely there?" He sounds puzzled.

"Are you too hot now?" I ask, distracted. "I can turn the fire back down?"

"Maybe a little," he answers, "but don't worry."

"You could take your coat off," I say, and look at him, my tone serious. "You've been here a while now, and I've made it warm. Too warm, apparently."

He doesn't say anything, just grins again. Buffoon.

I sigh, and head back into the living room, towards the fireplace, so I can turn down the heat. "There," I mutter. "That should help."

"Thank you, Alan." He moves across to the sofa now, and sinks down onto it, staring up at me. "Are you still feeling weak? Tired?"

I shake my head. "Always, but the tablets made it—"

He interrupts me quickly. "Maybe we should take these appointments back to the office; what do you say?"

"I can't leave here!" I answer, incredulous that he'd even ask. "You know that!"

"I don't, actually," he insists, and I notice he's getting paler, hiding his hand inside his jacket. *Why would he do that*?

"You used to like my office, remember?" He's wheedling now. I hate that.

"I still do," I retort, my tone sharper than I intended. "But I can't leave here. Not anymore."

There. There it is. I see it. The first sign. He's taken his hand out to run it through his hair, sweep back the strands falling over his forehead. The veins are darkening, just as they did with Sarah. As they did with me. The rot's creeping up his hand to his wrist, snaking under the cuff of his jacket sleeve. The skin itself is starting to decay. *Oh God, I've infected him, too.*

"Is there something wrong?" he asks, bemused.

Surely he can see it?

"Your hand…" I whisper, and point a shaking finger at the offending limb. "See?"

He lifts his hand in front of his face, turning it this way and that, stretching and clenching it like a decayed crab, the skin on his bony fingers splitting as he forces them to move. "What's wrong with it?" he asks.

He doesn't know! "It looks cold," I try, and it's such a relief when he smiles back at me and puts his hand back inside his jacket. I pretend not to notice the blackened threads rising out of his collar. *It's spreading so fast.*

"Well, yes," he admits. "I suppose it is. Not to worry, though. I have gloves if I need them."

I can only stare.

"I know your family relationships are...difficult," he goes on. "I know there have been words, to say the least."

You don't know the half of it.

"And I understand how that made you feel," he says, "I really do. It's hard, realising your family – your *haven*, if you will – don't understand what's going on with you. Can't help you."

"No one can help me."

"Oh, come now," he goes on, forcing himself to sound upbeat. He really doesn't look it. "I'm sure that's not true."

"Nothing works."

He sighs. "Well, now, we haven't tried everything, have we? We've tried various things. There are other medications we can try as you didn't tolerate the others well—"

"Nothing helps," I insist. "How can it?"

"There's something else we can try," he offers. "Have you ever heard of ECT? Electro-convulsive therapy? We've had very good res—"

"Liar!"

That stops him.

"Sarah said the same thing!" I cry, and before I know it my hand's over my mouth as I stare at this man, my doctor. My psychiatrist, standing there with his mouth flapping open like a blowfish, milk-blind eyes peering at me.

"She did?" he whispers.

"In the kitchen! I tried to tell her nothing works, nothing helps, but she wouldn't listen! She just kept on and on…"

He's rattled now, visibly shaken as he stands once more, starts shuffling slowly towards the living room door.

He wants to leave. They all do.

"You can see her if you want," I whisper, and swipe ineffectually at my eyes. They're leaking. "She's through there." I gesture towards the kitchen once more.

"She's in the kitchen?" he asks. "Did she come back, then?"

"No," I say. "She didn't leave."

"What? She's been staying here?"

"She's in the garden." We're in the hallway now, and I gesture once more, towards the back door.

He's inching towards it now, darting glances back at me every few seconds as he goes. I stay where I am, not wanting to frighten him more. It's safe enough. He can see her if he wants.

"The key's in the lock," I mutter, and sigh. "I'm so tired of the lies."

He doesn't answer me, just watches as I make my way into the kitchen and pull out a chair so I can sit at the table. Once he's sure I'm not moving any closer, he turns the key and pulls the door towards him, flinching as it creaks wide.

"Sarah..."

He's shocked. Of course he is. The rot's taken her over completely now. I knew it would. She's lying where I left her, on the sun lounger I used to love lazing on, to one side of the patio. She's even worse now. Her skin's bloated, and wet, and broken here and there. There are things crawling on her face, her blind eyes, in and out of her gaping mouth. At least she can't nag me anymore.

"Alan," he whispers. "What happened? What did you do?"

He's stepped out onto the patio, stopping a foot or so away from his nurse, Sarah. He has no colour at all now; he looks almost completely bloodless. I can almost...almost...see right through him.

"It's a good thing we're outside," I whisper, and smile at him. "At least you found Sarah." I gesture towards her, and my smile grows wider as he flinches backward. "Ask her. Go on, ask her."

"Ask her what?" he moans. He's starting to look... curdled.

"Ask her about this...ECT treatment. Whether she thinks it'll work."

"Alan," he whispers, and raises an arm in supplication. "She can't answer me, you know that, don't you?" He looks down at her again, and swallows. Hard. "She's dead."

"I know she is," I reply. "Of course she is. That's why she's out here."

"What?"

I'm not going to waste what little energy I have explaining. "I couldn't keep her in the house, could I?"

"You couldn't?"

He's walking towards me, hands reaching out, trying to placate me. "I can help you, Alan. I really can. This new treatment's had good results for other sufferers of—"

He can't talk anymore, once the shovel dislocates his bottom jaw. I don't want to hear it. He falls to the ground, grunting, and I recoil at the black, viscous fluid leaking from the ruin of his mouth. *He's more rotten than I thought. How long has he been decaying like this*?

He's hidden it well, up to now, or I would have seen it the moment I let him in. Thank God I got him outside, out of my house. A hand reaches towards me, barely more than skin and bone now, and I can't help moaning in disgust as I stamp on it. The finger bones break like dry twigs, and so does the skull when

I stamp on his head. I just keep kicking and kicking, wanting him to stop moving, to stop…coming at me!

And then it's done. And he's lying there, on the paving stones, black tar-like fluid spreading out around what's left of him. I couldn't have him inside. I just couldn't.

There's a ghost in my house.

And it's me.

Author Note

When the editors of this anthology, the lovely Lee Murray and Dave Jeffery, asked me for a story dealing with the theme of mental illness, I was delighted – and also a little bit stuck. I had some ideas, but wanted to find something I thought would be unusual – at least, I hoped it would be. I remembered hearing about a condition called Cotard's Syndrome, in which the sufferer believes themselves to be dead, often to the extent of denying the existence of their own body. They believe they can infect others, and the illness often includes self-starvation and delusions of immortality. Why do they need food, if they have no body? How can they die (again) if they have no body to do so? An episode of *Luther* featured a criminal who suffered from this syndrome, and I found the idea of it heartbreaking. I wanted to try and show the limitations this would place on a sufferer, from their point of view, and try to understand how scary such an existence might be – how such a person would react to someone, *anyone*, trying to alter that state, trying to 'fix' them when they didn't believe themselves to be fixable. I hope I've done the idea justice, and I hope you enjoy this story – if that's the right word.

The Book of Dreems

Georgina Bruce

IN THE BOOK OF DREEMS, a dog is a friend.

Fraser told Kate the dog was in her head. You imagined it, he said. The mind can play all sorts of funny tricks. But Kate was sure about the dog. It was the only thing she remembered: the little dog running around and through her feet as she tripped, stumbled, whirled in the darkness. A long vague slow sick wrestle with wet branches and thorny bushes, and the little dog tumbling at her feet, whining and yelping. After that – nothing. A lacuna, a drop of darkness in her mind. As if someone had reached in with thumb and forefinger and pinched out a little of her brain. An absence felt in the centre of her head.

Fraser said, the doctor said, everyone said – there was no dog. If there'd been a dog, it must have run away. The doctor told her strange things happen to brains when they black out. She explained it all in a calm voice. There's no damage, she said. It's common not to remember a traumatic event, the brain's way of protecting you. It's a good thing. You don't have to worry.

Yet there was an absence. A dark matter. A black hole with its chaotic corona, an event horizon over which tumbled thoughts and memories and intentions, if they drifted too close, got caught in its gravitational pull. When Kate tried to think about the accident, to imagine, to edge her thoughts towards that black lake, she lost herself horribly. She forgot. She sensed herself dissolving into the thick inky void, and was afraid.

* * *

While she was in hospital, the apartment changed shape. It moved through itself like a Necker cube, an optical illusion, turned itself inside out, doubled itself in rooms and hallways. Maybe it was a sleight of hand. Or maybe it was the twist in a Mobius loop, a different dimension on the same plane. Or maybe it was just broken. Kate tripped over its fracture lines. She walked into walls. She banged her knees on the table, trapped her fingers in the cupboard door, called Fraser to help her with the window that wouldn't come unstuck. She didn't know what to do with herself.

"Bed," said Fraser. He put an arm around her and walked her to the bedroom, pulled back the bedcovers for her, tucked her in like a child. It made him seem somehow fatherly, a thought that hadn't occurred to Kate before, despite their age difference, his forty-seven years against her twenty-two. But then, she hadn't known her father, so how could she compare? Fraser was so certain, so sure of himself and his place in the world. She was grateful for that, for everything he did for her. She wanted to be reassured by him, by his calm presence and the touch of his hand. But his fingers felt hard and cold, strangely repulsive. She thought they'd argued, before the accident. Had they? She remembered anger darkening Fraser's face, and something dark and wet slithering from his mouth, some black fluid leaking from his eyes and nose – but that couldn't be right, that was her broken brain talking. She drew his hand to her lips, forced herself to kiss his palm, though it felt waxy and stiff. Everything was a little strange; it was normal for things to be strange, when you'd been concussed. That's all it was, she told herself. She put his hand down on the bed, carefully, like it was a valuable object.

"What did we fight about? Before the accident, I mean. I can't remember."

"We didn't fight," Fraser said. "We never fight."

"Was it something to do with the program? Something to do with…those things?"

"The Dreemy Peeple?"

Kate hated them, those dolls or robots or whatever they were. She never told him that outright, but she did. She hated them. They frightened her.

Fraser smiled. That smile of his. "Sweetie, we didn't argue. Actually, we talked about going to the moon."

"Oh. But – I don't *think* I want to go to the moon…" She had to be so careful, when she disagreed, not to hurt his feelings. He was a very sensitive man. And he'd been under so much pressure lately, she didn't want to upset him.

"I know, my love. I know that now." He smiled sweetly. "I'll be a while, okay? Some emails I need to send. Sort out some glitches. Hate those glitches." He leaned down to kiss her. She kissed him back, tried to draw him into the kiss. But his lips were cold and rubbery; she didn't know how to kiss his lips when they felt so lifeless and numb. And he broke away. "You need your sleep."

"I'm not tired."

"I won't be long."

"Fraser?"

"What?" He stood in the doorway, waiting for her to speak, his hand on the light switch.

"What happened? I can't remember anything."

"Nothing happened. Go to sleep." He left the room, turning out the light and closing the door behind him. The darkness felt heavy, pressing down on her. What did he mean, *nothing happened*? Why wouldn't he tell her anything? How could he just leave her in the dark? It wasn't like him, she thought. Or maybe it was like him. She tried to remember Fraser, what he was like. She knew she was being strange. He was right there, in the other room, working. But it was strange, it felt like he'd gone. Oh, but she was being ridiculous. Fraser was Fraser. It was Kate who was wrong. Of course. Even before the accident, she had a terrible habit of being wrong.

When she woke in the early hours, Fraser had come to bed. He was sleeping, lying straight and neat as a pin. Distant, almost alien in his composure. His eyes were closed, but Kate suspected he was awake deep down. Awake somewhere inside himself. Maybe she could speak to him in the middle of the night. The real Fraser. Her love. She thought about loving him. Her body flooding with love for him. A stomach lurch, an electric jolt, a shiver when she thought of him. The real Fraser, not the strange one who brought her home today, who slept here like an empty doll of himself. Where was he? Could she wake him? Bring him back? She stroked the inside of his elbow, glanced her lips over his shoulder. Whispered. *Wake up. Kiss me. Touch me.* But he was gone. His breathing was regular, so harsh and monotonous it sounded machine-like. He lay completely still, his wanting self hidden away somewhere, inside another dream. Kate sighed and rolled away from him onto her back. She closed her eyes. *I want you to touch me. Not you. I want the real Fraser.* Why wouldn't he wake up? Where was he? It was as though he'd vanished, disappeared so completely she thought she must have imagined him, as if he had never been real in the first place. And still she couldn't bear it – the absence of his mouth, his hands, his hair in her hands, his tongue around her tongue – she couldn't bear the absence of him, and she didn't understand. He hadn't gone anywhere. He was there, right there beside her. But untouchable. As cold and distant as the moon.

* * *

Fraser left for the moon the next morning. He put the apartment keys on the bedside table, next to Kate's head. "I don't want you to dream anymore," he said. "While I'm gone, I want you to learn to stop dreaming. I hate it when you dream. It's so loud. It keeps me awake, and I need my sleep. I need to be on top of my game. You understand? No more dreams from now on." He kissed her cheek. "I'll call you from the moon."

It was a plane to Florida and then a shuttle to the Moon Unit Hotel and Resort. A long, long journey. Kate went back to sleep after he left, woke up in the early afternoon, in a panic, knowing she had defied him and dreamed something, not knowing what the dream was, but something she shouldn't have dreamed, something illegal. He wouldn't know, it would be okay, he couldn't possibly know. She was worried, though. She didn't know how to stop her dreams. They just came, or not, regardless of what Kate wanted. He must have been joking, she thought. He must know you can't stop dreams. He had a strange sense of humour at times.

She wandered around the apartment, Fraser's keys in her dressing gown pocket, swinging against her thigh as she walked. The apartment was definitely different from how she remembered. It was the weirdest feeling. Brain damage. That inky black lake in the centre of her head, sucking at her memories. It had taken them, taken the other rooms, the staircases and hallways. She didn't even know what the apartment was supposed to look like. It was as though she'd never been there before. Rooms upon rooms, and rooms within rooms. Some of the doors were locked. But there was a key for every door on Fraser's key ring, and she opened them all, one by one, to see what was inside. They were just ordinary rooms. Bedrooms, bathrooms, sitting rooms. A library. She spent some time in there, trying to read a book that kept all its secrets from her. She could barely even read the words, they were so faint on the page, broken whispers from another story. It was unsettling and she put the book away and left the library. She came back to the living room, curled up on the sofa in front of the television. She didn't want to go to bed in case Fraser called – he'd been travelling all day and night; it would be awful of her not to be awake when he found a moment to call. She sat upright on the sofa, biting the inside of her cheek to stop herself from sleeping.

When Fraser called, she answered on the first ring. She needn't have worried. He was in one of his tender moods, tired and tender, and she wondered why he couldn't always be this way with her. He said he missed her. He wished she had come to the moon with him. She promised him she would, one day. Next time. But she was lying – she was afraid of going to the moon, afraid of the shuttle, afraid the oxygen shields would fail, afraid of the Dreemy Peeple that wandered the hotel, served drinks in the bar, made the beds, waited tables. They were everywhere. In Fraser's room. She could see one behind him, a Dreemy Peep slumped over his bed, wires spilling out of its back. Broken. Its arms were dislocated and hanging from its shoulders. Its legs popped out at the hips. A strange misshapen thing. Its head was turned towards the screen and when Fraser moved aside, Kate got a glimpse of its face, a dented and torn raggedy hole in the plastic at its temple. It reminded her of someone, but she couldn't think who.

"I should have stayed," Fraser said. His image crackled over the screen. "You could be up to anything. Plotting, scheming, planning my downfall."

"Oh, that's all I do, all day long." Kate smiled.

"Don't laugh at me."

"I'm not. I'm sorry. It was just a silly joke."

"Yes, it's so funny. Your husband far from home, you think you can do anything you want. Don't be like those other bitches, Kate. Don't be a typical bitch girl. You're better than that."

There was the sound of popping plastic and synthetic voices from Fraser's room. The Dreemy Peep slumped over the bed was twitching and twisting, speaking in a strangulated blur of static. Kate tried to hear what it was saying, but it was too faint, too weirdly spoken, stuttering out of its wires and speakers. She thought she saw a glaze of despair in its eyes as they shuttered forward in its head. She must have imagined it. But Fraser had turned and seen the Dreemy Peep too.

"Glitches!" he screamed. "Hate these fucking glitches. I'd better go. Sleep time for you. And no more dreaming, don't forget." He signed off before she could ask if he was joking.

Kate turned the television on again. That stupid advertisement for Doctor Rain's Travel Gum. With the cartoon dog that ran around farting rainbows and singing.

When you're lonely and in pain
Make a call to Doctor Rain!
Chewchewchew! No longer blue!
Doctor Rain is here for yoooooooooou!

Kate couldn't figure out what the dog had to do with the jingle or even with the gum. Dogs like to chew things, she guessed. And they're happy. Or was the dog supposed to be Doctor Rain? It didn't make any sense. But there was something she quite liked about that little dog. The sweet way it bounced around, a silver key dangling from its collar. The way it winked at her, at the end of the advert. Its stupid, cute little face.

The advert ended and the screen went black, then gradually broke into a buzzing static blur. Rain, torrential rain. A little copse of trees and bushes, a deep wet green, water dripping from the branches and tips of the leaves. And under one of the bushes, a woman, naked, curled up in the wet soil. Blood poured from a cut on her head. Kate put a hand to her temple, felt the tender wound tied up with wiry stitches. On the screen, a boot swung towards the woman's face, smashed into her cheekbone. A caption flashed up: THROUGH THE NIGHT DOOR. Kate grabbed the remote control and turned the television off. She felt sick. She didn't like to see that kind of thing. But she was fine. She was fine.

Maybe she was dreaming. It was so late. She should go to bed. Bed was the best place for her now. Sleep. No dreaming.

But in the hallway, she lost her bearings. Somehow, impossibly, she walked the wrong way from the living room to the bedroom. She turned herself around in circles, not knowing which way to go next. The long, doorless hallway kept taking her around corners, tighter and smaller corners, until she found herself at the foot of a little wooden staircase that led up to a hatch in the ceiling which led… she had no idea where it led. She'd never been in this part of the apartment before. Not that she could remember. It was cramped and close at the foot of the stair, claustrophobically trapped by the angle of the corners that spiralled around it. So she went up. Up the little wooden stairs. Through the hatch. She climbed out into a kitchen, crawled out from underneath a table in the middle of the room. The only light came through the window over the sink. Kate could see it was twilight and raining. It was strange, so strange. She had a memory of this place. Like she'd been here before. All so familiar – the cheap wooden table, the photographs stuck to the fridge. Kate knew those people, the people in the photographs. But she couldn't place them, couldn't think of their names. Friends? Family? Was that someone she knew? But the longer she looked at them, the stranger they began to seem to her. Their skin, their faces – they looked wrong, too smooth, too shiny and stiff. Looking at them made her anxious. She wanted to open the back door, to let some air into the room. She reached up above the door frame and felt around until she put her fingers on the key she knew would be there.

The door opened into an overgrown garden. A sea of green, swaying and dipping in the rain. The water pummelled against her, soaking her through to the skin. Cold, shivery. And something not quite right. There was something out there with her. Something that crawled and mewled piteously under the bushes. A bloodied, moonstruck thing. Smashed in and broken. She was terrified of it, terrified and ashamed. She turned back to the door, but the door was gone, the house was gone. The light in the garden was failing, the rain coming down harder than before, and the moon drifted out from behind trees. A white eye staring down at Kate, transfixing her, pinning her to the spot. She wanted to move, to turn and run, but the next thing she felt was her knees buckling as she was hit from behind, a mud-caked black boot travelling towards her head.

* * *

The moon opened Kate. Traversed her. Translated her. Broke and rewrote her. Her face stretched out, the bones snapped and splintered, a sensation of her whole self being pulled forward, through her mouth. Her hands shrivelled, fingers melted together. The moon churned through her, a hundred new smells, her milk-sweet mother running in the grass between trees, in night's glamour, fresh cold rain dripping from leaves. The moon roared; it sawed through her, turned her inside out and silver bright. She tried to beg forgiveness, but she'd forgotten the moon's language. It was a prising apart of dimensions, it was two knives scraping each other to death. It was a whispering rustling creature in the leaves. She spoke, but her words came out stripped of meaning, in strings of saliva and bile. She spat and retched words into the dirt, and they crawled away like blind white maggots, and burrowed into the soil. She forgot the language of her own self, and when she cried, it was the whimper of a beaten dog.

Alone, alone, she was a creature hiding in the woods, in the cold rain, in the sharp grass and velvet-soft moss, not knowing herself at all. Lost in the dark spaces between things. But a voice spoke in her ear, spoke without meaning, and he was there, he was with her. And she was glad; she wanted him there. More than anything. Yes. She clung to him, wild panic let loose. Come back, he ordered her. Stop dreeming. He made the world for her again, pulled shapes from the darkness and built walls for her to live in. He covered her body with his own, held her down, crammed her into a person shape, pushing and moulding her body until it made sense again. He traced words against her skin, speaking in tongues, sharp tooth, soft lip, a fluid language that flowed inside her. He pressed his fingers to her, where she was tangled and wet, slipped and stroked inside. It was an entanglement of mouths, tongues, lips, it was a summoning, a gathering spell, bringing her into herself. She clung to his neck, breathing in the smell of his skin, his realness. (But how was he there? How had he returned from the moon so quickly? No, no, never mind that. Don't doubt him. Don't fear.) Yes, he was so real. And the bed was real, the room was real, everything was real and really there. It had never gone away. She had never gone away. Only maybe, maybe she had slipped, wandered a little too near that black lake of forgetting, the dark lacuna in the centre of her mind. She was afraid, but Fraser loved her, was loving her, holding her in the world with his own hands.

Yet his tenderness was a passing thing. He unpeeled her arms from around his neck. "Turn over," he said. He gripped her wrists and pinned her out across the bed, her face pressed into the pillows. "Do as I tell you," he whispered. "I have to fix this one little glitch."

She couldn't move if she wanted to. She was frozen in place, as passive and inert as one of those terrible

Dreemy Peeple dolls. And yet he was making her feel so real. So much more real than she was in that other place, with the rain and the dirt. The hallucination or whatever it was, the way her body had changed, turned inside out. That wasn't real. But this was. This felt so real. Painfully real. So real it hurt. He levered her open at the seam, pierced her with stiff fingers.

"You've been dreeming, Kate. What did I tell you about dreeming?"

She whispered, "I'm sorry. I'm so sorry."

"How can I trust you now? You're just like all the others, aren't you? Admit it."

No, no. Sorry. Please. How could he doubt her, after everything? But all his softness had leached away, into the darkness, into some other realm of himself. He was rigid and furious. He stabbed at something inside her, popped something in her back. She felt her wiring spilling out, pulled out in Fraser's hands. He wrenched her arms and legs from their sockets, made her a strange broken shape.

"No more dreeming. Swear to me."

She couldn't speak. She couldn't even move her head, let him see her eyes, to make him know how sorry she was. So sorry.

"Glitches. Fucking glitches. Don't think you can use them against me."

No. She wouldn't. Couldn't. Didn't even know what that meant. Just please, please stop now.

"Don't break my heart." He spat the words out, forcing her head down into the pillow, tearing her hair from the tender wound. "Don't be like all the others."

* * *

He went away again the next day, leaving Kate a long list of rules to keep to. He would know, he said. He'd know if she broke any, if she even thought about breaking any. *No dreeming, no listening to the moon, no screaming, no touching yourself, no opening the door, no running away*.

But Kate couldn't help breaking rules. And she couldn't help the moon from whispering its broken language into her ears. A fractured, jumbled language, words cracked open and drained of blood, bleached bone-white. It was wrong, it was terrible, of course it wasn't real. No. But she didn't know how to stop it. She couldn't silence the moon, so she silenced herself. She closed her mouth and stitched it shut. She knew she would never, could never tell Fraser. Not about the moon. Not about the strange television, or the dreeming dolls, or the night doors, or any of the other thousand tiny secrets she was keeping from him. He mustn't know anything. He mustn't know that she knew. That was the only way she might survive him. Keep everything secret and hidden away.

She was a closed case, her skin zipped tightly around a million unspoken words, a whole alphabet of herself, crazed little letters she had to keep still and quiet and contained within her body. They moved around inside her, spelling out blackbirds and spiders, ghosts and books and rotten apples, dead leaves and murdered girls and wrong music and long falls in the darkness. She felt chaotic inside, under her skin, stuffed tight and swarming with dirt. She couldn't stand it. She wanted to explode out of her body, unspool out of herself, unravel the tangled mess until she was nothing but one long thin strand stretched out across the universe.

But no. She would never be free. There would always be this pain, this bone-crushing pain in her head. She took a handful of painkillers, too many, she couldn't help it. Needed the pain to stop, couldn't take any more, couldn't stand the sawing at her bones. She screamed, knowing she was breaking his rules, not caring. The scream burst up from somewhere deep inside her, calling up some ancient vision of herself, her throat raw with the rush of air, emptying her lungs. She screamed and felt something break inside her head, a snapping of some connection. Then there was a brief loose emptiness, and she felt something warm and wet on her cheek. Something dark, spreading over the pillow. Blood. She was bleeding. Shaking, she got out of bed and stumbled to the bathroom. In the mirror she saw dark stains over her face and hands, streams of liquid running from both ears, dripping down her neck, her back, her breasts, everywhere. But it wasn't red. It wasn't blood. She wiped her fingers over the mirror. Black smears across her reflection. Black ink, leaking from inside her head.

Dreeming. I'm dreeming, and he'll know. He'll know. He'll come back and fix me, fix my glitches. He'll fix me and I'll be good again, I'll be his Kate again.

But she knew she wouldn't be good again. She knew this time he wouldn't forgive her, that in fact he was impatient for her to break his rules. Excited. He couldn't wait. And she knew that she was no good to him now, now that she'd broken the spell he'd cast over her. He would see it and be bored right away. He'd kill her. He'd turn her into a Dreemy Peep. Even if he couldn't tell by looking at her face, he'd see the ink all over the bathroom floor. All over the mirror. Smudged over her face and pooling at her collar bone. No, no. He was on the moon. He couldn't see her. He couldn't, could he?

She stumbled out of the bathroom and down the hallway towards the front door, trailing black droplets behind her. He was in the apartment somewhere; she could sense him. Coming after her with his tools and his hands, ready to fix her glitches, rewire her. Make her good again. Again? How many times? What even was she now – just a thing made of plastic and wires and spare parts? But it wasn't true. No, no. That's just what he wanted her to think.

The door was locked, of course. Kate went through Fraser's keys frantically, looking for one that would open it. But she knew she knew she knew there was one key he would never give her. The key to her escape. The keys failed, one after another, until she had tried them all. And yet there was something. A little something, dancing around her feet. When she looked, there was nothing there. But she remembered a little dog. A little dog with a key hanging off its collar. That had stayed with her. Stayed in her head.

Kate scratched at the bandage over her wound, pulled it away. She dug at the stitches, picked them apart with impatient fingers. Blood spilled over her hands, making it harder to grip the wiry threads and pull them out. When the wound was open, she stabbed inside it with her thumb and forefinger shaped like a beak, digging around in the broken skull, pulling out a bloodied silver key.

* * *

The door opened into Fraser's room on the moon. She knew it would, it must do. She was there already, too, broken and slumped over the bed, her back panel open and wires tumbling out. And Fraser standing over her yelling, "Fucking glitches! You're just like the others, full of disgusting glitches. Stop dreeming! Stop it!"

Kate came closer and he saw her and turned on her, grabbing her by the shoulders, slipping because of all the blood and the black liquid on her skin.

"What the fuck? What's this?"

He slammed her down onto the floor but couldn't get a purchase on her. The floor was slippery now and she was soaked. In the confusion, she managed to climb on top of him, press herself over him and hold him down for a moment. It was pouring from her now: the black ink rushed out of her, like blood from a severed artery, covering them both. It was a lake of ink, flooding out of her and into him. That black lake inside her head, that black lake of forgetting. It spilled out and out of her, and as it drained away, she remembered. Remembered how he had dragged her outside in the night. Dragged her by her hair. How he had kicked her, stamped down on her head with his big black boot. How she had screamed and begged for help, for someone to help, for the moon to fall down and rescue her. She remembered it all, and everything that had come before that, the slow silencing, the friends she had dropped, the job she'd given up. She wanted it all back now. She wanted her life. Her self. She would take it all back.

Black lake water flooded over Fraser, into his mouth and his eyes. It made him stutter and twitch uncontrollably. She saw blue sparks fizzing over his skin, heard the crackling of his insides, the liquid sloshing in his hollows. She slumped back on the floor and watched as he struggled to sit up. Still in his clothes, his smart leather shoes, his legs splayed straight out before him. His mouth stuttered open and closed. His eyes rolled back in his head. He was broken. If not, she would smash him to pieces. His smooth skin and his perfect hair, all sticky with blood and ink. And his moving parts, clogged up now and stuck. His mouthpiece twitched. A blue filament arced through his eye, leaving it black and empty. No. His eyes had always been empty. She saw her own self reflected in the glossy dead orbs. That was all she'd ever seen in him, after all: her own love, her own strength. She was the one who'd been real. Kate, and the others, the bitches with glitches. They were the real ones, humming with so much reality that Fraser couldn't bear it, would do anything to deny it, kill it. But it was undeniable. She felt it in herself now, in her aching, beaten body. She felt it thrumming inside her veins, thundering to her heart.

Author Note

This story is one of several I wrote about the Dreemy Peeple: women and girls who have been turned into perfect dolls for men to play with. In 'The Book of Dreems', Kate is literally dehumanised by Fraser, who makes these Dreemy Peeple dolls. I wanted to write about the labyrinth inside Kate's mind, how she comes to be trapped, and what great strength and sacrifice it takes to free herself. On the one hand, it's a fairytale – Bluebeard, with his rules and his key and his room full of dead wives. On the other hand, it's a classic science fiction story in the sense that it takes a current societal preoccupation – in this case, body modification – and projects it into a future where technology can deliver it to an extreme. The perspective is internal and claustrophobic, raising questions about consent and culpability. Why does Kate submit to Fraser in the first place? How is it that one person can invade and colonise another person's mind? But more importantly, how can you live when you have been gaslighted and mentally abused to the extent that you no longer have a solid grasp on reality? As with many of my stories, the question of what is real is paramount. Kate is able to enter into another reality in order to engineer a potential escape from her situation. But the true madness is Fraser's: he cannot accept any reality that he doesn't control. He doesn't tolerate women who don't conform to his view of what they should be and how they should behave. I hope the story exposes his misogyny as its own form of madness, along with his entire project of erasing nature in favour of manufactured perfection.

The Dark Gets In

Sean Hogan

COME IN, COME IN. Quickly, someone might hear!

God, I'm so glad to see you. Really, I am. I was beginning to think…

Oh, be careful where you step. I'm sorry it's so bloody dark in here. But I have to keep the curtains closed, and I don't dare run the electricity. I threw out all my electrical devices because…well, you just never know, do you? Here, let me light a candle.

That's better. Now I can see your face properly. See that it's really you. It *is* you, isn't it? Of course it is. Hahaha.

Did anyone see you walk into the house? Are you quite sure? You have to be so careful these days. I got a notice slipped under my door the other morning. I didn't see who put it there. But it said no one was allowed to leave their home, under threat of the strictest penalty. I don't know exactly what that penalty might be, but I can imagine, can't you? At first

I thought it might be a hoax, but it was on headed paper. Something official. Governmental, I'm sure.

At least, I *think* it was. The heading was blurred, as though it had been smudged in the printing. Or perhaps deliberately. Anyway, I couldn't read it properly. But I'm certain it said Ministry of…of, well, *something*. Who even knows anymore? They seem to make up new government departments all the time. As and when it suits them. So, you know, you were taking a risk coming here. They're probably watching the streets.

Still, you know what I think? When times are hard – and I think we can both agree that these *are* hard times, don't you? – we all have to stick together. And I say this as someone who, as a rule, treats other people with the suspicion they generally deserve. I mean, you can't really trust anyone these days, can you? You just don't know what they're thinking, or plotting, or where their allegiances lie. Politically or religiously or ideologically. You can't take these things at face value anymore. And so, before you know it, you're a pariah, or worse. Hounded online, mocked and shunned in your everyday life. Simply for the crime of being your own man. And you just know the government is listening to everything you say, watching every move you make. There's no privacy at all, now that we've given up all our hard-won rights. We'll never see *those* again. I'm not naïve about these things, not one bit. You can't afford to be these days.

And look, I've said it all along. My ex-wife – oh, of course, you knew Maggie, didn't you – always insisted that I was a crank, a soapbox paranoid. She used to laugh at me, and not in a nice way. Conspiracy theories, she said. She even went so far as to tell me I was full of shit. But just look out the bloody window and tell me I wasn't right!

I still write letters to her, you know. I tell her, Maggie, you must finally admit now that I was correct the whole time. About everything. Regardless of how much you mocked me, I was right on the money.

Of course, I can't post any of them because I don't know where she is.

Oh, just so we understand each other, I don't include you in any of this. You've always been my oldest and most trusted friend. I know we've had our occasional fallings-out, but my feelings about you have never changed. I've always known precisely what you're thinking. Our beliefs, our core principles, have always been entirely in tandem. We've walked through life in lockstep. We're practically attached at the hip, don't you agree? Like conjoined twins.

So if I confide in you, I know it won't go any further than these four walls. That goes entirely without saying. It's one of the fundamental tenets of our friendship, without which we'd never have made it this far. We do understand each other about this, correct?

Well? Look, I really need to hear you say it out loud. Just to be sure.

Okay, good. Of course I know I can trust you, but with times being what they are. Do you know, I haven't eaten in days? I heard the Government are meant to be leaving food parcels outside our doors, but I haven't received a crumb. I think someone has been stealing mine.

Sorry, I'm getting away with myself. What I really wanted to tell you was this: I went outside earlier. Just as it was starting to get light. I know we're not supposed to, that they say it isn't safe, but...well, you can't believe anything the authorities tell you, can you? And I speak as someone who doesn't normally set foot outside if they can absolutely help it. So when I'm told I mustn't under any circumstances leave the house, well, I start to wonder why. I start to wonder what's being kept from me.

So, first thing this morning, I crept out. I was very careful about it, believe me. I didn't put my shoes on until I was out of the front door, in case any of the other tenants heard me. Mind you, I haven't seen or heard a peep out of any of them recently. But I'm assuming they're still there, lurking behind closed doors. Listening. Have I told you about the other people that live here? They're a suspicious lot. Always whispering in the hallway. Eyes pressed to keyholes. Twitching curtains. You know the sort of thing. Not to be trusted. Not one bit.

Outside, it was a beautiful morning. I don't see a lot of mornings these days, but it was quite exquisite, take my word for it. The sky was as pink and rosy as a young girl's cheeks. I just wanted to take a short stroll and look around. Hardly a crime, is it? No matter what they'd have you believe. Of course, I was careful not to draw any attention to myself, stayed off the main roads and all that. I probably walked around for about half an hour or so.

And I didn't see a soul. Not a single solitary soul. The streets were as empty as...oh, a politician's promise. Now, what's so surprising about that, you might ask? We've all been told by The Powers That Be to stay inside, haven't we? That congregating outside is expressly forbidden. That it's Unsafe. So you wouldn't *expect* to see anyone, right?

But face it, we all know when someone's watching us, don't we? That little prickle you get? I certainly do. I've always had a sense for these things. A natural instinct. And I didn't feel anything. Not once. Now, it stands to reason *someone* would have seen me. Face it, the odds are that at least one person would have been idly glancing out of their window as I went by. And I'm telling you that no one did.

Because there's no one out there. No one at all.

You think that sounds quite mad, don't you? Well, I'll tell you this. I was so sure that everyone had gone, that not only were the streets empty but all of the buildings and houses were too, that I went and made absolutely certain, you see. I went around peering through windows and banging on doors and shouting through letterboxes. I made a hell of a racket, believe me. And nothing! Not a bloody peep. So where have they all gone?

I'll tell you what I think: they've all been moved en masse. Bussed away in the night. Taken God knows where. Somewhere safer, perhaps. Leaving me alone, to fend for myself. But why? Why wasn't I taken? Have I done something? What do they know about me? Have I been singled out somehow? Or was I just overlooked? Some kind of random clerical error?

I'm probably better off, anyway. I mean, where else would you put that many people but in some kind of camp, am I right? Just imagine it, being cooped up in there with all those others. No way out. The prying eyes, the staring faces. Every one of them a complete stranger. And look, we all know what happens in places like that. If history has taught us anything, it's this: when they put you in a camp, they've got you right where they want you.

Here's the thing. I knew, I just *knew*, that no matter how far and how long I walked for, I would still be entirely alone. That there would be nothing but empty streets and houses as far as the eye can see. I'll admit it; I got scared. I ran all the way home and locked the door up tight. That probably sounds ridiculous, doesn't it? Why in God's name are you locking the door, when there's no one else out there?

Well, I'll tell you. It was to keep the emptiness out.

That's why I'm so relieved that you're here. I need to know I'm not alone in all this. We all have to stick together, don't we? Especially two old friends like us. God, how long has it been? Can you even remember?

Listen. I've started to suspect something. It was her. That bitch Maggie. She informed on me. Everything I told her in confidence, all my private thoughts and fears, all my opinions, she told them. And now something dreadful's going to happen to me as a result. You know me, I normally play my cards very close to my chest. I mean, you have to these days, don't you? But I did let my guard down with her. Of course I did; I loved her. Trusted her. Christ, what an idiot I was! She was probably a plant all along. You hear about that sort of thing, don't you? Informers, sent out amongst the public to gather information and sniff out troublemakers.

That's why I threw out anything electrical. All those little devices and gadgets, anything could have been put inside them. Anyone could be listening.

But you always liked Maggie, didn't you? The two of you always got on very well, I thought. If I hadn't married her, I reckon you would have proposed. Am I right?

No, I don't mean anything by it. I'm just stating a fact. You two were very close. There's nothing wrong with that. Two people can be close without anything untoward going on, can't they? I mean, you tell me. I have to say, if I'm being honest, the way you're reacting makes me wonder…

No, I'm not accusing you of anything. And even if I was, it's all in the past. So it really doesn't matter now anyway, does it? It's all sewer water under the bridge.

So tell me truthfully, were you and Maggie having an affair? Don't get upset, it's just an innocent question. We're two old friends, we should be able to speak honestly to each other. There's a bond of trust between us. All I want to know is whether you fucked my ex-wife, and how many times. I don't need to know any more than that. I don't care how she liked it or how you liked it or any of that stuff. I'm not interested in intimate details. What do you think I am, some kind of pervert?

Why is it important? It's important because I need to know whether I can trust you. Because I have to know if Maggie has told them things about me, and whether you helped her. You could both be in on this together! Christ, how do I know you're not working for them? Oh sure, we're old friends, but what does that really mean when it comes down to it? The world is falling down around our ears out there, and it's every man for himself! I went out this morning and there was nothing! All the buildings were just empty doll's houses. So where are all the dolls? Are they all dead? Or just all hiding somewhere, laughing at me? Hahaha. Poor old Jerry, stumbling around like a rat in a maze, desperately searching for a crumb of cheese. Hahaha.

Are you laughing at me? Are you? I swear to God, I'll kill you if you are. I don't care how long we've known each other. And if I kill you, then they'll have to do something. They'll take me away and put me somewhere, somewhere there are other people, and I won't have to be alone all the time. I don't care where it is, just that they'll have to listen to me, speak to me. I can't be left alone like this anymore.

Please, tell them I'll do anything, say anything. I'm sorry for whatever I've done. I want to go with the others. Please.

I…excuse me. I'm sorry, I lost myself for a second there. I do apologise. That's why it's good that we're such old friends. I can be weak or stupid with you if I need to be. God, we've seen the worst of each other over the years, haven't we? I know I certainly have of you. But none of that matters now. Because when things get rough, we have to look out for our nearest and dearest. I know I'll always be looking out for you. These are dark times we're living through, but like I always say, it's at times like these when people really need each other.

Don't you agree?

Well, don't you?

Author Note

It probably comes as no great surprise that 'The Dark Gets In' has its roots in the UK lockdown of 2020. Indeed, it began life as a monologue written in the early days of the pandemic, something I was considering recording with an actor via Zoom. That plan never came to fruition, but the piece never quite left my mind. So, when the opportunity arose to submit something to this anthology, I dug it out again, wondering if there might be anything in it I could use or adapt. Reading it again, I realised that, although the story began life during lockdown, aspects of it still speak to a certain COVID-spawned mindset that continues to be very much with us. Sadly, one doesn't have to search too hard on social media for examples of this kind of thinking; the enduring notion that the world remains a deeply threatening and unsafe place, plagued by all manner of state-sanctioned conspiracies and malfeasance.

Although I ended up revising the story quite heavily for publication, I ultimately decided that the original monologue form seemed to translate quite well onto the written page. The direct address to the reader lends it (I hope) a feeling of uneasy intimacy that eventually blossoms into outright dread, as we increasingly find ourselves implicated in the narrator's paranoia and madness. As someone who started out in screenwriting, I'm always very concerned with the individual voices of my characters. Exactly how do they talk? Precisely what are they saying, and, perhaps more importantly, what are they not saying? I've always found paranoid characters very compelling to write, because in order to do them any justice, you have to present their way of thinking as reasonably and rationally as possible. However ridiculous what they're saying might appear to others, it makes perfect sense to them – so while I'm writing them, it has to make sense to me too. And besides, which of us hasn't occasionally entertained such thoughts? As William Burroughs famously almost said, "A paranoid is a guy who's just figured out what's really going on."

Eighty-five Per Cent, Give or Take

Alan Baxter

THERE'S DEFIANCE in his eyes. A latent anger. "I should be dead."

"But you're not."

"Shouldn't have survived."

"But you did."

Andy looks at the table, gently turning his pint glass in long fingers. Fingers that still make wonderful drawings. Thank fuck it was his left side that suffered some paralysis, not the right. Although he'll never play bass again, that fretting hand won't recover enough to find the right notes and timing. Not that we were ever going to be England's greatest rock band, but we had a small following. It was more than nothing. Still, given the doctors thought he wouldn't even walk again, ending up with "about eighty-five per cent normal function, give or take" is a remarkable recovery. Despite that, he's still lost so much. He'll never regrow the foot, a prosthetic below the knee for life now. A life he doesn't think he deserves.

"That fucker keeps eyeballing me."

Confused by the comment, I look up, follow his gaze. A guy in the corner of the pub is glancing uncomfortably our way every few seconds, nervous. Andy is a big guy, after all, long-haired, tattooed. He's an absolute teddy bear if you know him, though he looks anything but.

"Look at him, screwing me out."

"You're staring at him, Andy. I think he's wondering why."

"He started it."

I frown. "Did he? Maybe he glanced this way, then *you* started staring?" Andy seems to do that a lot lately, thinks everyone is sneering at him, 'eyeballing' him, 'screwing him out'. "You're being paranoid."

Andy pulls his gaze away to glare at me. "I'm not paranoid."

The guy in the corner talks quietly with his friend and they get up and leave. Andy watches them, eyes hooded, threatening, all the way out the door. "Probably going to get some friends. We need to watch it when we leave. Probably try to jump us."

"Mate, I think they left because they're worried *you're* going to jump *them*."

"Why would I do that? Might be for the best if they do. I should be dead anyway."

And here we are again. Around and around we go. He's not actually suicidal, just thinks he has no right to the life he's still got. How do you address that?

A couple more pints and he lightens up a little, glimpses of the old Andy shining through. The jokes, the wry observations, the ridiculous non sequiturs that somehow make sense with applied Andy-logic. The way he always used to be before the accident. The way only booze and weed makes him now, partially melting the wall of guilt and paranoia that cages him the rest of the time.

It's funny how the process has gone. Not funny "ha ha", of course. Funny like how fucked up life can be. When I rushed to the hospital at the news of my best friend's accident, I thought I was going to lose him. He threw his motorcycle aside to avoid the kid running across the road and went right under a car coming the other way. Sacrificed himself to save a teenager he didn't even know. Foot torn off – 'traumatic amputation' is the term they used – pelvis smashed into four pieces, head trauma causing full left-side paralysis. He spent days in an induced coma, and we all celebrated he'd lived while we tried to imagine the shape of his life with the consequences of that survival. Then his slow but continuous recovery over the following months. The seemingly miraculous leaps forward, all the way to "about eighty-five per cent normal function, give or take" and learning to walk again on a prosthetic leg.

He ranted and raved, of course. Cursed the kid for running into the road. But his determination was incredible. His focus to recover. From thinking we were going to lose him to watching him rise again, beyond all expectation. And now the physical recovery is largely achieved, I'm losing him anyway. The trauma an ever-present shadow no amount of rehab can alleviate, it seems.

We go back to his place after the pub, watch *Event Horizon* while smoking joints and marvelling at one of the greatest horror movies ever made. Mellowed by the abuse of various substances, Andy is more like his old self than ever. We chat in the slower moments of the film. We remember Glastonbury the year it rained so hard I lost a shoe in the mud. We remember the time at a New Year's gig at the Sovereigns when Andy and me got in a friendly wrestling match – until we rolled over dog shit in the pub garden and the landlord hosed us down before letting us back in. We remember a holiday together in Corfu and the torrid ten-day love affair we managed with a pair of German sisters. We'll always argue about who scored the better-looking sister, but we both know it was me. And then he remembers the guy in the pub, and his face darkens. The old Andy subsumed by the new.

"Wonder why that bloke changed his mind about jumping us?"

"What?" Takes me a moment to figure out what he means, drunk and stoned as I am.

"Probably couldn't reach enough mates in time or something."

Then I remember too. "Andy, he wasn't planning to hurt us."

He scowls at me. "You saw him screwing me out."

I have nothing to say, no point arguing, and blackness seems to move above and behind my friend. Like a distorted shadow of the man himself, pulsing and writhing in the dimness of the flickering TV screen with the rest of the lights in the house turned off.

I frown, trying to comprehend past the haze in my mind. What am I seeing here? The thick-limbed shadow leans forward, wraps its arms around Andy's neck and leans its head on the top of his. Kind of loving, kind of smothering.

"Fucking prick'll be waiting outside my house next time I go out."

"What? How? How could he possibly know where you live even if he did want to do that?"

Andy stares hard at me, eyes like polished agate. "Couldn't find any friends, so followed us back. He knows where I live now."

It doesn't make any sense.

Those shadow arms thicken and Andy settles back into them, draws deep on the joint and then holds it out to me.

"I'm good, thanks, mate. Had enough."

He smirks. "Lightweight."

I wake up in the armchair some time in the small hours, everything still and heavy, the TV dark and silent. Takes me a moment to remember where I am. I don't remember dozing off. Did we see the end of the film? Doesn't matter, I've seen it dozens of times. I cut my eyes to Andy's chair and a startle races my heart. He's staring hard at me, those glassy eyes, the tip of a joint glows as he draws deep. Then he grins.

"Lightweight."

I can't help a wry laugh escaping. "I'm gonna head home."

He tips his chin up once. "Catch ya later."

Where's my friend going? We've been like brothers for decades and now he's sliding away from me. That shadowy presence is still behind him, embracing him. It swells and I feel like it's watching me, daring me. Claiming Andy in spite of me.

I suck in a breath and push up out of the chair, grab my jacket and head out into the cold night. The streets are quiet as I walk the mile and a half home, past the pub we'd been drinking in, dark and closed now. Dark and closed like my best friend.

* * *

"These pricks have fucked up the oil change."

His first words when I get to his place after work

two days later and find him on the driveway. His eyes are darker than ever underneath. I look down at Andy's new bike, the back brake pedal set in a cantilever to the gear shift on the left side because his right foot is false now and he has no toes to press down on it. Although he says he can still feel the foot he lost. He describes exactly the injury despite not knowing anything about the specifics because he was unconscious. Phantom limb stuff is truly freaky.

"What do you mean they fucked it up?"

"Too much oil. They've blown the sump seal."

"That's annoying."

"I should have known better."

How could Andy have known anything? "Known better?"

"They blackballed me, these cunts."

My stomach drops. Here we go again. "You think it was deliberate? Didn't you say it was City Bikes that didn't like you? You took it to Street Performance this time, right?"

"Yeah, but they all talk to each other, don't they."

"What?"

"City Bikes told Street Performance to fuck me over."

"Andy, they're in different towns."

"So? They all talk to each other."

"Mate, why would one mechanic shop ever talk to another one about a customer? How would they even know where you went?"

“They all talk. I’m blackballed everywhere, I expect. Fuck knows how far I’ll have to go to get a decent service now.”

“Andy, that’s—”

He pins me with a gaze. “Don’t call me paranoid. You know I’m right.”

“I don’t think you are right.”

He scoffs. “You’re blind to it. Like everyone else.”

He heads into the garage and, as the shadows swallow him, I see that presence again. I blink, rub my eyes. Am *I* being paranoid? That can’t be real, surely? But it’s there, I can’t deny it. A huge, bloated silhouette of a person floating gently behind Andy as he moves about in the gloom of the garage, its thick limbs wrapping around him, massaging up and down. Andy pauses, stretches, seems to press into the presence like a cat against a person’s leg. Then he winces, shifts his prosthetic foot back and forth.

“Sores again?” I ask.

“Yeah. Need a new gel cup. It’s fucking gross in there.”

“I’ll go up with you. Get it fitted.” It’s a trek to the specialist limb unit, and always interminable wait times. Least I can do is go with him. It’s depressing how busy they get and how broken all the people are.

“Maybe later.”

“Make an appointment, at least.”

Andy shrugs. “I should just put up with the pain. I don’t deserve the comfort. Should be dead.”

"Mate, don't talk like that."

"They probably gave me a dodgy fit anyway."

I frown. "What, deliberately?"

"Yeah. They don't like me."

"Andy, that rehab nurse fucking loves you. And all the doctors are so impressed with your recovery."

"They have to say shit like that."

Andy has such rapport with the nurse, Annabelle. She's besotted with him. How can he think like this now? I feel like he reached a peak in recovery but didn't stay there. He's sliding back down the other side. There is no more recovery now, in the physical sense, no more fight back. This is simply life, indefinite, and he can't handle it. Without the physical battle, he's emptying inside, draining away.

It's hard to see clearly from outside in the bright daylight, Andy moving around in the shadows, but I'm sure the presence floating with him swells, grows, wraps him up a little more. Consumes him a little more.

"There he goes." Andy's scowling as he emerges back into the light, glaring across the road.

His neighbour opposite is walking out of the driveway, heading towards town. "What about him?"

"Dunno exactly. Him and the bloke next door were talking the other day, kept looking over here. Planning something."

I'm so tired of this. It's relentless. "Someone was chatting to their neighbour? Were you staring at them?"

Andy turns his glare to me. "Chatting and clearly planning something. I see the neighbours talking to each other all the time. Probably trying to find a way to drive me out."

"Neighbours talk to each other, mate. It's normal. You used to before the accident, for fuck's sake. You and Ben next door get along well, right?"

Andy spits a venomous, "Ha!"

I'm too tired to probe any further. It's so pointless.

We find ourselves heading to the local again that night. It's a ritual for us, always has been since we were old enough to go to the pub. Since before we were old enough, in fact, but now it's legal. I know the booze isn't helping, but I only get to see the old Andy when he's drunk.

I'm not so selfish that I'll accept that, of course. I've tried so hard to convince him to take a break from the drink and the weed, but he won't hear it. Pensioned off with a huge compensation payment, he doesn't even need to go to work any more, but that's not doing him any favours. He sits at home, day drinking and rolling joints. He always calls within half an hour of me getting in from work, then we usually hang out and he drinks more, smokes more. It's better if I'm with him, that's what I tell myself, though I make excuses here and there, to take a day off from it. He's been getting progressively worse these recent weeks in particular.

Even as I tacitly enable him, I tell myself he'd be doing it anyway, so it's better if I stick around. Try to help. Try to get him to accept help. But I'm watching the slow degradation of everything he was, everything that made him so special, and there's nothing I can do about it.

"Let's go to the Crown," he says, halfway there.

"We always go to the Sovereigns."

"They don't like me there."

"What?" I'm incredulous. "We've been going there for years, mate. You're a feature. They love us both. It's our second home." I laugh, but it's forced as I realise what that implies.

"Paid with a twenty last night and Caroline only gave me change from a ten."

"That's just a mistake. Why didn't you say anything?"

"It was a pretty clear message."

This makes no sense at all. If it happened, it was definitely just an error.

"Andy, Caroline's a doll. We've always got on. You and her even had a roll a while back. Why would she rip you off?"

"You fucked her too, once."

"Yeah, sure, a long time ago. But that's not really the point. She wouldn't cheat you. She likes you."

"She says that, but she shortchanged me. I stared at the money in my hand and she just smiled, like daring me to say something."

Or simply oblivious to her mistake. "Andy, these people are our friends. They wouldn't—"

"I don't care if you fucking believe me or not, that's what happened. I'm going to the Crown."

He turns at the junction, the Sovereigns only a block ahead, but the Crown another half a mile. I watch him go for a moment and in between one pool of street light and the next I see that presence, fat and hulking like a black cloud now, floating in his wake. Its arms reach around him, brush back over his head. As he reaches the next streetlight it fades, but it's still there, gossamer, an echo of itself.

I run to catch up.

"Well, they've clearly been talking to each other."

I put the two pints on the table and look back to see who he's talking about, but nothing is obvious. I sit down, take a sip. Andy downs a third of his in one draught.

"What do you mean?" I ask.

He nods towards the bar where a young guy is serving. "That cunt. Keeps giving me the eye."

I sigh, exhaustion a weight pulling at me. "You're staring at him."

The young barman glances over between customers, frowns at Andy's hard glare.

"Mate, stop staring at him."

"He keeps checking me out. Caroline must have rung around, made sure all the local pubs know not to treat me right. Did he give you the right change?"

"Yes! Why wouldn't he? As if Caroline would call around, Andy. That makes no sense."

It's quite bright in this pub, not nearly such a gloomy vibe as the Sovereigns, but I see the heavy presence around Andy all the same. It's above him and behind but through him as well. It's like Andy exists inside a dark cloud of himself and it's getting thicker. More opaque. Can no one else see this?

Am *I* the one going mad?

"I bet he shortchanges me. Drink up, I want to check."

"I've only just sat down. Barely had two sips."

Andy makes a noise of annoyance and downs the rest of his pint. He's up and heading for the bar before I can say anything. The barman watches him approach, Andy's gait just slightly hitched from the prosthetic. The barman is understandably guarded. Andy's thick shadow trails off him as he moves, not only wrapping him up, consuming him, but tailing him like a wake now as well. There's a lot more cloud than Andy.

There's a moment of heated conversation at the bar, then the barman is gesturing, Andy's voice is rising. I gulp down another mouthful then jump up and hurry over.

"—had one pint so far!"

"I'm sorry, sir, I can't serve you."

Andy turns to me. "Cunt's accusing me of being drunk!"

"Antisocial behaviour is unacceptable. We have the right to refuse service."

"Caroline told you all about me, has she?"

"Caroline who?" The barman looks at me for help, confused. Concerned.

"You know exactly who I fucking mean!"

I pull on Andy's arm, half turn him away from the bar. He resists, muscles taut under the sleeve of his jacket. He's always been strong, still scarily so despite the injuries. Still fit, powerful. Powerfully alive in spite of himself.

"Let's go, mate! Get some cans from the off-licence and go back to yours. Watch *The Thing*."

"Fucking prick!" Andy spits the insult like a verbal punch and the barman takes a step back, face souring. I see the calculation. He's wondering if he can take Andy. He wants to so badly. He glances down and I can tell he clocked Andy's gait, suspects the false leg.

"Andy, let's just go. Yeah? Get out of here."

Pub security have noticed. Two burly guys usually stationed at the door heading over. This is going to get ugly any minute. I pull hard on Andy's arm and force him around, nod towards the problem.

"Pricks!" Andy snaps again, then starts moving with me.

I hold up a placatory hand. "We're leaving, we're leaving!"

I guide Andy past, praying he won't take a swing at anyone.

The cold night hits us as we leave, fresh and stunning.

"You see that fucker?" Andy asks as we walk. "He was gonna have a go."

I don't know what to say. I can tell Andy exactly what happened, but he won't believe a word of it. His internal narrative of the situation is entirely unique.

"So that's all the pubs around here fucked then," he says. "Guess it'll save me money. Just stay home instead."

Far from a healthy option. Andy needs help. But I need help to convince him. I think I'd better call in some of our other friends, try to arrange some kind of intervention. It's usually just me and Andy during the week, but it's Friday tomorrow. I can get Grant around, and Tim. Maybe Claire and Emma too. Try to arrange a bit of a get together. If they'll come. Everyone has said how angry Andy is becoming. How negative, surly, unpleasant. They always make excuses, have plans they can't change. But I'll ask, see if they'll come, see if we can't all pull together, convince Andy to go to a professional who can help him.

The one thing he always refused in rehab was the counsellor.

"Fucking shrinks just mess with your brain," is what he said. "They'll have you convinced of all kinds of old shit. I know my mind. I know better than someone else what's in my head."

The irony of it isn't lost on me. I think he's scared a psychiatrist will convince him it's okay to still be alive, to be a survivor. Then he'll have to stop assuming everyone else, every*thing* else, is out to get him as some kind of twisted karmic justice.

I blink, can't see too clearly, like there's a fog come up suddenly. Then I realise I'm walking close enough to Andy that the dark presence encompassing him is partly over me too. A wave of negativity passes over me, through me. A sensation of raw fury. I take a stagger step to my left and feel a moment of resistance, of drag, then I'm out of it.

We pick up a six-pack each and head back to his house. When we get there, I ask him to humour me, come upstairs to the bathroom.

Andy laughs. "You getting freaky on me, mate?"

"I just want to check something, yeah?"

"I've definitely got a bigger cock than you, just accept it."

I can't help laughing despite my concerns. But glimmers of the old Andy like sunbeams through storm clouds only further highlight the darkness.

He cracks a can and chugs it as we walk up the stairs. One down, five to go. He turns the bathroom light on and looks at me, one eyebrow raised. "What's going on, weirdo?"

I smile, turn the light off again. The light from the landing is enough. We look at ourselves in the big rectangular mirror over the sink, uncanny in the gloom. Andy's shadow is massive, hulking. It encompasses him totally and half blocks my vision. I feel its presence, like cobweb I can't brush off, tightening my breath, curdling my gut. I want to move away, but force myself to stay, at least just a moment longer.

"What do you see?" I ask through gritted teeth.

"Two dickheads standing in the dark."

"Can you see anything around you? Anything different?"

"Like what?"

Why am I the only one who can see it? "Anything! *What* do you see, Andy."

"Someone who should be dead and his annoying mate."

"Andy, please. You need help. I'll come with you, we'll find a good—"

"There are no good shrinks! Is that what this is?"

"There are! I think you're scared of what they'll reveal. That they'll prove you're not—"

"Fuck off, mate. Out of the way." He elbows me aside, rough, painful. Like he's pushed away everything and everyone else. "You either believe me or *you're* against me too." That hurts more than the elbow. He heads down the stairs, his not-quite-a-limp more pronounced in his anger. "I need a fucking joint."

When I get downstairs, after taking a moment to gather myself, to hold back the tears, he's in his chair, another beer open beside him. He's rolling a joint, a big one, packed with too much weed. And I can't see his face, or even really those long, talented fingers, so covered is he in the thick, cloying shadow that's consuming him.

My throat tightens.

I can't see my friend any more.

Author Note

It's always fascinating to me, and absolutely terrifying, how mental illness can be such a slow but devastating creep in a person's life. So much so that, in my experience, it's often not even noticed at first, both by the affected person themselves and the people around them. It can be an incremental corruption of 'normal' that those around the person eventually start to perceive even as the person affected doesn't realise anything untoward is happening. In that process, the most well-meaning friends often don't have the necessary tools to support people when they're struggling and can even enable the affected person's further descent through inaction or incorrect action. Mental illness is isolating in more than one direction – for the person affected, as they feel more and more that others don't understand what they're going through, and for that person's close friends and family, feeling helpless to stop the slide. Both unable to help and unable to find help from elsewhere by the time they realise a serious problem is arising. It can be a vicious cycle of ongoing descent, a kind of vortex with the affected person at the centre and everyone around them either drawn in or pushed aside.

People are often unused to asking for help, unused to needing help, therefore at risk of becoming trapped in their own mind. Even a supposedly strong experience like survival can trigger a spiral in the most stable people. In many ways, the normalising of asking for help early, of accepting that it's not weak to *need* help, could curtail so many of these situations long before they become a real problem. And that, perhaps, is the biggest challenge for all of us, as we're all at risk of becoming the centre of that vortex one day.

The Carousel

Stephanie M. Wytovich

I sweat medication the way I
inhale prayers, the sting of urine
hot on my thighs, rosary beads
clenched in my fists.
                    It's been a week
of saying yes to cold showers, to
scrubbing blood from my clothes.
I rip my hair out in clumps, high-
pitched ringing cracking the bones
in my neck.

I live in rigor, my muscles starved,
ghosts soaking blank eyes. I try
to wake up, to write my name
in the sound of fog, a fever dream
lodged like death in my throat.
                    It's been a month
since I saw my reflection, texted

my therapist *there's a crow at*
my door, a skull in my cup, the nightmare circling my bed, its breath hot,
sour like mother's milk.

I count my steps, triple triple triple
lock the door. My head a carousel
of burnt houses, a blood-born
hallelujah poisoning the pills
I can't afford.
It's been over a year
since I sewed myself shut, the scars a
phantom zipper, a memory from when
they opened me up.

Author Note

After the birth of my daughter in January 2020, I suffered from an intense bout of Postpartum Depression (PPD), which eventually led to diagnoses of Obsessive-compulsive Disorder (OCD), Post-traumatic Stress Disorder (PTSD), and a panic disorder. When I try to explain what it means to *be stuck*, to struggle with a type of paralysis of sorts, people tend to have a lot of questions, especially because, logically, I understand that what I'm going through doesn't make sense.

For instance, I get stuck in my house some days. That's not to say I don't want to leave, or that I haven't tried, but that I physically just can't leave sometimes. One time before work, I got stuck for a half hour before I could walk out the door, and when I did, I sat in my car for about another twenty minutes. My intrusive thoughts caused me to spiral. I checked things repeatedly – locks, windows, the coffee pot, our stove – and by the time I did make it to work, I was so mentally exhausted that I was slamming down espressos just to stay awake.

On the flip side, there are other days when I feel wired and almost manically productive. I'll make to-do lists and organize my workload, check one thing off after another, work 14 to 16-hour days. I'll write poetry, edit manuscripts, detail clean my bathroom, and while that might sound great, it's just another calling card of my anxiety. Hyperfixation is a big crutch for me, a way for me to dissociate from the actual problem.

In the poem, I reference ripping my hair out, and that's a response that sometimes happens in these moments. Same with the phrase 'exist[ing] in rigor', which is a reference to how my body feels, especially my calves, when I go stiff and get frozen in the moment.

Truth be told, I've felt like a clenched fist for most of my life.

That said, my mental health journey has been just that: a journey. I've taken medication that didn't work, pills that made me sick, done treatments that turned me into a zombie. I continue to process trauma and express vulnerability in the hopes of finding stability and peace, and I'm thankful I have a fantastic support team and routine that helps me stay on track. Every day I get healthier and better at setting boundaries and advocating for my health and my wellbeing, and even though some days are better than others, I've learned to accept and honor the way my brain works, responds, and creates, because while there has certainly been horror, there's also been a lot of beauty, too.

Resources

Readers in countries not listed below can access their dedicated mental health resources by using the following Global Checkpoint link: checkpointorg.com

Australia

Health Direct Website:

healthdirect.gov.au/mental-health-helplines

Canada

Open Counseling Website:

blog.opencounseling.com/hotlines-ca

India

The Health Collective India:

healthcollective.in/contact/helplines

Ireland

Mental Health Ireland:

mentalhealthireland.ie/get-support

Italy

Samaritans Onlus:
suicide.org/hotlines/international/italy-suicide-hotlines.html

New Zealand

Mental Health Foundation:
mentalhealth.org.nz/helplines

United Kingdom

Mind Charity:
mind.org.uk/information-support/guides-to-support-and-services/seeking-help-for-a-mental-health-problem/mental-health-helplines

The National Health Service (Mental Health):
nhs.uk/nhs-services/mental-health-services/where-to-get-urgent-help-for-mental-health/

USA

Mental Health Gov:
samhsa.gov/find-help

About the Authors

Kayleigh Dobbs is an author, editor, and playwright from South Wales, who also runs a book review website called Happy Goat Horror, with a focus on independent horror. Her recent short story collection, *The End* (Black Shuck Shadows), was a 2023 Imadjinn Award Finalist. She lives with her husband and cats in a house in which the books on her TBR pile seem to multiply every time she turns out the lights. She can be found on Facebook, Instagram, and at: happygoathorror.com.

Jonathan Maberry is a *New York Times* bestselling author, five-time Bram Stoker Award® winner, and comic book writer. His vampire apocalypse book series, *V-Wars*, a Netflix original series starring Ian Somerhalder (*Lost*, *Vampire Diaries*), debuted in early 2019. He writes in multiple genres including suspense, thriller, horror, science fiction, fantasy, and action; and he writes for adults, teens and middle grade. His works include the Joe Ledger thrillers, *Glimpse*, the Rot & Ruin series, the Dead of Night series, *The Wolfman*, *X-Files Origins: Devil's Advocate*, *Mars One*, and many others. Several of his works are in development for film and TV. He is the editor of high-profile anthologies including *The X-Files*, *Aliens: Bug Hunt*, *Out of Tune*, *New Scary Stories to Tell in the Dark*, *Baker Street Irregulars*, *Nights of the Living Dead*, and others. His comics include *Black Panther: DoomWar*, *The Punisher: Naked Kills* and *Bad Blood*. He is a former board member of the Horror Writers Association and the president of the International Association of Media Tie-in Writers. He lives in Del Mar, California. Find him online at jonathanmaberry.com.

Emily Ruth Verona is the author of the novel *Midnight on Beacon Street*, published by Harper Perennial in 2024. Her upcoming novella, *Shiva*, is expected from Dark Matter Ink in 2026. Emily received her Bachelor of Arts in Creative Writing and Cinema Studies from the State University of New York at Purchase. She is a Pinch Literary Award winner, a Bram Stoker Awards® nominee, and a Rhysling Award Finalist. Her work has been featured in magazines and anthologies that include *Under Her Skin*, *The Ghastling*, *The Jewish Book of Horror*, *Under Her Eye*, *Monstrous Futures*, *Coffin Bell*, *Monster Lairs*, *Rust & Moth*, *Strange Horizons*, and *Nightmare Magazine*. She lives in New Jersey with a small dog.

Stephen Volk is best known as the writer of BBC TV's notorious (some say legendary) Halloween mockumentary *Ghostwatch* starring Michael Parkinson and the award-winning ITV paranormal drama series *Afterlife* starring Lesley Sharp and Andrew Lincoln. His other screenplays include *The Awakening*, *Shockers*, the miniseries *Midwinter of the Spirit*, and Ken Russell's cult classic *Gothic* starring Natasha Richardson as Mary Shelley. He is a BAFTA winner, a two-time British Fantasy Award winner, a Shirley Jackson Award and Bram Stoker Award® finalist, and the author of four collections of short stories: *Dark Corners*, *Monsters in the Heart*, *The Parts We Play* and *Lies of Tenderness*, while his acclaimed *Dark Masters Trilogy* consists of three novellas featuring Peter Cushing (*Whitstable*), Alfred Hitchcock (*Leytonstone*) and Dennis Wheatley (*Netherwood*) – with a guest appearance in the latter by Aleister Crowley. His most recent books are *Under a Raven's Wing*, featuring the duo of a young Sherlock Holmes and Edgar Allan Poe's master detective C. Auguste Dupin, and *The Good Unknown and Other Ghost Stories* from Tartarus Press. stephenvolk.net

Cynthia Pelayo is a Bram Stoker Award® and International Latino Book Award-winning author and poet. Her novels include *Vanishing Daughters*, *Forgotten Sisters*, *Children of Chicago* and *The Shoemaker's Magician*. In addition to writing genre-blending novels that incorporate elements of fairy tales, mystery, detective, crime, and horror, Pelayo has written numerous short stories, the poetry collection *Crime Scene*, the story collection *Loteria*, and is editor of the upcoming *Ghosts of Where We Are From, An Anthology of Latinx Horror*. She holds a Master of Fine Arts in Writing from the School of the Art Institute of Chicago. She lives in Chicago with her family. For more information, visit cinapelayo.com.

Grace Chan (gracechanwrites.com) is an award-winning speculative fiction writer. She writes about brains, minds, and space. Her critically acclaimed debut novel, *Every Version of You*, is about staying in love after mind-uploading into virtual reality. It won the NSW Premier's Literary Awards People's Choice Award, and was shortlisted for The Age Book of the Year and longlisted for the Stella Prize and the Indie Book Awards. It has been optioned for a film adaptation by Cognito Entertainment. Her short fiction can be found in *Clarkesworld*, *Lightspeed*, *Escape Pod*, *Black Cranes: Tales of Unquiet Women*, and many other places. She won the Aurealis Award for Best Science Fiction Short Story in 2022. Grace was born in Malaysia and now lives on the unceded lands of the Boonwurrung and Wurundjeri people. In her other life, she works as a psychiatrist.

Freddie Bonfanti is a London-based filmmaker and writer with an unyielding curiosity for stories that challenge, unsettle, and provoke. His work often dwells in the borderlands of dark and weird, where familiar worlds twist into disquieting shapes and the human experience is thrust into unsettling new contexts. Whether navigating futures warped by technological dread, or diving deep into the psyches of those bracing against extraordinary pressures, Freddie's writing is driven by a commitment to honest, prose-forward storytelling.

As a filmmaker, Freddie brings the same raw, unfiltered spirit to the screen, translating his literary instincts into vivid visual narratives. In all his work, he strives to remind audiences that even the darkest corners of existence can yield moments of connection, empathy, and hard-won understanding.

Sayan J. Soselisa is a neurobiologist and professional troubleshooter whose stories tend to be either funny, tragic, or both. They enjoy exploring odd places and perspectives in their fiction, and try to shed a new light on the things we believe to be familiar. As a non-binary person of mixed heritage, Sayan tends to root for the underdog, the (sometimes) unjustly vilified; the outcasts, outsiders and everything and everyone that doesn't neatly fit into a box. They have a fascination for the darker side of existence, and a strong will to find joy in there nevertheless. When not writing or complaining about their day job, they are probably preoccupied with one of their many, many hobbies, or can be found in one of Vienna's many coffee houses.

C.D. Vázquez is a debut author and tech entrepreneur born and raised in Puerto Rico. A creative technologist by day and storyteller by night, his writing draws from his love for vintage horror and his research. While 'Calm Springs' marks his debut in the literary world, he has authored scientific publications presented at premier conferences on Human Computer Interaction and Computer Vision. Vázquez is also the co-creator of the sci-fi fantasy Fyat Lux universe. He currently resides with his partner in Camuy, Puerto Rico, where he finds inspiration in the island's rich culture and beautiful beaches.

Callum Rowland is a UK-based writer and co-founder of charity publisher TL;DR Press. He writes across all genres, although science fiction, fantasy, and horror are closest to his heart. When not writing he works in the medical supply industry, is parent to the protagonist of his and his wife's story, and fights a losing battle against the ever growing to-be-read pile of books. A finalist in the Writers of the Future competition, his stories can be found in: *Daily Science Fiction*, *Aphelion Webzine*, *ExoPlanet Magazine*, *Bandit Fiction*, and a number of other markets and anthologies.

A Bram Stoker Award® finalist, **L.E. Daniels** is an American author, poet, and editor living in Australia. Her novel, *Serpent's Wake: A Tale for the Bitten* (Interactive Publications) is a Notable Work with the HWA's Mental Health Initiative. Lauren edited Aiki Flinthart's legacy anthology, *Relics, Wrecks and Ruins* (CAT) with Geneve Flynn, which won the 2021 Aurealis Award. With Christa Carmen, she edited the 2022 Aurealis finalist, *We are Providence: Tales of Horror from the Ocean State* (Weird House Press) and the 2024 release, *Monsters in the Mills* (Interactive Publications). Recent publications include 'Silk' in *Hush, Don't Wake the Monster* (Twisted Wing Productions), 'Darkness Repeats' in *Monsters in the Mills*, and 'Hangman's Coming' in *Where the Silent Ones Watch* (Hippocampus Press). Lauren runs Brisbane Writers Workshop.
Website: brisbanewriters.com
Facebook: facebook.com/laurenelisedaniels
Instagram: instagram.com/lauren_elise_daniels

The *Oxford Companion to English Literature* describes **Ramsey Campbell** as 'Britain's most respected living horror writer', and the *Washington Post* sums up his work as 'one of the monumental accomplishments of modern popular fiction'. His awards include the Grand Master Award of the World Horror Convention, the Lifetime Achievement Award of the Horror Writers Association, the Living Legend Award of the International Horror Guild and the World Fantasy Lifetime Achievement Award. In 2015 he was made an Honorary Fellow of Liverpool John Moores University for outstanding services to literature. Among his novels are *The Face That Must Die*, *Incarnate*, *Midnight Sun*, *The Count of Eleven*, *The Darkest Part of the Woods*, *The Overnight*, *Secret Story*, *The Grin of the Dark*, *Thieving Fear*, *Creatures of the Pool*, *The Seven Days of Cain*, *Ghosts Know*, *The Kind Folk*, *Think Yourself Lucky*, *Thirteen Days by Sunset Beach*, *The Wise Friend*, *Somebody's Voice*, *Fellstones*, *The Lonely Lands* and *The Incubations*. His Brichester Mythos trilogy consists of *The Searching Dead*, *Born to the Dark* and *The Way of the Worm*. His collections include *Waking Nightmares*, *Ghosts and Grisly Things*, *Told by the Dead*, *Just Behind You*, *Holes for Faces*, *By the Light of My Skull*, *Fearful Implications*, and a two-volume retrospective roundup (*Phantasmagorical Stories*) as well as *The Village Killings and Other Novellas*. His non-fiction is collected as *Ramsey Campbell, Probably* and *Ramsey Campbell, Certainly*, while *Ramsey's Rambles* collects his video reviews, and *Six Stooges and Counting* is a book-length study of the Three Stooges. *Limericks of the Alarming and Phantasmal* is a history of horror fiction in the form of fifty limericks. His novels *The Nameless*, *Pact of the Fathers* and *The Influence* have been filmed in Spain, where a television series based on *The Nameless* is in development. He is the President of the Society of Fantastic Films.

Ramsey Campbell was born in Liverpool in 1946 and still lives on Merseyside with his wife Jenny. His pleasures include classical music, good food and wine. His website is at ramseycampbell.com.

Sumiko Saulson is a Bram Stoker Award® Finalist for Poetry for *The Rat King* (2022, Dooky Zines) and *Melancholia* (2024, Bludgeoned Girls Press), and an Elgin Award Nominee (2022 and 2024), 2018 Afrosurrealist Writers Award-winner, and 2021 Ladies of Horror Readers Choice Award-winner. Their novel *Somnalia: The Metamorphoses of Flynn Keahi* is available from Mocha Memoirs Press. See more at sumikosaulson.com.

Amanda Cecelia Lang is a horror author and daydreamer from Colorado. Her scary stories haunt the dark corners of many popular magazines, podcasts, and anthologies, including *The Deadlands*, *Ghoulish Tales*, *Uncharted*, *Cast of Wonders*, and *Darkness Beckons*. Her short story collections *Saturday Fright at the Movies: 13 Tales from the Multiplex* (Dark Matter INK) and *The Library of Broken Girls: Stories of Survival* (Gateway Literary) are available everywhere books are sold. You can follow her work at amandacecelialang.com.

Alma Katsu is the award-winning author of eight books and numerous stories in a variety of genres, including horror. Her next horror novel, *Fiend*, will be published by GP Putnam's Sons in fall 2025.

Ryan Cole is a speculative fiction writer who lives in Virginia with his husband and snuggly pug child. By day, he reviews contracts and wields the mighty red pen of a paralegal. His work has appeared in *Clarkesworld*, *PodCastle*, *Factor Four*, *Gallery of Curiosities*, and *Voyage YA by Uncharted*, among others, and has been nominated for the Pushcart Prize. Find out more at ryancolewrites.com.

Tim Waggoner has published over sixty novels and eight collections of short stories. He writes original dark fantasy and horror, as well as media tie-ins, and his articles on writing have appeared in numerous publications. He's a four-time winner of the Bram Stoker Award®, a one-time winner of the Scribe Award, and he's been a two-time finalist for the Shirley Jackson Award and a one-time finalist for the Splatterpunk Award. He's also a full-time tenured professor who teaches creative writing and composition at Sinclair College in Dayton, Ohio. His papers are collected by the University of Pittsburgh's Horror Studies Program.

Sara Larner (they/she) is an award-winning author and screenwriter based out of Los Angeles, where they write predominantly YA fantasy with frequent dalliances in horror, often playing with the unreliability of one's own mind and body. Their work has appeared in *Trollbreath Magazine*, premier horror podcast Pseudopod, and *Dandelions on Mars*, among others. When not writing, they spend their time painting, losing to one of their partners at Magic: The Gathering, talking superheroes with their other partner, and trying to mediate the war between their cat and all of the houseplants.

Marie O'Regan is an award-winning author and editor, based in Derbyshire. She is the author of three collections of short fiction, a supernatural novel, *Celeste*, and her short stories have appeared in magazines and anthologies in several countries – including *The Mammoth Book of Halloween Stories*, and *Best British Horror* among others. To date, she has co-edited fifteen anthologies, including the bestselling *Hellbound Hearts*, *Mammoth Book of Body Horror*, *A Carnivàle of Horror – Dark Tales from the Fairground*, *Exit Wounds* (four stories from which have been shortlisted for a CWA dagger for Best Short Story), *Wonderland* (nominated for a Shirley Jackson award and BFS award), *Cursed*, *Twice Cursed*, *The Other Side of Never* (nominated for a British Fantasy Award), *In These Hallowed Halls*, *Beyond & Within Folk Horror Short Stories*, *Death Comes at Christmas*, *The Secret Romantic's Book of Magic* and *These Dreaming Spires*, as well as the charity anthology *Trickster's Treats #3* (nominated for an Aurealis award). More are forthcoming in 2026. She is also the sole editor of bestselling *The Mammoth Book of Ghost Stories by Women* and *Phantoms*. An ex-Chair of the British Fantasy Society and the UK Chapter of the Horror Writers Association, she also ran several FantasyCons, as well as ChillerCon UK, which took place in Scarborough in May 2022. Marie is also Managing Editor of PS Publishing's award-winning novella imprint, Absinthe Books, novellas from which have won the Shirley Jackson award (alongside several nominations) and the World Fantasy Award for Best Novella. It has also garnered several nominations for the British Fantasy Awards, the Aurealis Awards and the Bram Stoker® Awards.

Georgina Bruce is a housesitter who also purports to be a writer. Her latest story collection, *The House on the Moon*, is available from Black Shuck Books. She writes a weekly humorous column on her substack, The Distractionist.

Sean Hogan is a writer and filmmaker based in the UK. He has published several books of cinema metafiction, including *England's Screaming* and its sequel *Twilight's Last Screaming* (each named as one of the five best genre novels of their year by the *Financial Times*), *What Screams May Come*, *Three Mothers*, *One Father*, and *That Fatal Shore.* His latest novel, *The Corpse Road*, was published in 2024. His feature film credits include *The Devil's Business*, *The Borderlands*, the documentary *Future Shock! The Story of 2000AD*, and the acclaimed folk horror *To Fire You Come at Last*, which recently debuted on Shudder as the first instalment of an ongoing series of Christmas ghost stories,

The Haunted Season. He is currently in production on his next film, *Scenes from a Young Girl's Disappearance*.

Alan Baxter is a multi-award-winning British-Australian author of horror, supernatural thrillers and dark fantasy liberally mixed with crime, mystery and noir. This Is Horror podcast calls him 'Australia's master of literary darkness' and the Talking Scared podcast dubbed him 'The Lord of Weird Australia'. He's also a martial artist, a whisky-soaked swear monkey, and dog lover. Alan grew up in the UK and now writes his dark, weird stories deep in the valleys of southern Tasmania. Find him online at alanbaxter.com.au.

Stephanie M. Wytovich is an American poet, novelist, and essayist. Her work has been featured in magazines and anthologies, such as *Weird Tales*, *Nightmare Magazine*, *Southwest Review*, *Year's Best Hardcore Horror: Volume 2*, and *The Best Horror of the Year: Volumes 8 & 15*. Wytovich is the Poetry Editor for Raw Dog Screaming Press and an adjunct at Western Connecticut State University, Southern New Hampshire University, and Point Park University. She has received the Elizabeth Matchett Stover Memorial Award, the 2021 Ladies of Horror Fiction Writers Grant, and the Rocky Wood Memorial Scholarship for nonfiction writing. Wytovich is a member of the Science Fiction and Fantasy Poetry Association, an active member of the Horror Writers Association, and a graduate of Seton Hill University's MFA program for Writing Popular Fiction. She is a two-time Bram Stoker Award®-winning poet, and her debut novel, *The Eighth*, is published with Dark Regions Press. Her nonfiction craft book for speculative poetry, *Writing Poetry in the Dark*, is available now from Raw Dog Screaming Press.

Follow Wytovich at stephaniemwytovich.com and on X/Twitter, Threads, and Instagram @SWytovich and @thehauntedbookshelf. You can also sign up for her newsletter at stephaniemwytovich.substack.com.

About the Illustrator

Greg Chapman is an illustrator and graphic designer based in Queensland, Australia, specialising in the horror field. Trained as a graphic designer and visual artist, Greg has provided artwork for various magazines, comics, graphic novels and promotional designs for the Horror Writers Association and the Australian Horror Writers Association. He also specialises in book cover design and has created cover art for many authors and publishers. The graphic novel he illustrated, *Witch Hunts: A Graphic History of the Burning Times*, written by Rocky Wood and Lisa Morton, won the Bram Stoker Award® in 2013. Greg is also a Bram Stoker Award, Australian Shadows Award and Aurealis Award-nominated author. You can find out more about his writing at darkscrybe.com.

About the Editors

'Lee Murray is a powerful voice in horror.'
– *Interstellar Flight Magazine*

Lee Murray ONZM is a writer, editor, poet, essayist, and screenwriter from Aotearoa New Zealand. Her country's only recipient of the Shirley Jackson Award, she is a thirteen-time Sir Julius Vogel, four-time Australian Shadows, and five-time Bram Stoker Award® winner, and an Aurealis and British Fantasy Award nominee. A *USA Today* bestselling author with more than forty titles to her credit, including novels, collections, anthologies, nonfiction, poetry, and several books for children, her notable titles include the *Taine McKenna Adventures*, *The Path of Ra* (with Dan Rabarts), *Grotesque: Monster Stories*, *Black Cranes*, *Tortured Willows*, *Unquiet Spirits*, *Hellhole*, *Despatches*, *Remains to be Told*, *Baby Teeth*, and *Battle of the Birds*. Her short fiction appears in prestigious venues such as *Weird Tales*, *Space & Time*, and *Grimdark Magazine*. Lee holds a New Zealand Prime Minister's Award for Literary Achievement in Fiction, the first author of Asian descent to achieve this, and is an Honorary Literary Fellow of the New Zealand Society of Authors. In 2024, *The Listener* named her as one of New Zealand's fifty most inspiring people. An advocate for the speculative and horror communities, Lee is especially proud of her work in the areas of mentorship, Asian diaspora narratives, and mental health in horror. She is a judge of the 2025 World Fantasy Awards. Recent works include horror-comedy feature film *Grafted*, which premiered in August 2024, and NZSA Cuba Press Prize-winner *Fox Spirit on a Distant Cloud*, a prose-poetry collection blending fiction, memoir, and myth from The Cuba Press. Read more at leemurray.info.

'Jeffery has a connoisseur's eye for the
grotesque and mind-bending.'
– Stephen Volk, writer of *Ghostwatch* and *Afterlife*

Dave Jeffery is the author of eighteen novels, two collections, and numerous short stories. His *Necropolis Rising* series and yeti adventure *Frostbite* have both featured on the Amazon #1 bestseller list. Other work includes the critically acclaimed *Beatrice Beecham* supernatural mystery series for young adults, and the *A Quiet Apocalypse* series. His *Campfire Chillers* collection made the 2012 Edge Hill Prize longlist, and his screenwriting credits include award-winning short films *Ascension* and *Derelict*. He is a long-time contributor to *Phantasmagoria Magazine*, a final reader for *Space and Time Magazine*, and a regular book reviewer for *The British Fantasy Society*. Prior to retirement in 2019, Jeffery worked for thirty-five years in the National Health Service (NHS), specialising in the field of mental health nursing and risk management. He holds a BSc (Hons) in Mental Health Studies and a Master of Science Degree in Health Studies. During this time, he has worked with Whurr International, Wiley & Sons, and the Royal College of Nursing's *Mental Health Practice Magazine*, writing academic papers and research articles. Jeffery is also co-editor of *Deafness and Challenging Behaviour* (Wiley & Sons). His literary criticism has been published by Bloomsbury Academic and Peter Lang Publishing. *Finding Jericho*, Jeffery's contemporary mental health novel, has featured on both the BBC Health, and Independent Schools Entrance Examination Board's 'Recommended Reading' lists. He is a mentor on the Horror Writers Association's Mentorship Scheme, and the 2023 recipient of the HWA Mentor of the Year Award. For three years Jeffery was co-chair of the HWA Wellness Committee. Read more at: davejefferyauthor.com.

Acknowledgements

We would like to extend our sincerest thanks to everyone who contributed to the development of this book: our wonderful authors, including those who participated in the submission call, reviewers, readers, and signal boosters, and to Nick, Gillian, and the Flame Tree team for producing this gorgeous volume. Special thanks to our families for their unrelenting support while we stayed up (or got up early) to do editorial Zoom calls in our pyjamas.

Beyond & Within

THE FLAME TREE Beyond & Within short story collections bring together tales of myth and imagination by modern and contemporary writers, carefully selected by anthologists, and sometimes featuring short stories and fiction from a single author. Overall, the series presents a wide range of diverse and inclusive voices, often writing folkloric-inflected short fiction, but always with an emphasis on the supernatural, science fiction, the mysterious and the speculative. The books themselves are gorgeous, with foiled covers, printed edges and published only in hardcover editions, offering a lifetime of reading pleasure.

FLAME TREE FICTION

A wide range of new and classic fiction, from myth to modern stories, with tales from the distant past to the far future, including short story anthologies, Collector's Editions, Collectable Classics, Gothic Fantasy collections and Epic Tales of mythology and folklore.

•